About the Author

Scott Rule was born in East Kilbride. He studied Humanities at Thames Polytechnic London and has previously written radio and television sketches with The Comedy Unit for various BBC programmes. He is a member of the pub rock band The Moes.

The Milk Boys is his first novel. He lives in the South Side of Glasgow with his wife and son.

Instagram: @scott.rule.75
X/Twitter: @Rule685564Scott

SCOTT RULE

The Milk Boys

AUSTIN MACAULEY PUBLISHERS™
LONDON • CAMBRIDGE • NEW YORK • SHARJAH

Copyright © Scott Rule 2024

The right of Scott Rule to be identified as author of this work has been asserted in accordance with sections 77 and 78 of the Copyright, Designs and Patents Act 1988.

All rights reserved. No part of this publication may be reproduced, stored in a retrieval system, or transmitted in any form or by any means, electronic, mechanical, photocopying, recording, or otherwise, without the prior permission of the publishers.

Any person who commits any unauthorised act in relation to this publication may be liable to criminal prosecution and civil claims for damages.

This is a work of fiction. Names, characters, businesses, places, events, locales, and incidents are either the products of the author's imagination or used in a fictitious manner. Any resemblance to actual persons, living or dead, or actual events is purely coincidental.

A CIP catalogue record for this title is available from the British Library.

ISBN 9781035849765 (Paperback)
ISBN 9781035849772 (ePub e-book)

www. austinmacauley.com

First Published 2024
Austin Macauley Publishers Ltd
1 Canada Square
Canary Wharf
London
E14 5AA

Dedication

For Joanna and Harry.

Acknowledgements

I would like to thank all of the people who have encouraged me to write this book, including Kenny, Carol, Maria, The Moes, Graham and Graeme, and Janey.

Thanks to Jacquie Lyons for listening.

Thanks to my extended family for always being there and the biggest thanks to my wife Joanna who has always supported me and my son Harry who inspires me every day.

Also, in memory of Kenny, Hugh, Drew and Gus.

I would like to thank Walter Stephenson and all at Austin Macauley for their support in producing this book.

CHAPTER ONE

1970

TOMMY LOY MOVED to East Kilbride in 1959, aged 14, along with his newly widowed mother, Agnes. The New Town was 12 years old and beginning to boom. Tommy was a war baby, which was a bit of a miracle, not because his father was involved in the war effort overseas, but because he was in and out of jail throughout the entire conflict. The Loys were born and bred in The Gorbals, a tough working-class area of Glasgow renowned for its poverty, violence and deprivation. Moving to East Kilbride was a new start for Agnes and Tommy, a chance to put everything behind them and make a life for themselves.

They moved into one of the brand-new flats above the shops at The Calderwood Square and, for Agnes, it was a palace; two bedrooms, a living room, a kitchenette and most importantly, an inside toilet. Compared to the room and kitchen they had been in before, it was incredible. Tommy's dad, Jimmy, had died two years earlier of a heart attack while serving a six-year stretch for robbery in Barlinnie. He had broken into a bank via the roof, dropping down directly into the vault, but hadn't thought about how he was going to get out again. He was discovered the next morning, fast asleep next to the safe, when the staff came in to start their shift. The Victorian built prison, housing the most dangerous men in Glasgow, was no place for someone with poor health.

Jimmy had been a bit of a clown and he had left his family with nothing. Agnes was determined to give young Tommy a better start in life than she or anyone else in her family had been given before. Tommy was already involved in gangs by the time they left The Gorbals, and she dreaded the idea of him following in his dad's footsteps to a life of crime and violence. Jimmy had been part of The Beehive Boys, a local gang who took their name from the draper's shop on the corner of Cumberland Street and Thistle Street and had graduated from fighting rival gangs like the Bridgeton Billy Boys and The Norman Conks over territory nobody wanted, to being a member of an organised band of armed robbers and petty thieves. Jimmy was in jail more often than he was out and she had no doubt the lifestyle he led had been the death of him. Agnes wanted better for Tommy.

On moving to East Kilbride, Agnes started working in Laird Portch, the factory exporting tartan kilts, skirts and shawls to the world. She loved the camaraderie of the factory and the money she brought in. Life was sweet, but Tommy was a constant worry. He had never been one for going to school before they moved so she had relented and didn't register him, denying him the chance of furthering his education in East Kilbride. The problem was, although there were plenty of jobs available in the factories of the industrial estates surrounding the town, Tommy wasn't interested. Agnes was soft on her son and didn't want to stifle him. The open spaces of East Kilbride were like a playground for Tommy and after the start he had endured to his young life in the dark, dirty streets of The Gorbals, Agnes felt he deserved a bit of freedom. In short, she spoiled him rotten, and let him get away with pretty much anything.

The Calderwood Square was Tommy's playground. It had a chippy, a café and all the shops anyone could possibly need. And there were kids of all ages everywhere. It wasn't long before Tommy was running with a crowd of boys, playing football, hide and seek and all the games it had been difficult to play in the confines of the busy Glasgow streets. There were fights, too, and this was where Tommy's reputation began to flourish.

There was a local boy called Stevie Larch who terrorised all of the other kids. He was two feet taller than everyone else and built like a brick shithouse despite his young age. Nobody dared challenge him when he decided he was going to spoil everyone's fun by kicking the ball away or cutting down the rope swing that hung from every second tree. If anyone complained, his favourite way of dealing with it was to push the aggressor over and simply fall on top of them. His bulk would squeeze the air out of his victim, leaving them choking for a breath and incapable of giving any kind of resistance. One day, a group of boys, including Tommy, were playing kick the can in the car park behind the Square when

Stevie appeared and stomped on the can, flattening it and making it useless for the purposes of the game.

"Fuck off Larch, ya big mongol."

The boy who had reacted and made the brave move to voice his disgruntlement realised immediately that he had maybe overstepped the mark.

"What did you fucking say?" Larch loomed tall over the smaller boy, his shadow dwarfing him. Before the boy could offer an apology, Larch pushed him with both hands, easily forcing him to the ground. He was about to follow up with his trademark move of flopping down on top of the boy when Tommy spoke.

"He said, 'Fuck off Larch, ya big fucking mongol'."

Larch stopped and turned to face Tommy, his eyebrows raised in surprise that someone was daring to challenge his authority. All the other boys took a step back, just as surprised as Larch was, leaving Tommy to face the giant on his own. Larch let out a wee giggle.

"Have you got a fucking death wish, Loy?"

"Aye, ah wish you were fucking dead, ya ugly big fanny." Tommy was standing with his hands by his side, not flinching an inch.

"Ya cheeky wee fucker..." Larch started to move towards Tommy, but before he had got one step closer, Tommy jumped up and swung his right hand round to smash a concealed half brick off the side of his massive head. Blood started to pour from the wound immediately. There was an audible intake of breath from all the boys watching and Larch stopped in his tracks, a look of confusion on his face as to what was happening. Tommy didn't wait. He followed up the initial blow with two more rapid strikes, the second one catching Larch full on the face, spreading his bulbous nose. Tommy quickly grabbed Larch by the hair and pulled him down to the ground, kicking him repeatedly in the head and body until there was no more resistance. Eventually, Tommy leaned down and lifted the prostrate giant's head up by the hair. He put his face as close to Larch's as he could without getting blood on himself and shouted:

"If I see you round here again, I'll fucking kill you."

Tommy threw Larch's head back to the ground and kicked him full on the face, causing a tooth to come flying out with a fresh spurt of blood. Tommy turned to the group of boys, all open-mouthed and in shock.

"Let's go."

Tommy walked away and every one of the other boys followed him. From that day, the boys would follow Tommy wherever he went. His legendary status was confirmed.

As the fights became more regular and the violence fiercer, Tommy and his friends were christened The Woodie Boys, later shortened to just The Woodie when they had outgrown the 'boys' part.

There were rival gangs from other areas of the town, but Tommy and his crew were unparalleled in the ferocity of the violence, with Tommy always front and centre when anything kicked off. The Olympia bowling alley in the centre of town was used as a battleground and when it converted into a ballroom, attracting big names like The Kinks and The Small Faces, the skirmishes often got more attention than the advertised events. It was at The Olympia that Tommy met Mary. Mary was young and easily impressed with Tommy's standing amongst his peers. When he asked her out, all her friends were jealous, and she enjoyed the respect her peers bestowed on her. They were both seventeen and within six months, Mary was pregnant. Tommy did the 'right thing' and they married, moving into a council flat in Geddes Hill, a short hop from The Calderwood Square. Agnes hoped marrying Mary and becoming a dad would help Tommy settle, but his change in circumstances domestically did nothing to temper his ways.

He was already robbing the shops below his old flat at The Square and then offering protection to the shopkeepers to stop the burglaries happening. The shopkeepers knew Tommy was the one behind the robberies in the first place, but none of them dared challenge him about it. It was easier to pay him five pounds a week to keep him from stealing from them, and if anyone else was daft enough to steal from them or threaten them once they were under his protection, Tommy always made sure retribution was swift and severe. It wasn't long before he targeted the many small factories in the town too. Tommy would always wonder why anyone would want to get a job in one of the factories when it was much more profitable to rob them all. The same protection was offered to the factory bosses that the shopkeepers received, and they were happy to pay. Any who chose not to accept the offer of protection would find windows smashed, stock disappearing and in some cases, nobody willing to work for them until Tommy received his weekly stipend. Money was flowing in, and Tommy used it to create a life for him and his family. Mary never asked where the money came from, perhaps out of naivety, or maybe because she was too busy creating a loving home.

Mary had a second child two years later, another boy, and everything was running smoothly for Tommy. Although Tommy was happy to be the loyal family man in public, women were throwing themselves at him and he enjoyed it to the limit. There were girlfriends all over town and Mary never complained about him disappearing for days on end, as long as there was food on the table and the flat was kitted out with everything she needed. Every now and then there would be some friction in the marriage, but a gentle backhander was usually enough to shut her up until the next time. By 1970, Tommy was at his violent peak. Money came and went, but it was plentiful. He had started lending cash to local residents who preferred his low-interest rates to those of the banks. The only downside was that the money had to be repaid on time or the consequences were unthinkable. If Tommy was honest, he often lent money to people he knew had no chance of making the repayments, so he could use them as an example to others as to what would happen if you didn't pay up. Slashings, broken bones and general beatings were handed out on a regular basis, and it was Tommy's favourite part of the job. He was spending less time with Mary now. The boys were six and eight and Tommy had no interest in them whatsoever. Kids got in the way. Eventually, Tommy had enough of Mary's moaning and when she told him not to come back after he had dished out a heavy beating, he was happy to comply. He was ready to take his criminal career to a new level, and a young family would only get in the way.

The only gang who could rival Tommy were the guys who ran Blantyre. Blantyre was a small town a couple of miles down the road from East Kilbride. It was a tough, working-class place and the people resented the money East Kilbride attracted as a 'New Town'. Jobs were scarce in Blantyre while East Kilbride flourished, but in criminal terms, the Blantyre boys were streets ahead. There had been many showdowns between the youths of the towns over the years, with stabbings and severe doings handed out on both sides. Tommy liked nothing more than getting one over the Blantyre boys. He got involved with a few girls from Blantyre, just to wind up the locals, and recently he had tipped off the police about a robbery he had heard about from a Blantyre girl, resulting in a few of the major players from the town going down for a while. They had no idea Tommy had stitched them up.

Tommy's new idea was drugs. Smoking pot was becoming a major pastime for the youth, encouraged by the stories of peace and love all over the news the past few years. The problem Tommy had was he didn't have a contact, a way in. He had no idea where to go to find a supplier. When he found out that Sammy Graham, one of the Blantyre crew Tommy had grown up fighting as a teenager, was supplying the few people in East Kilbride already enjoying their own Summer of Love, Tommy knew he would need to bury the hatchet with his rivals and go into partnership with them. Tommy had been seeing Sammy's sister, who lived in East Kilbride, off and on for years, even since before he married Mary, so he got her to reach out to Sammy and arrange a meet to discuss a partnership. A couple of weeks later, Tommy got a phone call.

"Is that Loy?"

"Who's this?"

"Sammy will see you tonight. Crossbaskets at seven. Come on your own. If anyone else is with you, we'll see them and the meeting's off."

Tommy didn't recognise the voice. "Who is this?" The line went dead.

Tommy was delighted. Sammy Graham was a prick, and all the cloak and dagger stuff was typical of him, but Tommy knew he would need to bite his tongue until he got his foot in the door. Once he had contact with the main man, he could get rid of Sammy and run the organisation himself. Tommy would need to treat Sammy with respect for now.

Tommy got some kids to wash his car before he headed down for the meeting. He wanted his Ford Capri to be sparkling when he met with the Blantyre lot, letting them know how well he was doing without rubbing their noses in it. First impressions were important, and Tommy wanted the suppliers to know they were dealing with someone important. He didn't imagine the main man would be there for the first meeting, but you never knew. Tommy put his suit on and shined his shoes. He had never been for a job interview before, but he reckoned this would be as close as he would ever come. He resisted the urge to get there early and drove down Stoneymeadow Road to Crossbaskets, arriving dead on 7pm. Tommy loved driving on Stoneymeadow Road. The narrow road, with tight bends and dips, gave him the opportunity to put his foot down and show off his prowess at the wheel. There were no streetlights, adding to the danger, but he slowed down a few bends before the rendezvous point, so as not to come across as a boy racer. A clapped-out Vauxhall Viva was sitting by the side of the road when he arrived. Tommy smiled to himself, happy that he had got the Capri washed. You couldn't hide class.

Two men got out of the Viva as Tommy parked in front of them. They both had Crombie coats on and one of them was wearing a trilby hat. The one on the left was huge, well over six foot and the other was much smaller, but stocky. Tommy didn't recognise either of them, so his hopes of meeting the main man rose as he jumped out of his car and greeted them.

"How you doing?" Tommy held his hand out to shake but withdrew it when none was offered in return.

"Are you Tommy Loy?" The smaller of the two men spoke.

"Aye. Is Sammy joining us?" Tommy hoped the answer would be no.

Both men ignored his question. The tall one stepped forward. "I'll need to search you."

"What for?" Tommy wasn't used to being under suspicion.

"Weapons."

The tall one started patting Tommy down. He finished and nodded to the smaller man.

"I don't bring a weapon to a business meeting." Tommy smiled, hoping to break the tension he could feel in the air.

"You fucking should have."

The voice behind Tommy belonged to Sammy Graham. Tommy spun round, but as he did, the tall guy grabbed him from behind, pinning his arms behind his back. Simultaneously, Sammy punched Tommy in the face, the knuckleduster he was wearing breaking his nose. Tommy's legs buckled, but the goon pinning his arms held him up. Sammy punched Tommy twice more, once on the side of the head and the second in the solar plexus, knocking the wind out of Tommy's lungs. Sammy paused long enough to be sure that Tommy was still conscious.

"Did you really think you could wander down here and take over my business and I would just roll over and let you tickle my arse?" Sammy wasn't angry. There was control in his voice. Tommy spat out a mouthful of blood before he could reply.

"I don't want to take over, ya daft cunt. I just want to help you expand." Tommy felt that some of his teeth were loose, but so far none of them had fallen out.

"Bollocks. You can't stand to see anyone do well apart from yourself. You're a fucking rat, Loy." Sammy punched Tommy again. "You sold out the boys doing that linoleum factory."

"What are you talking about?" Tommy felt his world collapse. Dealing with the police had been a gamble, but it was one he had been willing to take.

"Deny it all you like, rat. You think I don't have coppers in my pocket? I heard it straight from the horse's mouth. You tipped them off." Sammy jabbed his finger in Tommy's face.

Tommy cursed the police. You couldn't trust anyone.

"They were on my patch. I don't come robbing down here. They should have stayed away or at least let me know what they were doing. I've got a reputation to keep." Tommy's only hope now was to brazen it out, take the beating and get his revenge at a later date.

"Your patch? You don't come down here because you wouldn't fucking dare, but you fuck my sister, you slap her around and treat her like shit. You think I'm just going to sit back and let that go? I've got a reputation to keep too, and mine is bigger than yours." Sammy couldn't hide his anger when he spoke about his sister.

"She's a fucking slag." Tommy wasn't going to be scared. He would go down with a fight, even if he was struggling to stand up. Sammy punched Tommy again. "You'd better kill me, Sammy, because if you don't, I'm coming for you and when I find you..."

Tommy didn't get to finish his sentence. Sammy grabbed Tommy by the hair and lifted his head up to expose his neck. "What a good fucking idea." Sammy pulled a blade from his coat pocket and stuck it in Tommy's throat, drawing it all the way across until the head was almost severed completely. Tommy's dead body dropped to the ground, blood spreading across the road.

"Fuck's sake, Sammy. You've killed the prick." The biggest goon's eyes were almost popping out of his head. Sammy threw the knife into the bushes at the side of the road.

"Who gives a fuck?"

Sammy and his two cohorts got into the Viva and drove off, leaving Tommy dead at the side of the road.

CHAPTER TWO

1979

BILLY LOY HEARD the alarm clock going off in his mum's bedroom. The bedrooms were at opposite ends of the flat but at 3.45am the sound had no problem filling the air. Billy wondered if the Nicol family who lived downstairs would hear it and complain about the noise. They complained about noise a lot.

The bedroom stank of the stale booze coming from his brother Brian's every snore. The alarm was not going to trouble his slumber, even though he lay only two feet away from Billy in their shared room. Brian, 17, was two years older than Billy, the man of the house since their dad had died when they were both very young. Billy didn't really remember his dad but there were lots of pictures and plenty of stories he had heard over the years which gave him the feeling that he knew him as well as he wanted to. In Billy's mind his dad had been a bit of a flawed character, a ducker and diver, but essentially a good guy.

Billy heard his mum go into the kitchen, put the kettle on and pad down the hall before giving a gentle knock on his bedroom door. Billy sat up in his bed as his mum entered.

"Are you up, son?"

"Aye."

"Okay, do you want some tea before you go? It'll be cold out there..."

Billy laughed. It was the middle of the night in December. It was cold in the bedroom, never mind outside. The condensation on the wooden-framed window was frozen solid and he could see his mum's breath as she spoke.

"Do you think?"

"Are you sure you want to do this, son? It's awful early and you really don't need to. You'll be knackered going to school."

Billy knew his mum meant well but the truth was, he wanted

to have his own money. Brian was a labourer at the Rolls-Royce factory, but he didn't earn a lot of money. O Levels had been beyond Brian at school, so an apprenticeship was never on the cards. Billy didn't know how much his brother passed to his mum from his weekly wage packet but the number of times he was out drinking with his pals couldn't leave much. The bedroom was littered with scrunchedup, losing betting slips, some of which were for amounts Billy could only imagine. Billy had to earn his keep if he wanted to do all the things he had planned, and he didn't want to rely on handouts from his single mum.

"I'll be fine, mum. Loads of guys at school do the milk and none of them are knackered. I'll be home by sixish so I can go back to bed if I need to." Billy hoped a reassuring smile would put her mind at rest.

"Well, okay. If you're sure. But if you don't like it, just say. You didn't like the paper round because it was so early..."

That wasn't completely true. Billy hadn't minded the paper round he did for only two weeks in the summer, and it certainly wasn't the getting up early bit that had made him stop. The problem was the wages he earned. Two pounds a week plus tips had sounded fair until he realised he was never going to get any tips. Very few of the people he delivered to were awake when he was at their door, so the chance of getting a tip was rare. When he pointed this out to Mr Conti, who ran the newsagents, he was given short shrift. Billy asked the other paper boys how much they got in tips and none of them got any. Except at Christmas. Christmas was when you made your money as a paper boy, but Billy wasn't willing to get up early seven days a week, humph a heavy bag around for two hours for two pounds a week and the promise of a Christmas bonus. Billy already delivered the *Evening Times* after school but at least people were awake when he delivered that, so he collected regular tips which brought his money up to £2.50 a week. It was a thin newspaper and he only had thirty customers, so it barely took him half an hour to finish the round. And there wasn't a Sunday edition, so he managed to have a day off.

Delivering milk was the best job you could get as a schoolboy in 1979. £5.50 a week plus tips. One of the guys from school, Andy, said you could get as much as a fiver in tips every week when collecting the money on a Friday night. Andy had been on the same milk float for a year now and let Billy know that a space had come up if he wanted it. Billy knew it was hard work, but that didn't worry him. Hard work was worth it if the money was right, and Billy reckoned between delivering the milk and the *Evening Times*, he could make £10 to £15 a week. Even after giving his mum half, he would still have enough money to make life a bit more comfortable.

"Don't worry, Mum. This is much better than the paper round."

"Okay. Come on then, up you get and get plenty of layers on. I'll make some tea."

Billy pulled back the bed covers and smiled again. He was fully dressed already.

"Ta-DAH!"

Billy's mum laughed as she left the bedroom. "Well, you're certainly keen enough, son."

Billy wondered if 'keen' was the right word, but the excitement coursing through him was new and he hadn't slept a wink, so there was certainly something going on. Margaret Thatcher had been Prime Minister for six months or so now and she was always on the telly saying that the good times were just around the corner. 1980 was going to be the year of jobs apparently, just in time for Billy to leave school and pick up a good one. In the meantime, delivering milk to the good people of East Kilbride would keep things ticking over.

Billy looked at himself in the mirror to make sure he didn't look tired. His blue eyes were crystal-clear and the spot he had squeezed on his chin the other day was clearing up nicely. He gave himself a smile and flattened his auburn hair as best he could without putting water on it. He planned on wearing a woollen hat, so it didn't matter, but Billy liked to look good.

"Tea's ready." The call from the kitchen snapped Billy out of his self-admiration. He gave himself a final smile and padded down the hall to be fussed over a bit more.

Mary closed the front door quietly as Billy set off. She never had to worry about Billy. He was quite a serious laddie, but he was clever, and he seemed to know his own mind already. Brian was already beginning to show signs of being a bit of a dreamer, but Mary was happy with the way her boys were turning out, considering what they had been through. Mary struggled with the demands of being a single parent. She would do anything for her boys, and tried to make sure they wanted for nothing, but it was difficult. She was both mother and father to them after their dad died, making sure there was love and discipline in equal quantities. Not that Tommy would have been any good when it came to showing love or handing out discipline. He had been handy with his fists, but it took more than that to keep boys in check without turning them into little monsters.

Mary could see their father in both the boys. The serious, level head of Billy and the lack of direction or motivation of Brian were the exact characteristics Tommy had shown. He was a good provider, but it was always best not to know exactly how he was providing what he did. He was a chancer of the highest order. He would come home with boxes of stuff to sell. Hats, coats, bread bins, tins of paint, anything he could get his hands on. He even came home with a live pig once. He stored it in the shed but had to move it on when Mrs Nicol threatened to call the police if he didn't stop it squealing. Those were the funny stories she told the boys about. When they were wee and wouldn't go to sleep, she would tell them about innocent adventures featuring Tommy as the hero. Mary wasn't telling them many lies; she was just embellishing the character of the father the boys had barely known when he died. There were too many other stories she couldn't tell them, but she was sure there were plenty of people in the town who wouldn't be slow in letting them slip into conversation when the boys were older. Some of the stories were legendary in East Kilbride. And every tale had grown legs in the years since he died.

Mary could sometimes sense others in the street or at the shops whispering as she walked past.

"That's Tommy Loy's missus."

Tommy had been dead nine years and it still happened at least once a week. Mary ignored it every time. All of Tommy's friends who had assured her they would see her right after the funeral had disappeared within a week, so Mary knew exactly where she stood and that was on her own with two small kids to look after. The truth was, Tommy hadn't had any real friends, just people who feared him and others who were indebted to him in some way. Mary quickly put her old life with Tommy to one side and moved on. She had to find work. Tommy had never let her get a job before, so she didn't have experience doing anything other than cleaning, the one thing she was an expert at.

She applied to the library and got the job cleaning. Within weeks she was cleaning the dentist's and the lawyer's office in the same block. It wasn't long until the manager of the pub next door asked if she could do the cleaning there too. She was out the door at 5am every day to do the office and the dentists, popping home at 8am to get the boys' breakfast and see them off to school before heading back to clean the library. Only then did she take a break to drink a cup of tea from her flask before heading to the pub. By 11am she had finished and headed home to clean her own house with the same vigour she showed in her job before it was time to welcome the boys home from school. She was good at it, and she earned a good wage. There were always a few shifts behind the bar available in the pub if she needed money for something in particular. She was doing okay, considering.

Now that Brian was working and Billy was nearing the end of school, Mary had started to dream about having a life again. Time was ticking and she got lonely. Friends were hard to keep when you had the legacy of being Tommy Loy's missus, but she was only in her mid-thirties and had plenty of life left in her yet. Mary had tried the other pursuits of her peers, but bingo held no interest for her, and when Mrs McGraw in the next block of flats had suggested lawn bowls, it had taken all of her self-control not to flatten the old sow. Just because Mary was a widow, she wasn't ready to start acting like a pensioner.

Every now and then she would let herself think about the notion of settling down again. She was still a good-looking woman who turned heads; she would see it happening until someone whispered in the ear of an admirer to let them know they were handling fire when it came to the Loys. She had managed a couple of dates with one of the young dentists, but he stopped calling when he found out about Tommy. He claimed it was because he wasn't keen on taking on somebody else's kids, but Mary knew the real reason. He had been scared off by a ghost. Nine years he was gone, but Tommy Loy was still ruining her life from beyond the grave.

CHAPTER THREE

Shagger

"WHAT'S THIS NEW guy called?"

"Billy."

Hugh Davidson expertly manoeuvred his electric milk float up to the dairy loading bay. He was 24 years old and good-looking in a kind of third-tier footballer kind of way. His centre-parted ginger hair had a shine to it that showed he looked after his appearance, even if it may not be immediately apparent in the dark at four in the morning. The dairy boilersuit didn't flatter but years of carting crates of milk around had toned his muscles to make it bulge in the right areas.

"Billy what?"

"Loy."

Hugh looked at Andy with a frown.

"Loy? Is he anything to do with Tommy Loy?"

"I don't know…"

Hugh stopped the float perfectly in line with the loading bay. He turned round and looked at Andy. "Well, that's the kind of thing you should be sure about before you say he can work on the float."

"Tommy Loy was his dad." Mark was sitting in the cab, wrapped up in his coat with his bobble hat down over his eyes.

Hugh turned sharply to Andy.

"You're bringing Tommy Loy's boy onto my float? Ah'm not sure about that." Hugh shook his head.

Andy didn't know what to say. He looked to Mark for support.

"He's nothing like his Da." Mark was barely awake.

"How do you know what his Da was like?" Andy didn't even realise that Mark knew who Billy was.

"Everyone knows about Tommy Loy. Apart from you, apparently…" Mark yawned and hugged himself against the cold.

"I know what his Da was like! He was a fucking nutter! Is this boy a nutter? Cos if he's a nutter he can get a job on Oggy's float or better still, he can fuck off to Kojak's. We're lovers, no' fighters on this float..." Hugh was struggling to hide his discomfort.

"He's no' a nutter." Andy wasn't just defending his friend, it was true. Billy wouldn't harm a fly.

"Right, well, the first week is a trial. Make sure he knows that..." Hugh moved to get out of the cab. "Come on, the float's no' gonnae load itself, ya lazy wee pricks."

There was an art to loading the crates of milk onto the milk float. You had to make sure there was room for the boys to work, two on the front and the other two on the tailboard at the back. Each boy started with two empty crates close to where they stood, with the full crates piled up behind but within easy reach. Everybody had their individual customers, and it was their job to load the empty crates with the required amount of milk for each foray away from the float. The whole thing was planned with precision and timing was everything. If a boy was slow delivering to one street and didn't make it to the desired pickup point before the float got there, it could knock the whole process off course. The boys had to be fit because they were expected to run, carrying up to 40 pints of milk in crates at a time, before jumping back on and making sure they were appropriately stocked for the next drop-off. They had to make sure the empty bottles they had collected from the doors were stacked away, making sure the full crates were always to hand. You had to be organised. After a week, the boys were expected to know what every customer wanted each day on their run; and after a month, they would know the numbers and routes for every run on the float. It always sounded daunting to people starting the job, but it was amazing how quickly they picked it up. When you considered that the float very rarely came to an absolute halt throughout the process, the boys had to catch on quick how to jump off and on, laden with milk crates. Broken bottles came out of your wages, so the quicker you learned the better it was for everyone.

East Kilbride had two dairies serving the town, Wisemans and Hamiltons. The rivalry between the float drivers could be fierce but it rarely spilled over into how the boys treated each other. They all played football, went to school and generally hung about together so there was no rivalry on their part. Some of the drivers tried to instil some kind of loyalty among the boys, but the truth was they were only interested in getting paid. On the other hand, the competition between the drivers was real. And not just because of the milk. There was pride in completing your round the fastest, having the most customers, even having the best footballers on your float. There was a pecking order that was computed who knows how by who knows who. Hugh had his own version of the pecking order just like all the other drivers. If you asked him, he was the fastest. His crew were a good bunch of boys, good at football but not as good as the boys on old Bunnet's float. Two of his boys were playing on S Forms at Motherwell FC and even though Motherwell were shit, it was better than any other boy was doing. Okay, Mark on Hugh's float had a trial for Clyde once, but nobody wanted to play for Clyde, for fuck's sake. Hugh's dead gran could get a game for them. No, Hugh had a category all of his own for the pecking order. His float was the best looking. Obviously, he brought the average up quite high himself, but Mark was quite handsome when he ever put his hood down and Andy wasn't a complete mong. Hugh had to admit Johnny was a weird-looking character. Johnny's nickname was Sandy because he looked a bit like Sandy Shaw, and not in a good way. But he was a grafter, and he knew every part of the round like the back of his hand, so his peculiar looks were tolerated. Hugh hoped he would flourish and become a swan, just as he had at around the same age.

And now he was sitting outside a flat on Geddes Hill waiting on Billy Loy to show his face. It wouldn't matter what he looked like; he was Tommy Loy's boy, so that would be enough to make plenty of women go weak at the knees. Women loved a bad boy which meant Oggy, who drove the next route to Hugh, and Kojak, who did the Hamiltons route around the same area, had ranked pretty high in the success with women category, even though Kojak was as smooth as a billiard ball because of alopecia. He was a fucking nutter who was involved in all sorts, maybe drugs, and Hugh was pretty sure that Oggy took protection money from the prostitutes who hung around the bus station, and he was mental too. But none of them did as well as Hugh with the ladies. At least that was the impression everyone had of him, so who was he to say any different?

Hugh watched Billy come out of the flat. He had too many

clothes on. It was always the same: the mums would dress the boys like they were heading to the North Pole and within 20 minutes of work the layers would be peeled off before they sweated away to a greasy spot. He would learn that as his first lesson. Billy walked over to the float.

"Alright, Billy?" Andy was standing on the back step of the float, getting his first few orders organised so he would be ready for the first street.

"Aye."

Billy didn't know where to go. You could enter the cab of the float from both sides, but Mark and Johnny were already in there. Andy motioned to Billy to join him on the back.

"No, the newbie's in the cab for the first week at least." Hugh didn't turn round to look at the boys when he spoke.

"Who's going on the back, then?" Mark sounded like he already knew the answer.

"You. And don't start fucking complaining about it."

Mark knew better but he still gave his best teenage pout as he jumped off and moved round to the back of the float to join Andy.

"It's better at the back anyway." Andy believed it to be true.

"Fuck up, Puppet." Mark quite enjoyed working on the back too, but he wasn't going to show it.

"Come on son, jump on, we're ten minutes down already." Hugh finally turned round and looked at Billy. He was a good-looking boy. If his trial went well, and depending on him not being a nutter, having him on the float would increase the handsome quota.

Billy jumped on and Hugh immediately set off, putting Billy off balance for a second.

"Have you done the milk on any other float?" Hugh was watching the road again.

"No but Andy told me all about it." Billy was holding onto the rail with both hands but let go when he realised the other boys were balancing themselves unaided.

"Aye, well, ah wouldnae listen to what he says, he's the slowest on the float." Hugh looked in the mirror to make sure his barbed comment registered with Andy in the hope it would speed him up a bit. "You work with Sandy this morning. He'll show you what to do. You're Billy? Have you got a nickname?"

"No."

"Well, we'll need to give you a nickname."

"Why?" Billy didn't follow the reasoning.

"Because everyone who works on the milk gets a nickname. It's tradition." Hugh looked at Billy again, wondering what innovative name he could come up with.

"Colin and Kev on Bunnet's float don't have nicknames." Mark was still pretending to be in a huff.

"That's because Bunnet's an old arse." Hugh liked Bunnet, but he was so old compared to everyone else and he never mixed with the other drivers. Hugh had heard Oggy saying he didn't trust Bunnet because he wasn't one of the lads and it was dangerous to be considered untrustworthy by guys like that.

"Your pal back there is Puppet, not just because he's called Andy like Andy Pandy, but because he runs like a fucking flowerpot man." Hugh smiled in the mirror at Andy on the back step.

"Fuck off." Andy took it in good fun and laughed as he swore.

"Mark is called Birthy, because he's a birthmark." Hugh was proud of the clever reasoning he had used to christen the boys on his float.

"That doesn't even make sense." Mark didn't share Andy's good humour over the nicknames.

"And Sandy is Sandy just because it suits him." Hugh didn't know if the boy knew the real reason for his nickname, but he was sure he didn't care.

Billy looked at Sandy, expecting a response but he was concentrating on moving milk bottles from one crate to another. Billy wasn't sure if he was even listening.

"Ah'm no' sure I want a nickname." Billy was still standing watching Sandy work.

"Aye well, if you last the week and pass the trial, we'll see about that. Right, boys, two minutes until the first drop. You'd better all be fucking ready." Hugh knew when to stop the joking and get the graft under way.

"What's your nickname?" Billy shouted over his shoulder to Hugh, not taking his eyes off what Sandy was doing.

"Shug!" As Hugh spoke, a Hamiltons milk float flew past them. Kojak and his motley crew were all giving the finger and catcalling towards their rival float.

"Come on, Shagger! Get that heap of shite out of our way. The people need their milk." The driver made a wanker sign towards Hugh and laughed as he sped past.

Hugh gave a half-smile, which couldn't hide the mix of contempt and fear he always felt when Kojak or Oggy treated him badly in front of the boys.

"Shagger?" Billy couldn't help but laugh.

"Just get fucking ready. Let's go." Hugh didn't slow at all at the first drop off, making it difficult for the boys to jump off with their laden crates. They would have to work hard today now that he was in a bad mood.

CHAPTER FOUR

Oggy

OGGY FUCKING HATED East Kilbride. It was a Scottish new town that was slowly dying after its bright start, but the people hadn't realised it yet. The hordes who lived there thought they were so much better than the people from the surrounding towns because they had a shopping centre. They were that shallow. Oggy lived in Hamilton, just five miles down the road and he preferred the Lanarkshire attitude to life than the pampered self-righteousness of the fabricated society East Kilbride had created for itself. The multitude of factories in East Kilbride that were bursting at the seams in the 1950s and '60s were beginning to slim down considerably, whereas Lanarkshire had the steel works, which gave the towns a glow. The job centre in East Kilbride was doing a roaring trade, but the growing numbers of unemployed engineers being dumped on the scrapheap as the smaller factories struggled to keep up, looked down their noses at the jobs on offer. Lanarkshire folk, on the other hand, went wherever the work was and didn't mind what they were asked to do as long as there was a wage at the end of it. Oggy heard stories about print workers in the *Radio Times* factory going to the dancing when they were on nightshift and people in Rolls Royce deliberately going slow because the unions had such a grip on the bosses. That mad cow Thatcher looked like she couldn't wait for a fight with the unions, who had held the whole country to ransom for most of the 'seventies. She would sort them out and make it more difficult for the lazy fuckers to earn a living. Oggy wasn't interested in politics. He was only interested in looking after number one, and earning money was the only thing he focused on. And he was willing to work for it. Nobody should be getting anything for nothing.

Oggy always loaded his own float in the morning. He knew some people, like Shagger, had the boys do it, but Oggy wanted it done properly and he knew how to do it properly. It was a good work-out, too. He wasn't daft enough to think he was blessed with movie star looks but nobody could say he wasn't fit, and one thing Oggy had to be was fit. If he didn't keep his physique impressive, he knew he would be open to attack. Nobody was going to shit themselves at the prospect of a beating from their pimp if the pimp was a toothless wee wimp. Muscles were good when you wanted someone to do something they didn't really want to do.

It was being out and about at an ungodly hour which led to Oggy becoming a pimp. On his way up to EK one morning, Oggy had witnessed a guy assault a woman just across from the bus station. Without thinking, he had slammed his brakes on and jumped out of the car even though he had no idea what he was going to do.

"Hoy ya cunt, what the fuck are you doing?" Oggy walked straight to the man bent over the woman.

The man looked up in surprise, as if he hadn't noticed the car stopping and was only aware of Oggy's presence when he spoke. Oggy didn't pause. In one move, he reached the man and grabbed him by the chest of his shirt, pushing him back and away from the woman on the ground.

"Do ye fancy yer chances against somebody a bit bigger, ya prick?" Oggy sprayed saliva into the man's face.

"Fuck off, son, she's a hooker." The man spoke as if it was all a big misunderstanding. He was clearly drunk.

"Ah couldn't care less what she is, you don't hit a fucking woman." Oggy wasn't backing down.

"She was trying to rob me!" The man began to push back a bit but knew immediately he was never going to win with a show of strength against Oggy.

"I was not robbing him." The woman had got up onto her knees and was spitting blood.

"Listen son, ah thought ah had just landed lucky on my way home and then she starts demanding money off me! Ah thought she was going to attack me! Ah just pushed her away and she fell." The smell of cheap whisky on the drunk's breath made Oggy hold him at arm's length away from him. He looked over to the woman without letting go of the man. She was on her feet now.

"What have you got to say?" Oggy wasn't sure what to do next; the adrenalin beginning to fade.

"He's right, I'm a hooker, but he knew exactly what he was doing. He's never away from here. None of the girls like him but I take his money the same I do all of them. Tonight, he decided he wasn't going to pay any more. He fancies himself as a pimp, but he's not got the bollocks."

"Ya lying bitch..." The man made a lunge towards the woman, nearly taking Oggy by surprise. The lunge wasn't strong enough to break Oggy's grip.

"Are you okay? Do you want me to get the police?" Oggy couldn't stop looking at the woman. He now noticed the short skirt, high heels and the leopardskin coat but she exuded class in some kind of scummy way. She laughed.

"Fuck no, don't call the cops. They'll more likely nick me and give me a slap on the way to the station than they will arrest that fucker."

"What do you want me to do then?" Oggy felt a bit daft standing in the road holding on to the guy now that things had calmed down.

"Ah'll take a lift up the road if you're going my way. He was the last one for the night anyway. I'm knackered." The woman smiled, licking the blood on her teeth away with her tongue. Despite that, she was attractive.

Oggy couldn't believe how casual she was. This obviously wasn't the first time she had been beaten up in the street by an angry punter.

"Aye, fuck off to your hovel..." The guy wasn't fully backing down.

Oggy looked at the man, then back to the woman.

"So does he still owe you money?"

"He does, but I'm sure he doesn't have any on him. He'll be back next week, full of apologies and willing to pay double for his hole. And he will!" She said the last sentence directly to the man.

"Fuck you, you're getting nothing from me..."

Oggy turned quickly back to the man and tightened his grip on the jacket. His face contorted into a menacing snarl.

"Have you got any money?" The man cowed away from Oggy's ferocity.

"No! I don't have anything on me." He tried to scowl in his reply, but it just made him look demented. Oggy slapped the man across the face with his right hand, the left keeping him on his feet as he nearly fell over.

"I'll pay her double next week!" The man realised he was out of his depth and had lost any cockiness he may have had before the slap.

"Are you here tomorrow night?" Oggy looked over his shoulder towards the woman.

"I'm here every night." It was the first time the woman had shown any regret in her persona. Oggy turned back to the man.

"You be here tomorrow night with her money."

"I won't have it until next week..." The man was beginning to sound frightened.

"Tomorrow night! And if she disnae get it, I'm coming for ye." Oggy put his face as close to the man's as the smell allowed.

"Aye alright! Just let me go, mate. It's not worth all the fuss." Oggy pushed the man away roughly.

The woman walked over to him.

"What's your name, love?"

"Oggy."

"Oggy? What kind of name is that?"

"It's a nickname."

"Okay, Oggy, let's be having that lift then. It's cold out here with no knickers on." The woman smiled at Oggy and started walking towards the car. "My name's Brenda, by the way." As she passed the man, she couldn't stop herself from giving him a smug smile.

"Fucking slag." The man mumbled as she drew level. Without missing a step, the woman swung a perfect left hook which caught the man square on the jaw. He crumbled to the ground, moaning. Oggy watched her get into the passenger seat of his car and then back at the man lying prostrate on the ground.

"Come on then, Oggy, we'd best get the fuck away from here in case the cops do turn up." Brenda laughed as she put her seatbelt on.

CHAPTER FIVE

Hands Up

SCHOOL WASN'T A priority for Billy. School wasn't a priority for anyone, even the teachers. If some of the kids came out of it with a couple of O levels it was regarded a success and if anyone went on to do Highers it was unusual. University was a pipedream, even if there were plenty of kids who could have done it if they had the finances or the encouragement. Hunter High School was a production line to supply the factories of East Kilbride with enough people to churn out the various shit they produced. Nothing more, nothing less.

Billy was clever. He had passed all his prelim exams with flying colours, much to the surprise of pretty much everyone, and was going to make sure he studied enough to pass the O levels too. His determination was partly a response to the way he was treated by the teachers. The teachers at Hunter High were a mix of strict disciplinarian types, some of whom had fought in the war and despised the current youths with their long hair and privileged upbringings, and inexperienced nonentities who epitomised the old saying, those who can, do and those who can't, teach. The one thing all the teachers had in common was that they could control the kids with the belt, a thick leather strap with two or three prongs at one end, that they would use to thrash any indiscipline out of any child. At primary school, the belt was rarely used, a rap across the knuckles with a steel ruler usually being enough of a deterrent for any unruly behaviour. Billy had been belted once at primary school when he was wrongly accused of setting fire to the wooden hut in the swing park at the back of the school. His pal Danny got away with it by crying in front of the headmaster when he was accused. Billy was never going to cry, especially over something he didn't do, so he took the punishment of six strikes of the belt, three on each hand. It had hurt really badly, but still Billy didn't cry. That miscarriage of justice was nothing compared to high school.

On his first day, Billy was standing in line with his friends, excitedly looking at their timetables, wondering what delights they were about to experience now and for the next four years, when the deputy headmaster grabbed him by the scruff of the neck and sent him to stand against the wall of the technical block along with a dozen others he had taken an instant dislike to. In front of the whole school, the deputy head walked along the line of boys, lashing each of them twice with his trusty belt, which he kept over his shoulder underneath his jacket, handy to whip out at any given moment. He was a big man and the pain from the strikes was like nothing Billy had ever experienced. A bruise developed on his left wrist almost instantly, showing an imprint of where the two prongs of stiff leather had struck him. The first lesson hadn't even begun yet and already Billy was wondering what the hell was going on. By the end of the first day, Billy had been belted by three different teachers and his hands were red raw. When he complained to his brother that night as they lay in bed about the injustice of it all, he got no sympathy.

"Welcome to Hunter, wee man. Get used to it." Brian laughed at Billy's naivety.

The next morning, when Billy was wondering if it was worth going back, Mary didn't have any sympathy either.

"Why did the deputy belt you?"

"He said I was talking in the lines."

"Were you?"

"We were looking at our timetables." Billy couldn't believe Mary was blind to the injustice.

"Lesson learned, then. Don't talk in the lines and you won't get the belt. The teachers won't belt you for nothing..."

Mary was wrong of course, but Billy learned very quickly there was no point complaining about the abuse. Nobody cared and the teachers knew it, so they could dish out as much violence as they wanted, without anyone blinking an eye.

There were some good teachers. Billy enjoyed English, Art and Speech and Drama and it wasn't a coincidence that he was rarely belted in those classes. Mr Black, the English teacher, was a cool dude who shared a love for David Bowie with Billy and would often sit on the edge of the desk and talk about the genius of 'Hunky Dory' or 'Alladin Sane' when he should have been droning on about *Macbeth*. He even asked Billy if he could borrow his Clash album when he heard him talking about it excitedly, taking it home, taping it and bringing it back the next day.

"I can see what you mean, Billy. It's exciting. You should listen to The Stooges; you'd like them too."

Speech and Drama was the one class you were allowed to have a laugh in. In one lesson, Miss Conway was teaching them about breathing, so she had pushed all the desks to the side of the room and had the whole class lying on the floor. She turned the lights off and had them shut their eyes, breathing in slowly through their nose and out through their mouths. Billy had never felt so relaxed and was in danger of dropping off when a massive fart ripped through the air. Giggles began to spread round the room until the delayed smell overpowered everyone. Miss Conway had to usher them all out into the corridor to get away from the rancid stink, everyone crying with laughter, including her.

Playing truant, or dogging it as it was called at Hunter, was part and parcel of everyone's education. Some started dogging it very early and some never came back, but it wasn't something the teachers kicked up much of a fuss about. Billy dogged it once. Double maths and double French on a Friday afternoon was a terrible way to end the week, so Billy and his mate Danny decided to leave at lunchtime and wander round the shops in the town centre instead. They spent a pleasant afternoon rifling through the records in Impulse, the coolest place to hang out and the only record shop where you could get things other than the shit in the charts. They made sure they were home at their normal time, so nobody suspected a thing. That night while sitting having dinner, the local news was on telly and a report came on about the rise of big shopping centres killing off local shops. They cut to a reporter talking to shoppers.

"Look! That's the town centre!" Mary's excitement got Billy's attention. As they watched the reporter ask his mundane questions, there in the background was Billy and Danny, walking down the street towards Impulse. Billy froze, hoping Mary would be too immersed in the reporter's questions to notice her son and his pal trading jokes in the background. He was out of luck. "What the...?"

There was no time to think of an excuse. Billy couldn't believe neither he nor Danny had noticed the TV camera. He had no idea what a TV camera would look like, but he was pretty sure it was something he should have noticed.

"Right! Bed! Now!"

Mary was livid. She barely spoke to Billy for the whole weekend, her silence being a worse punishment than anything else he could think of. On the Monday, she gave him a note to hand into school saying he had taken unwell on Friday and come home. The shame of him dogging school was too much for her to admit. Billy handed the note to his registration teacher on Monday morning and watched as he read it, then tossed it in the bin. The teacher didn't care, but Mary had shown that she clearly did, so Billy didn't dog it again. He would go and he would try hard, and he would put up with the apathy his efforts received from the teachers, but he was going to leave as soon as he could.

CHAPTER SIX

Fuck Off John

BRENDA HAD ALREADY been working the streets of East Kilbride as a hooker for eight years when she first bumped into Oggy. The town planners had generously designed the place with lots of foot tunnels under the plethora of roundabouts and they had made sure there were plenty of wooded areas for God alone knows what. At night they all became areas where the girls could work away from the cold and rain that seemed to be the permanent weather report for the town. After midnight it was the bus station that attracted them. Apart from the bus drivers being regular and mostly respectable punters, there were always drunks being poured off buses from Glasgow and the various towns in Lanarkshire who were either horny or so drunk they would have no recollection of what they had been up to. The back of the station could be lined with as many as a dozen girls entertaining their punters at any one time. Between midnight and 4am was when the girls made most of their money. And the best bit about the bus station was the hot drinks machine. Although you were sheltered from the worst of the weather at the back of the station, the chicken soup from the drinks machine had saved Brenda many a time when the cold seemed to be eating her from the inside out.

Brenda was a good-looking woman. Voluptuous would be the best way to describe her. Although she was in her thirties, time had been kind and she often passed for much younger. Her natural blonde hair was always immaculate and the piercing green eyes, paired with the leopard skin jacket she always wore when working, gave an aura of sophistication the other girls could only dream of. Brenda preferred to go with the drivers and conductors who worked in the station. They were mostly good guys who just wanted to let off a bit of steam at the end of a long day and you didn't have to stay out in the cold when you went with a driver. The back seat of the 77 bus was much better than banging your bare arse off the bitter corrugated iron of the back wall. Conductors were the most regular punters, a bunch of cocky young guys who had been flirting with the passengers all day without any success and were desperate to sow their wild oats. Brenda was kind to them and made sure they enjoyed themselves so they would always come back. A lot of the girls would deliberately make the sex clumsy or uncomfortable as some kind of penance for the punter because they paid for it. They hated their punters. Brenda had got to the stage where she had enough regulars that she didn't have to get involved with anyone she didn't know. And in most cases, the sex was good with her regulars. She had an old guy called Davy, an ex-driver, who still had the respect of the current drivers so that they would gladly lend him their bus for half an hour to show Brenda a good time, and it was the best sex Brenda ever had. He must have been in his seventies, but his cock was huge, and he definitely knew how to treat a lady. The other girls would tease Brenda about going with a grandad and how she should be careful in case she killed him while on the job, but Brenda knew it was more likely that Davy would finish her off with the going-over he gave her. And he always paid his cash in a small brown wage packet. Brenda felt good about getting a proper wage packet.

There were about twenty girls who worked regularly at the bus station, twice the number there had been a couple of years before when Brenda had graduated from the roundabout tunnels to the relative safety of bus back seats. Drugs had become a major problem in the last couple of years, so more than half of them were junkies. Young girls who seemed to have aged ten years every birthday because of the rubbish they put in their veins. Who knows what had happened to them in the past that they felt obliterating their bodies with that muck was a better option. Brenda had tried to help one or two of them at the start, but she quickly realised there was nothing she could do. They were the only ones who could decide if this life was their best chance, not Brenda. All she could do was keep an eye out for the more vulnerable ones and make sure they were relatively safe. The next biggest demographic was the single mums who couldn't get work and would do anything to support their families. The single mums were the most vulnerable. They didn't want to be there, and they hated the men who used them, but they needed the money. On any night Brenda would find herself consoling at least one girl who had broken down, hating herself for what she was doing. Brenda would always tell them the same thing. Go home and don't come back. Find another way. But they always came back.

The two who didn't fall into the category of single mum or junkie were Brenda and Joan. Joan was an enigma. She was just sex-mad. She couldn't get enough. It was rumoured she had paid a punter to have sex with her when she wasn't getting enough on a quiet night. Joan was married, but she said her husband couldn't keep her fully satisfied, so she came out to find some more and when she realised she could get paid for doing her favourite thing, it was a no-brainer. Joan was there every night and always went home with a smile on her face.

Brenda had been married young, but her husband had been a petty criminal who had been in and out of borstal and prison his whole life. He died when he tried to graduate from petty thief to safe cracker and succeeded in blowing up an entire shop when attempting to open the safe. He was a fucking idiot. Brenda was thirty then, had no job and no friends or family. She noticed girls in the underpasses and wondered if she could cope with the life they led, so she befriended a couple of them, and they taught her everything she had to know. The money on offer seemed out of this world and Brenda enjoyed sex, so why not? Her first punter had been a sweet young guy, about 18, who was a virgin and wanted to have some practice before his upcoming wedding night. He was bashful, handsome and quickly became very competent thanks to Brenda. After that, she had every one of his pals seeking her out for the same tuition and her career took off. One of the lads was still a regular punter ten years on.

Brenda had her first experience of a pimp when she worked the tunnel under the Queensway dual carriageway. His name was Dav Hogg, and he was nothing more than a local tearaway who had put the fear of death into the girls one night, telling them there was a group of vigilantes talking about chasing the girls out of town. For a cut of their takings, Dav promised the girls would be safe under his patronage and he would scare the mob away. There were only four girls working the underpass and the protection fee was one pound each a night so nobody really complained too much, and things were quiet, so it was worth it. The problems started when a vigilante group *did* show up and threatened that if the girls were there the next night, they would be breaking bones. The girls phoned Dav and told him they needed his help. He was never seen again. He had been all mouth and no trousers when it came to it.

The only other pimp had been Joan's hubby, John. He had come down to the bus station to pick Joan up one night and all the girls were standing outside in the pouring rain. The bus station manager tolerated the girls hanging around the station but none of them were allowed to come in and shelter from the elements. John went in and spoke to the manager for ten minutes then came out and called Joan over. He whispered in her ear and Joan went into the bus station. John came over to the girls.

"I've got a wee proposition for you girls. I've had a word with the boss guy in there and he's willing to let youse use the station when the weather's bad." John spoke like he was running for mayor.

"Wow, thanks, John. The weather's always fucking bad..." The girls all laughed.

"What's the proposition, John?" Brenda could tell John wasn't acting out of the kindness of his heart.

"Well, Joan tells me youse have had a few dodgy punters recently, not paying, slapping you around... Maybe it's time you had someone organising things a bit, looking after youse a bit?"

"And you think you're the man for the job?" Brenda was doubtful.

"Well, you all know me. You know I'm not going to rip any of you off..."

"How much, John?" Brenda didn't want to hear his shite; she had heard it all before.

"Ten per cent?"

"Fuck off!" The girls all gave the same reply.

"Tell you what, John, if we can all step in there when the weather is shit and you can keep the few nutters we get at bay, we'll all give you fifty pence a week. That's about a tenner a week when you add it up. What do you think, girls?" Brenda knew it was a done deal.

"Can we go in there now? I'm freezing and the thought of a cup of tea...." The girls would have promised anything to get out of the cold.

"It's a deal and yes you can go in there now and pretty much any time you want. Joan's up there closing the deal as we speak. Just don't make a nuisance of yourselves and if anyone is caught shooting up or bevvying or anything like that then you'll have me to deal with because that's a deal breaker. Is it a deal?" John seemed excited by the prospect of his new business venture.

The girls were already jogging through puddles towards the relative heat of the station.

"Okay John, it's a deal. You'll be paid every Friday night. But if there's any trouble or you don't give us value for money, you'll be gone."

Brenda wasn't sure John would be up to the job, but if it got them some cover from the elements for a while, she was willing to give it a go. John laughed at Brenda's veiled threat but when he looked up and saw the look on her face he quickly stopped. She was serious.

"Of course, I just want to look after you all..." John knew any tough talk would be wasted on Brenda.

Brenda rolled her eyes as she walked towards the comfort of the station and the welcome prospect of a chicken soup out of the drinks machine. She didn't have any confidence that John would be any good if things got tough, but she was willing to give him a go if it meant they could be warm tonight.

He only lasted three weeks. John had a weird compulsion for order and organisation. He was a foreman in one of the printing shops, so he was used to getting his workers in order. He started making the girls stand in certain areas and thought he could decide who went with each punter. He even brought a stopwatch one night to make sure the girls weren't giving more time than was paid for. The final straw for the girls was when he turned up with name tags. Revolution was growing in the ranks when the punters took the action required out of the girls' hands. It was only a Wednesday night, which was always the quietest night of the week, but around thirty punters turned up, all at the same time. But not one of them was looking for business. They stood and smoked nervously, as though they were waiting for something to happen.

"What's going on, lads?" Brenda could see the men were nervous.

"We're protesting." Jim Baird seemed surprised that he was the spokesman.

"What against?"

"John. And all his stupid rules. Look, Brenda, we don't want any trouble, but this is getting ridiculous. I came down on Sunday night for my regular with Sharon and John said I couldn't because it wasn't her turn! He told me to come back in an hour! It's not on." Jim was as angry as anyone had ever seen the quietest, most polite man in East Kilbride.

"You're quite right, Jim. You should let him know." Brenda tried to hide her amusement.

"We've got a banner. Actually, we don't have it to hand. Old Sammo was making it but he's not here yet…" Jim looked over Brenda's shoulder hoping to see Sammo coming over the horizon. Brenda couldn't stifle a laugh.

"You shouldn't laugh, Brenda; we're going on strike until John leaves. This affects you too."

Brenda straightened her face and tried not to smile. The crowd started to part as John made his way over from the bus station.

"What's going on? There's too many of you here. Half of you'll need to fuck off for an hour and come back later." John had a clipboard in his hand.

"Oh, they're not here for business, John, they're on strike. Protesting against you, in fact…" Brenda was enjoying herself.

"What?" John spun round to face the men. "Strike? Are you fucking mental?"

"You've got too many rules and regulations, John. You've killed the vibe of the place. If you don't leave, we're going on strike." Jim kept looking round at the other men to make sure they were still standing behind him.

"The vibe? It's a fucking bus station, ya stupid cunt! Fuck off the lot of you before I start cracking heads." John knew he was never going to be able to do that, but he reckoned bravado would be enough to see off Jim fucking Baird.

Not one of the men moved.

"Can you believe this?" John turned round to Brenda, looking to see if any of the girls were going to back him up.

"Actually, John, I'm surprised you've lasted this long. The lads are right, your rules and regulations are a pain in the arse and if

I see that stopwatch one more time, I'm going to shove it where the sun doesn't shine. We can't earn a wage while the lads are on strike, so I think the best solution would be you standing down."

Brenda didn't flinch at the sight of John's petted lip. He turned to the other girls.

"Do you all think that?" John was almost pleading.

"Yes." Everyone replied in unison.

"Well, okay. I had no idea. I thought I was licking you all into shape..." John looked devastated.

"We're not a production line, John. The punters are looking for a good time, not a shift down the mine. It's time to move on." Brenda was being kind. She didn't mind John, but he was never going to be good in a crisis and his rules were ridiculous. He had to go.

"Okay, okay, I don't want to stay where I'm not wanted. Come on, Joan, we're leaving." John started to leave.

"Naw, *you're* leaving." Joan turned to the punters, all looking on in disbelief at their plan coming to fruition. "Are all you boys looking for yer hole?" The men all shifted their feet and looked at the ground, almost embarrassed that their plan to oust John was working and shy about admitting that they did indeed want their hole. Joan looked back at John. "Aye, I'm going to be here all night seeing to these, lads, so it's probably best if you just shoot up the road and I'll see you in the morning. Bye."

John looked defeated. He stared at the ground and then walked off with all the dignity he could muster, which wasn't a lot when he'd just been sacked by a group of prostitutes after a rebellion held by a bunch of misfit punters. Everyone watched as he walked to his car, got in and drove away without looking back once. Nobody spoke. The silence was broken by the sound of old Sammo wheezing as he ran up to join his comrades.

"Sorry I'm late, lads, the wife widnae let me use one of the bedsheets to make a big banner so I've just done it on this." Sammo held up an A4-size piece of paper with some writing on it. In the yellow gloom of the single streetlight, it was impossible to make out what it said.

"What does it say, Sammo?" Brenda was squinting but still couldn't read it. Sammo looked at his sign and back to Brenda.

"It says 'Fuck Off John'." Sammo read the sign like it was the only thing that could be on it. Everyone laughed.

"Well done, Sammo, it worked. John has fucked off."

The men all cheered, and Joan started to pair them off with the girls. Brenda went into the station for a cup of soup and a pre-arranged bunk-up on the 77 bus.

CHAPTER SEVEN
Dick

AS OGGY TURNED the corner into the first street of the round, he could see Dick already waiting outside his flat. Dick was always ready, and he was a really good grafter so Oggy had no idea why the lad was held with such contempt by everyone. Oggy rarely got involved when the nicknames were being handed out, so he had nothing to do with him being christened Dick.

"Why Dick?" Oggy liked to know the origins because some of the lads had a good sense of humour. Currently, the boys on his float were called 'Jaws', because he looked like Tam Forsyth, the current Glasgow Rangers hardman, 'Goosey', whose real name was Zander hence Goosey Goosey Zander, and Robert got called 'Damned', which was something to do with him being a punk. Dick was Dick.

"Because he's a fucking dick!" All the boys laughed. The disturbing thing was, Dick laughed too. He accepted the name and its origins without batting an eyelid. Oggy had even heard the boy's mother calling him Dick, for fuck's sake. And he always had a smile on his face. Oggy knew the boy had nothing to smile about but he was there every morning, fresh as a daisy and ready to graft, with a happy disposition and a smile. The boys were right, he was a fucking dick.

"Morning, boss!" The smile was there.

Oggy parked the float and got out of the cab. He grabbed a pint of milk and started towards the flats.

"Is your maw up?"

"Aye."

"Right, go and do the set-up for the first bit while I grab a cup of tea with her." None of the other boys would do what Oggy asked of Dick. He would have to take crates full of milk to various drop-off points on the surrounding streets and start delivering the route all on his own.

"Can I take the float down? I'll bring it back before I start." Dick added puppy eyes to the smile as he asked the question. Oggy stopped and turned round to look at him.

"You're getting to be a lazy wee cunt; do you know that? Awright, take it but if it's not here when I get back, you're dead. And if you crash or get stopped by the polis, I'll tell them you stole it and I'll be forced to press charges."

"Cheers, Boss!" Dick jumped into the cab and drove off.

Oggy had no qualms about letting him drive the float. An idiot could drive it, especially around the streets at 4am when nobody else was around. Dick was destined to be a float driver in the future. Every float had one. That weird Sandy Shaw looking kid on Shagger's float was one too. They delivered milk and they were good at it. They were never going to pass any exams, so the dairies would recognise their worth and give them jobs as dairymen or drivers. Kojak was the perfect example of the process. He had started out as a boy on Bunnet's float and then worked at the dairy when he left school and now, he had his own float. Such was the progression of a good milk boy.

Oggy watched Dick drive round the corner then entered the flats. He walked to the first door on the ground floor and walked in without knocking.

Dick loved driving the float. Every opportunity he got, he would jump in the cab and set off. He knew Oggy thought he was daft for doing his job for him, but Dick had no misconceptions about where his future lay. School had already given up on him, and he it, but working on the milk and doing jobs at the dairy gave him a real sense of achievement. This time next year he could go full time at the dairy and start to properly look after his mum. It wasn't her fault they were in the position they were. Because Dick had been born out of wedlock, to a dreadful father he had never known, the extended family had ostracised him and his mother; and without any support, she was never going to cope. Dick would see his cousins every now and then, and they were always kind to him, but his mum had broken the family code and she was never going to be forgiven. The cousins would tolerate Dick, but his mum was persona non gratis as far as the rest of the family went.

What Oggy didn't know was, Dick had ten of his own customers on the first part of the run. They were all one pint a day, and because Oggy was always in blagging cups of tea from his mum instead of doing his job, Dick was the one they went to when they wanted to join the clientele. Dick didn't tell Oggy about them, which meant he pocketed the cash from them each week. Floats were always overstocked in case of breakages or notes left in empties asking for extra pints, so ten pints a day was nothing. Float drivers had their own customers where they pocketed the cash rather than the dairies, so why shouldn't Dick? He was sure he would be a driver eventually, so there was no harm getting his own customers in place just now. Dick smiled as he stocked up the crates and dropped them off for the boys to get started when they turned up. He wasn't as daft as they all thought he was.

"Put the kettle on, Shirley." Oggy shouted down the hall to the living room as he went into the toilet. "Fuck me!" Oggy got a fright as he saw Shirley sitting on the toilet seat, a syringe in her hand and her bare arm exposed to the needle.

"Get fucking out!" Shirley was angry that Oggy had walked in on her. Oggy left her to it, muttering threats under his breath as he walked up the hall to the kitchen.

By the time Shirley came out of the bathroom, Oggy had made and almost finished his tea.

"Fuck's sake, Shirley, your boy's barely left the house and you're sticking that shit in your arm..."

"Mind your own fucking business." Shirley was slurring her words, but she didn't care. She lit a cigarette and sat at the dinner table, defiantly staring Oggy down.

"You are my fucking business and don't get fucking lippy with me." Oggy couldn't stand the junkies on his payroll. In the state she was, Shirley was no match for Oggy and she knew it. She dragged on her cigarette and looked down nervously at the floor. Oggy walked over to stand in front of her.

"What have you got for me?" Shirley reached over and grabbed her purse. She took out two notes and held them up for Oggy to take. She didn't look at him once. "A tenner? A fucking tenner?" Oggy was shouting in her face.

"It was a really quiet night..." Shirley knew her excuse wasn't good enough halfway through saying it.

"Naw, Sunday night is one of the busiest nights of the week! I expect forty, fifty quid. A fucking tenner!" Oggy was raging at Shirley.

"Some of the punters have got a vendetta against me. They tell everyone I'm not worth it..." Shirley couldn't hide the hurt she felt.

"No fucking wonder! Look at the state of you! Your eyes are fucking yellow, and your clothes are a mess and somehow you still manage to be about fifty stone. You should go for the world heavyweight junkie title, there can't be many others with your habit your size. The punters come to you because they're after their hole, not a shot on a bouncy fucking castle." Oggy was being deliberately aggressive, hoping to get a reaction, because the truth was, there was hardly an ounce of fat on Shirley.

Shirley jumped from her seat towards Oggy but he was one step ahead of her and easily side stepped the lunge. He grabbed Shirley by the lapels and drove his head into her face, the headbutt driving the fight out of Shirley. Her eyes were going black before she hit the ground. Oggy bent over Shirley and growled quietly into her ear.

"I want fucking double by the end of the week."

"I can't afford it!" Shirley knew her act of defiance was over.

"You can afford to buy fucking heroin. You can afford to buy fags and booze. You can afford to pay me. None of the other girls give me as much aggro as you do, Shirley. I even give your useless wee twat of a son a job..."

"Leave him out of it." Shirley could always muster a flicker of defiance when it came to her son.

"Aye well, if you can't come up with double by the end of the week, I'll be taking his wages as well as yours." Oggy checked his face in the mirror and then headed off down the hall, shouting back as he went. "Pull yourself together, Shirley!"

Oggy took a deep breath of the cold morning air as he left the flats. Despite what he had said, Shirley wasn't the only junkie he had on the books, and he had similar problems with them too. Oggy knew the others would hear about Shirley getting a slap so hopefully it would make sure they paid on time for a couple of weeks at least. Until the next one needed a slap. Oggy wished all the girls were like Brenda. Brenda was a businesswoman. She had a solid clientele that she trusted, and she never gave him one problem.

The first time he had been forced to give one of the girls a slap, he had sought out Brenda to explain why he had done it but there had been no need. Brenda knew he would have to keep discipline and junkies weren't renowned for following the rules, so some of them would need to be reminded of who was boss. She didn't have a problem with it, or certainly never mentioned it, because she was never going to be on the end of it.

Oggy jumped in the float and set off to pick up the other milk boys while Dick was doing the first part of everyone's run for no extra pay. The boys had named him well.

CHAPTER EIGHT

Kojak

DREW COCHRANE LOVED living in East Kilbride. His parents had moved there when he was three years old and everything about his childhood had been idyllic. Apart from when all his hair fell out. He was thirteen when that happened and, if he was honest, it had changed his life completely. Alopecia was the diagnosis, and the treatment was 'just get on with it'. Getting on with it was made more difficult when everyone Drew met couldn't believe what they were seeing.

"You're bald!"

Drew very quickly got sick of hearing it. They say kids can be cruel but there were very few who were crueller than Drew once he got into his stride.

East Kilbride had been filled with families from the poorer areas of Glasgow and the wonder they must have felt when they got their shiny new houses in their shiny new town must have been something to behold. Drew didn't remember his first three years spent in Easterhouse, but he still saw cousins every now and then and he couldn't help but notice how they treated him as some posh kid when his parents were probably struggling for money just the same as everyone else was. Living in East Kilbride gave you more prestige. The problem was, a lot of the families brought their baggage with them. There was still bigotry and rivalry alive and well in every household. For the kids, this manifested itself in gang warfare.

East Kilbride was divided into local areas. There was Calderwood, East Mains, West Mains, St Leonards, The Murray, Westwood and Greenhills. Every area had its own gang, but the four main ones were The Woodie (Calderwood), The Murray Rebels, The Kilby (Westwood) and The Himshie (Greenhills). The other areas dabbled, as kids do, but the main four were deadly enemies.

Drew was a Calderwood boy, so he had joined The Woodie as soon as he was deemed old enough. Or hard enough. It was only a matter of weeks after his hair fell out when he was invited along to a rendezvous with the older members of The Woodie. The older guys were legendary, with tales of battles fought throughout the years, and Drew was wary of meeting them as he had been told stories of the various things boys had been asked to do as initiation into the gang.

"This is Drew Cochrane. We should be taking him with us to the meeting." Drew was being introduced by Stu Morgan, a recognised Woodie leader who lived in the same street as him.

The group of boys standing outside the chippy at the Calderwood Square looked over at Drew and started sniggering.

"What, is he your fucking grandad? He's bald!"

"Aye his hair fell out but he's some scrapper. He kicked fuck out of Danny Harper last week." The boys raised their eyebrows with dubiety. Danny Harper wasn't associated with any of the gangs directly, but he was well known as a brawler, and he must have been at least three years older than the scrawny bald lad they were looking at now.

"You battered Danny Harper?" There was disbelief in the question.

"Ah did, aye." Drew looked around him at the best The Woodie had on offer and thought he could probably kick fuck out the lot of them too. Danny Harper was bigger and stronger than Drew, but he was soft in comparison. Harper should have won the fight, but it was Drew who was willing to go the extra mile when it came to dishing out violence. Drew never held back when others would.

"Awright Kojak, we're meeting the East Mains team down at the Whirlies tonight. Be here at seven and you can tag along." The boys turned away from Drew and laughed, congratulating themselves on how clever they had been at coming up with a humorous nickname. That night, after Drew had demolished three members of the East Mains gang on his own with a ferocity that most of the boys had never seen before, he was anointed to be the new 'leader off' for the Krazy Young Woodie, whose members were deemed to be the apprentices of the older main gang members. From that day he was a Woodie boy and even now, fifteen years later, although he didn't hang around the shops and fight the other gangs anymore, he had the respect of his peers, and he was legendary amongst the young guys who now ran the streets. The name Kojak had stuck but Drew didn't mind. Kojak was a cool, American tough guy detective. Drew was a shit name.

And so began Kojak's life as a street fighter and petty criminal. He rose quickly in the gang hierarchy due to his nonchalance at going the hard mile when it came to fights. He took a few doings, but they were always administered by groups of people. Nobody ever beat him in a square go, and it was that reputation he thrived on. School was never going to do anything for him and his mum's attempts at getting him involved with the church via the Boy's Brigade was a definite non-starter. He just stopped going to school. It was easy to intercept any letters sent home because both his parents worked, and they didn't give a shit anyway. Drew had been disruptive in class but when he became Kojak, the teachers were glad when he stopped showing up. Not one of them reported it in case someone took any notice and dragged the boy back.

Kojak already knew his future. The minute he started working on Bunnet's milk float, he knew it was the job for him. Instead of going to school, he would go to the dairy after he had finished his round and hang around there. It wasn't long before the dairymen were getting him to do odd jobs for them and finally started putting in a full shift. Kojak was learning the dairy business from the bottom and the more he learned, the more he became convinced that the job of float driver was his ultimate aim. Bunnet had been no help whatsoever. Fair enough, he had given Kojak the job on the float, but he always tried to discourage him from hanging around the dairy.

"Go to school, son, get a few qualifications and then a trade. The dairy life is really tough."

Bunnet didn't understand. Maybe the dairy life was too tough for him, but Kojak knew what he wanted, and he went and got it. He already had his own flat directly across the road from the Square. It only had one bedroom and it was three flights of stairs up, but Kojak was proud as punch when he first got the keys. He bought all his furniture from the 'Saturday Snips' in the *Evening Times*, which kept him happy for a while. When his sofa proved not to have been worth the two quid he paid for it, he decided it was time to move up the dairy ladder and start earning some real money.

Davie Sneddon had been the float driver before Kojak took over. He was in his forties, and he hated the job. He had been a van driver before taking the float on but the organisational skills and ability to deal with the public you required as a float driver were never things he mastered. And he didn't care what anyone thought. He walked around the dairy telling anyone who would listen that he was looking for another job and how much he hated being where he was. Kojak hated him. The guy was doing Kojak's dream job and all he did was moan about it. Kojak was ready to take the float on when Sneddon left but the problem was, it was taking too long to happen. Sneddon was one of those guys who moaned constantly about his job, his pay, how he should be doing something else because this was beneath him, but he never did anything about it. He just fucking moaned.

One Friday night, the dairymen were all in the Salmon Leap pub when Kojak finally snapped. Sneddon was moaning as usual, trotting out the same old pish about how he used to get double what he's getting now when he drove vans.

"I'm telling ye, there's no way I'm taking any shit. They'd better be putting my money up or I'm off."

The other men nodded their agreement that everyone needed a pay rise, but it was with a boredom at hearing the same old story from Sneddon.

"Why don't you just fuck off then?" All eyes turned to Kojak. Nobody engaged Sneddon in conversation about him leaving. The fucker would be talking about it for ages now. Kojak knew the rules.

"Oh, I will. I just need to get something lined up and I'm out of here." Even Sneddon didn't know if he could be bothered going into his usual spiel.

"You say that, but in my experience people who say they need to get something lined up, generally need to stop saying that and get off their arse and actually get something lined up." The men were all staring at Kojak because he had started talking again when Sneddon had given him an out. Sneddon was laughing.

"In your experience?" Sneddon looked round to the other men, mistaking their concerned looks as support. "You're just out of short trousers, ya wee prick. What experience have you got?" The men standing around Sneddon visibly took a step back away from him. Bunnet could see the danger that lay ahead.

"Okay, let's not let this get out of hand." Bunnet moved Sneddon down to the other end of the bar, hoping the other lads would calm Kojak down. Kojak assured everyone he was calm and had no intention of doing anything to Sneddon. He didn't take his eyes off him though. Half an hour later, Kojak announced he was going home, and everyone was glad to see him go. Sneddon waited another twenty minutes to make sure the young tearaway would be well out of the area before he left too. In true Sneddon fashion it would be half an hour after he left that everyone would remember it had been his round.

Sneddon had no idea how some of the guys could drink that much on a Friday night and still manage to get up and do the double run on the Saturday. It took great effort for Sneddon to do it after a couple of pints but some of those lads would be there until closing time. Sneddon's main vice on a Friday night was a fish supper with a pickled egg. The chippy at the Calderwood Square was the best one he had ever been to, and that was saying something because he had tried them all. And he loved the staff, too. They all knew his name and they always looked pleased to see him. It was the highlight of his week, which was sad when he thought about it, but he didn't care.

"Is it a song youse are wanting?" This was how Sneddon entered the chippy every week, arms outstretched and smiling like he was walking on to the stage. The three women behind the counter all smiled and cheered.

"Here he is! How's it going, Davie? Are you after your usual love?" The enthusiasm of the greeting was through gritted teeth, but Sneddon never noticed.

"Yes, thanks, Jean. Another week over and another honest buck earned." The patter could have been scripted. It was the same thing every week.

"It'll be a couple of minutes for fish." Sandra was frying tonight.

"Not a problem. It means I get to spend more time with you lovely ladies." The women maintained their smiles without giving away the discomfort of their skin crawling. Jean got a fright as someone came flying in through the open door and without pause grabbed Sneddon by the coat, punching him full on the nose. Sneddon flew up to the top end of the shop, landing on his arse. The speed of the attack had left him confused as to what had actually happened. When he realised it was Kojak coming at him, Sneddon knew he was in big trouble.

"Fuck off, ya nutter. Girls, call the polis." Despite his tough words, Sneddon was terrified. Kojak kicked him on the side of the head, smashing him against the wall with force. Kojak knew the girls wouldn't be phoning anyone and even if the police showed up later, they would swear neither Sneddon nor Kojak had been near the place all night. The Calderwood Square belonged to Kojak because he was a Woodie legend.

"Time to move on to something new, Sneddon. I'm sick of hearing you slag off the dairy, so as of tonight, you no longer work there. Have you got that?" Kojak punctuated the question with a vicious blow to Sneddon's left ear.

"I'll leave. I'll get something else..." Sneddon was defeated.

"No, you won't leave. You've left. Now." Kojak stood over Sneddon menacingly.

"Ah cannae just leave..." Sneddon was pleading.

"I know, it's terrible news but hey ho. You turn up tomorrow and I'll finish you." There was no doubt that Kojak was serious.

"No way! Who do you think you are?" Sneddon found one last piece of defiance but as he stood to face Kojak, the younger man was already pushing him back. Kojak headbutted Sneddon and dragged him round behind the counter. The three women moved down to the front, well out of harm's way. Kojak grabbed Sneddon's arm and plunged his left hand into the deep frier for two seconds. The scream Sneddon let out could be heard far down the street, but everybody would be deaf if they were asked about it. The smell of burning skin filled the air but was quickly replaced with the usual aroma of salt and vinegar. You could roast a whole man in the frier before it completely replaced the salt and vinegar. Kojak dragged Sneddon back round to the front of the counter and bent down to speak right into his face.

"If you so much as phone the dairy tomorrow then the next time I'll cut your fucking hand off first and batter it, do you understand, you horrible cunt? I'm doing your job now. You can fuck off." Kojak dragged Sneddon out of the shop and delivered a few more kicks to the head to make sure Sneddon had got the message. When he was done, he went back into the chippy.

"I'm sorry you had to see that girls, but he's been slagging everyone off for ages and I just got sick of it. If you give me the mop out here, I'll clean up. He's bled all over your floor." Kojak was calm, like nothing had happened.

"Don't worry, son, we didn't see anything. He was a real pain in the arse." Sandra handed over the mop and bucket while the other women busied themselves making up the cardboard cartons they would need for the fish supper rush when the pub closed. "Do you want a bag of chips?"

"Aye, that would be nice." Kojak smiled as he mopped up Sneddon's blood.

Sneddon didn't come back to the dairy, and nobody spoke about him again. Kojak took over the float the next day and he had been doing it ever since.

CHAPTER NINE

Teenage Vice

FOOTBALL WAS KING in East Kilbride. There were loads of teams for all age groups, along with school teams, boys brigade teams and, most importantly, street teams. Billy's street team was called Red Star and they weren't bad, although none of them were anything special. You had guys like Ian Fenwick, whose nickname was Pele, who played for EK Burgh, the 4th Boys Brigade, the school team and he was on S Forms at Motherwell and even he still played for his street team who were called Blue Hill. It was all the guy did. Billy was sure he wouldn't be good enough for Motherwell, even if he put in the same amount of time but he wasn't that interested.

The good thing about street football was the chaos. It was never eleven-a-side. Everyone who turned up, played. Red Star could muster 28 players if they had to and the average turnout for any game was in the high teens. And if you had 20 players when only 12 of the opponent's team turned up, then that's what happened, 20 would play 12. Nobody moaned about it, they all knew the rules. There were no age groups either. If you were aged 8-16 and you lived in the street, you could play. That's what Billy really enjoyed about the games, watching some of the younger ones who were obviously going to be great players putting defenders nearly twice their age on their arse. In street games, there was no passing or tactics or any of that shit. You got the ball and you headed for goal, trying to beat every player in front of you while your teammates ran alongside shouting for a pass in vain and the defenders would line themselves up to be next to take you on. Scottish football was littered with great dribblers and tough defenders, all brought up on street football. If you got near the goal, you shot but it wasn't often Billy got near the goal because he wasn't much of a dribbler. He preferred to watch.

Only a year ago Billy would have been excited about a big game, but music had become much more important than football. Punk had lit something up in Billy. Before punk, he hadn't really been interested in music. He liked Bowie and he liked Suzi Quatro but that was about it. It was actually Brian who first let Billy hear a punk single. He had bought 'Orgasm Addict' by The Buzzcocks, probably because he thought it was a sex single or something. The last single he had bought before that was by the fucking Nolans. From the first crash of Steve Diggle's guitar and the higher than expected, melodic whine of Pete Shelley's vocal, Billy was mesmerised. Brian insisted Billy had to buy the single from him before he would let him listen to it again, but he gladly paid. Billy must have listened to the song twenty times before he realised that, of course, there was a B-Side. He quickly turned it over and steadied himself. The A-Side had caught him by surprise, but he was ready this time. By the time 'Whatever Happened To' had finished, Billy knew what had been missing in his life.

The *New Musical Express*, or *NME* as it was commonly known, and *Melody Maker* became Billy's bibles. He would read about bands nobody had heard of, read the singles reviews of songs he would probably never get to hear, to see what he should be listening to and generally immersed himself in the punk rock ethos. The 'John Peel show' was essential listening. Through Peel, Billy could listen to the singles he had read about in the music press and finally decide which ones he would buy. Billy was lucky that his mum loved music and would always be happy to give him 50p for a single. As far as she was concerned, if they were buying singles, they weren't buying cigarettes or cider. Billy didn't believe his mum when she said she liked each new single he bought. When he bought Wayne County's 'If You Don't Wanna Fuck Me Baby, Baby Fuck Off', he thought better of letting her hear that one. But she never complained and never asked him to turn it down, so she must have liked some of it a wee bit.

And then Billy saw a poster at The Calderwood Square announcing a gig upstairs in The Salmon Leap. The picture of the band on the poster looked punky and the names of the bands were just like the bands Billy was reading about. The Sinister Turkeys supported by Teenage Vice. The weird thing was the time. The gig was from 1pm to 3pm on a Sunday afternoon. That didn't sound very punk rock, but Billy knew he was going to go from the second he saw the poster. Bands didn't play in East Kilbride so he would go to help encourage more to follow in their footsteps, even if they were shite. Nobody mentioned the gig in school and Billy didn't mention it either. He wasn't sure if he was ready to nail his flag firmly to the punk rock mast just yet. There was one punk in school, and he was a twat, but he had been a twat even before he made his hair spiky, so Billy wasn't inclined to align himself with someone like that. He would go to the gig, see who else turned up and take it from there.

Surprise number one was Billy recognised the drummer of Teenage Vice! This was an East Kilbride punk band, and he knew one of them! And they were younger than Billy. The drummer was the wee brother of a girl in his year and although Billy had no idea what either of their names were, he knew them! They weren't very good but that didn't matter. The other surprise was how busy the place was. It may have been a Sunday afternoon in the upstairs room of an East Kilbride boozer, but it felt like a Saturday night at The Roxy or at least that's how it felt to Billy. He had read about gigs and now he was at one. He was bursting with excitement.

The Sinister Turkeys were much better, but Billy couldn't stop looking at the bass player as he was sure he knew him too. They did a great version of 'New Rose' by The Damned.

After the Turkeys had finished, Billy walked over to where the members of Teenage Vice were standing talking to a group of the punters. Some of the punters were in their twenties but nobody was talking down to the young guys in the band. Everyone was talking about music. It didn't matter what team you supported or what school you went to or what you looked like. If you liked the music, then you belonged. Billy very quickly felt like he belonged too. He caught the drummer's eye and instantly a name popped into his head.

"How you doing, John? That was great by the way..." Billy hoped the younger lad would recognise him.

"Cheers. We made a bit of an arse of a couple of songs but fuck it..." He didn't seem younger than Billy.

"I'm at school with your sister..." Billy was never prepared when he started a conversation. He was always more comfortable listening. He needed an assurance the guy knew he wasn't just some random talking to him.

"Aye. It's Billy, is it?" Billy nodded, glad to be on firmer ground. "I didn't know you were a punk?"

"Well, I didn't really know it myself until tonight." Billy laughed, letting his excitement overflow. "I mean I've got a few singles and I listen to Peel and all that, but I had no idea there was an EK band. Where do you play?"

"We practice three times a week, in Allers, Long Calderwood and Maxwellton."

"The primary schools?" Billy couldn't make the connection.

"Aye. At the youth clubs." John could see Billy wasn't following. "The youth clubs aren't just for primary school kids. While they're all running about playing tig, we're upstairs in a classroom practising. At Long Calderwood we use the medical room."

"Wow. I had no idea." Billy was blown away. "And how did you get a gig with these guys?" A couple of The Sinister Turkeys had come over and joined the general throng.

"They practice at Maxwellton too."

"Fuck off!" Billy could hardly contain himself. "They're from East Kilbride? They're about 18, how do they get into a youth club?" The penny dropped on why the bass player had seemed familiar.

"You need to get it out of your head that youth clubs are for wee kids, man." John was laughing. "There are loads of bands in EK. There's us, The Turkeys, The Electrix, New Town Scum, The Stilettoes, First Priority, Neutral Blue... There's fucking loads and they all use the youth clubs. They're there for everyone. You should come along one night."

"Fuck, I think I should..." Billy's head was spinning. On the way home, all he could think about was forming his own punk band and hanging around with the crowd he had just met. His own friends were fine, but they seemed like little kids compared to this new crowd. Why had he not realised there would be bands in East Kilbride? Punk was for everyone. He was coming to it late, but Billy was ready to make up for lost time.

Billy went along to the youth club at Long Calderwood Primary School the next Tuesday. Teenage Vice were there, along with New Town Scum and The Feds. Two of The Feds were in the same year at school as Billy and he'd had no idea they were into punk. He didn't know either of them personally. They were guys who didn't play football, weren't in gangs and generally moved in different circles to Billy. They were only interested in one thing. Music. They weren't swots or anything like that. They might not have mixed with the wrong crowds, but they were instantly cooler than any of the twats who thought they were.

It was weird being in his old primary school again, especially when Billy went into the medical room. It was full of drums and amplifiers, but it was still the old medical room. Billy remembered having to go there when his head was split open with a rock while playing war fights under the huts in the playground. Aspirin Annie they called the nurse. Billy remembered she had been kind to him, and he had tried not to make fun of her when the others did, but peer pressure made it impossible.

The classrooms seemed tiny. It was hard to believe Billy fitted on the small chairs not so long ago. And going for a piss in the infants' toilets was a scream. The urinals were at knee height and if you needed a crap, you were sat so low your knees were at your chin.

When the club finished, Billy was invited to a couple of the other boys' houses to listen to records and before long they were talking about forming a band themselves.

Billy started going to The Apollo in Glasgow regularly. The other boys knew their way around, so Billy felt safe, even when some of the gigs turned a bit rowdy, which they did on a regular basis. Since the summer alone, he had seen The Buzzcocks, Joy Division, The Stranglers, Sham 69, The Skids and The Damned. Then he saw The Jam and things changed again.

Sid Vicious died, and punk along with him, at the start of the year. Some of the bands looked like they were going to survive but the Mod thing was happening now, with The Jam being the new poster boys. Later in the year Billy was going to see The Specials, so maybe ska was the next thing. It was getting complicated. Billy still loved Bowie and Quatro too, but he thought he could never admit it in case the punks all laughed at him.

Billy eventually bit the bullet and formed a band. His mum let him order a bass guitar from her Kays Catalogue that he could pay up at £1 a week and he set about learning how to play it. It was hard to say how good he was because he refused to play with anyone else until he felt he was competent enough to expose himself to the others. When he finally asked Andy Hall and Rab Taylor to join him, he was ready. Andy had a cheap sunburst guitar of no name that everyone had. It was the cheapest one in every mum's catalogue, so it was a popular choice. Rab didn't own drums, but Billy knew there were only about three drum kits in the band world of East Kilbride. Everyone borrowed, begged and shared, so there was always one available from somewhere.

"What's the band called?" Andy and Rab were sitting with Billy in the Long Calderwood medical room.

"Handclap." Billy looked at the other two boys for a response but all he got was raised eyebrows. Billy had been thinking about this for months and after disregarding ideas like The Smelly Farts, The Window Lickers and many others that were instantly forgettable, he had landed on Handclap. Not The Handclap. To stand out, he thought the band shouldn't have 'The' at the start, like every other band out there.

"So, if you're playing bass, who's the singer going to be?" Andy was keen to get started.

"It has to be a woman." Billy knew what he wanted.

"Why?"

"Because Debbie Harry, Siouxsie, Chrissy Hynde…"

"I don't think any of them are going to be interested." Rab smiled but Billy wondered about his commitment.

"Not them, obviously. But it needs to be a female…" Billy wasn't going to be questioned.

"Do you know any females?" All three of them laughed. "And more importantly, can they sing?"

"Leave it with me." Billy smiled knowingly.

A benefit of hanging round with the punk crowd meant Billy was in the company of girls, which you didn't often get at the street football. Sometimes Gordon Jones' mum would bring them a drink of diluting juice at half-time but that didn't count. The girls Billy was mixing with were there for the music. Okay, some maybe only showed up to be near the guys in the band and weren't interested in talking to a hanger-on like Billy, but some would at least nod him a hello every now and then. Being in a band would help in getting to have a conversation at least. But it was a Catch-22, because Billy would first need to have a conversation with one girl if he wanted a female singer in the band. And he knew exactly who it should be. Lisa Collins.

CHAPTER TEN

Lisa

LISA HADN'T SEEN either of her parents for about eighteen months. She spoke to them on the phone every now and then, but the truth was, Lisa didn't care if she saw them again. Her sister, Carol, was eighteen so she was the head of the household and although Lisa and Carol could have a fractious relationship, they got along by generally staying out of each other's way. Her parents made sure money was plentiful for the girls. They had careers that took them all over the world (Lisa honestly didn't know what they did) and they made sure they were available on the other end of the phone whenever they were needed. Lisa could still hear the speech her father had given the girls two years ago, explaining how he and his wife had devoted their lives to their jobs and how they couldn't give up the opportunity that had arisen to grow their business life. Why their kids couldn't be included in the 'special journey' they were about to go on was never discussed. Lisa was thirteen and Carol sixteen when their parents left and neither of the daughters cared if they were coming back.

Carol was desperate to be free of the shackles of looking after her young sister. Lisa would be sixteen next year and Carol was counting the days until she could move out and leave her dysfunctional family behind for good. Until then, she made sure there was food in the house and the bills were paid. Her parents had set up a bank account for each of their daughters and the money was in there every month, but it wasn't enough for Carol. She felt let down by her parents, but not because she missed them. Even when they lived in the family home, they had been working all the time or they were out socialising in the pursuit of more business. Carol had always been relied upon to look after Lisa and now it was getting close to the time when she could spread her wings and leave her sister to get on with things on her own.

Carol wasn't worried about leaving Lisa. Her young sister had a wise head on her shoulders and the unconventional upbringing the girls had endured meant they were better prepared than most people their age to go out into the big bad world. Lisa did her share of the cooking, cleaning and general household duties and she helped manage the budget well. In fact, she was probably better at that kind of thing than Carol was. Carol hated East Kilbride. Lisa liked East Kilbride, and that was the divide that ensured the girls wouldn't be living together after the approaching sixteenth birthday. Carol already had her eye on a flat share in Shawlands where two of her friends were already living the high life.

Lisa was angry with her parents. Not angry because they had abandoned her, although that was a factor. Lisa was angry that her parents had decided to have kids at all. Her mother explained once that being married to her father had been a tactical decision, aimed at ensuring their rise through the social echelons of their industry. Once married, the pressure to have kids became a thing. People trusted you more if you had kids. So, they complied, and Carol had been followed by Lisa. They hadn't been interested in having kids before and they were even less interested when the girls came along. Lisa couldn't remember ever laughing or having fun with her parents, but she had friends who supplied that emotional side of her life. Her friends were important, but being fifteen seemed to be tougher for her friends. They would get upset and cry over tiny things, taking offence at the slightest and most trivial of matters, ones that Lisa would brush off without a thought. When it came to maturity, Lisa was streets ahead of any of her peers. At least, that's how it looked. There was no point giving in to her insecurities, because there was nobody around to help her deal with them.

The punk rock crowd were different. They were all outcasts from society in one way or another, but any baggage was parked at the door when you entered the punk world. The music was exciting, and the gigs were great but the best part of it for Lisa was being part of something. They were becoming a community within the community as their numbers grew, and the number of bands springing up showed how quickly this utopian ideal was spreading. Some of Lisa's friends shunned the new way of life she chose, frightened by the rubbish written in the papers about how punks were the devil incarnate who were all out to bring down society. If what they were doing brought down society, Lisa was proud to be at the forefront of it. Society wasn't for her, because she felt she had been let down by it. Smashing the system was a genuine prospect and Lisa looked forward to it all coming to fruition.

Lisa had received a few offers to join bands, but she always felt she was being asked because boys were more interested in getting into her knickers than they were in hearing her sing or play. She couldn't play an instrument, which shouldn't have been a problem because most of the boys couldn't play properly either, but when you're a girl, the normal rules don't apply. Lisa looked good and she knew it. Being at the forefront of the band was where she belonged, like Poly Styrene in X-Ray Spex. Lisa refused to audition for any of the bands. If somebody wanted her, they wouldn't need an audition, they would ask her to join and that would be it.

There was one boy in the crowd, Billy Loy, who seemed to take it as seriously as she did. He played bass but nobody knew how good he was because he didn't want to play anywhere before he was sure it would blow everyone away. That seemed perfectly reasonable to Lisa. If you were going to do something, it was important to do it right. Of course, Lisa would never put herself forward for a band but if Billy asked her to join when he finally decided he was good enough to assemble one, then Lisa was sure she would say yes. It helped that Billy looked like he belonged in a band. He was attractive, in a punky kind of way, although he wasn't Lisa's type at all. Boyfriends hadn't been a factor in Lisa's life until now. She was becoming attracted to the bad boys of the town and Billy didn't fall into that category. He had a certain kudos because his dad had been some kind of nutter in the past, but Lisa wasn't interested in a boy. She wanted the real thing. The Woodie boys were against the punks, but Lisa was confident she could turn one of them on to the music if she could get them interested and they were certainly interested in her. Plenty of them were sniffing around and Lisa was happy to encourage them, as long as they accepted her punk outlook on life and supported her fully in her dream of being in a band. Lisa didn't have to dig too deep to realise her preference for the local bad boys was a direct challenge to everything her dad stood for, but she was cool with that. Now all she needed was Billy to get the confidence he needed to write some songs, form a band, ask her to join and ultimately become an important part of Lisa's life. Things moved quickly in the punk world. Lisa hoped Billy would get his finger out soon so they wouldn't miss the boat.

CHAPTER ELEVEN

Bunnet

KEN GODMAN HAD been a float driver for twenty years. When he started, he had been the only driver covering the whole Calderwood area of East Kilbride, but the town had grown so much in the last twenty years, there were now four floats, from two dairies, covering the same area. Probably a hundred boys had worked for him at some point over the years and he was proud that most of them would still stop him in the street to say hello, always reminding him of some funny story or another that he didn't remember.

With the surname Godman, the other dairy workers had toyed with various nicknames for him like 'God', 'Chief' and 'Saint Ken' for a while. The one that finally stuck was Bunnet. Ken didn't mind it because he did always wear a bunnet to keep his bald head warm and they could have come up with something horrible. Now everyone knew him as Bunnet, to the extent you would be hard pushed to find someone who knew him as Ken. His wife, Linda, had called him Ken but she was long gone now, the divorce papers being finalised almost ten years ago. Ten years. Bunnet still missed Linda terribly. When she left there was nobody more surprised than Bunnet. She said it was boredom that drove her away and Bunnet had come to realise that she was probably right to leave. It couldn't have been much fun living with someone who was in bed by 8pm six days a week and on the one day he didn't have to work, he would spend most of Sunday running his boys' football team. Linda wasn't even a close third behind the milk and the football, but Bunnet had still been surprised when she left.

"Why?"

Linda was standing with her suitcase in the hall of the flat they shared when Bunnet had arrived home.

"Ken, when we met you were fun. We would go out, we would laugh. We had plans. Now we're six years down the line and we're still living in this pokey wee flat. I can't remember the last time we went out and the only plans we have are making sure you get enough sleep! It's boring and I've had enough."

Bunnet had tried to talk her round, but she was right. Life had become boring to a certain extent, but the thrill he still got from driving the empty streets with a team of boys, teaching them about a work ethic and doing what he could to help steer them down the straight and narrow was all Bunnet needed. Linda worked part-time in Bullochs, the off sales, but Bunnet knew she hated it. Linda's life was boring because she didn't have a good job. And she didn't have a hobby like Bunnet did with the football, unless you counted drinking Babycham and watching telly as a hobby. She was lazy and wanted Bunnet to create an exciting life for her. Well, that was never going to happen. Linda was right to leave. She was living in Eaglesham now, married to an insurance salesman. Bunnet wondered if her life was less boring now and he doubted it. He still missed her, though.

1979 had been a tough year. Bunnet was an active member of the Scottish National Party and regularly attended the meetings at the Calderwood/St Leonards branch. They only had about ten regulars so in the run up to the referendum vote, Bunnet found himself out knocking on doors with leaflets when he should have been resting (who's boring now, Linda?). It wasn't an experience he had enjoyed. The apathy he was met with on the doorsteps had dented his faith that the Scottish people would grasp the chance of devolution being offered to them, and so it had come to pass. The majority who voted had wanted it, but the UK government had made sure it would never happen by stipulating the majority of the whole electorate would be needed to endorse the result. Every person who didn't vote was counted as a no vote, making it impossible. It had been a terrible blow for Bunnet. He had put so much into trying to get the people interested in the future of the country, but it had all been in vain and now he was suffering from some kind of post-referendum hangover. He hadn't been to a branch meeting since and he doubted he would ever go again.

Linda had been wrong about one thing: the flat they lived in wasn't pokey. It only had one bedroom, but that was never going to be a problem because they had known only six months into their marriage that they were never going to have kids. Linda had gone and had tests done and the results meant within the year she had had a hysterectomy. Bunnet had wanted kids, but he didn't stop loving Linda just because they couldn't. The bedroom in the flat was huge, with plenty of built-in cupboard space, and the living room was big too. The kitchen wasn't very spacious, but Bunnet didn't need a big kitchen. He only ever cooked for himself. The bathroom had what was required and there was a huge walk-in cupboard in the hall where the immersion heater went. Bunnet would dry his clothes on a little washing line he had set up inside the cupboard. It wasn't a palace, it was true, but Bunnet loved his flat and couldn't imagine living anywhere else. The neighbours were mostly nice, but Bunnet had noticed the number of single mums getting flats was increasing all the time. He didn't grudge them having somewhere to live, but where were the fathers? All Bunnet knew was that if he had a kid, he would make sure he was there for it. Young people didn't seem to have the same morals at the end of 1979 as they did ten years ago.

The float driver from Hamilton – his name was Angus, but everyone called him Oggy in homage to Angus Ogg – had started sniffing around one of the young single mums in the next block to Bunnet. Bunnet couldn't say he disliked Oggy, but he knew enough that he didn't trust him. It was the same feeling he got from Drew, or Kojak as he liked to be called. Kojak was a thug, he always had been, even when he worked on Bunnet's float as a boy, and Oggy spoke like he was cut from the same cloth. But there was something else. Bunnet didn't know what else the pair of them got up to but he was sure they were up to something. Bunnet would kid himself on that he would keep his eye on the pair of them and only act when he knew for certain that they were up to no good, but he wondered if he would have the strength to challenge either one of them. It was a dilemma Bunnet would have met head-on twenty years ago, but for now, he was happy to push it to the back of his mind. The quiet life was comfortable, and rocking the boat didn't seem so attractive after the disappointment of losing the referendum.

CHAPTER TWELVE

Physical Woodwork

BILLY WISHED HE had never taken woodwork or Technical Drawing at school. If he had known in second year, when you decided what subjects you were taking as O level subjects, that you could make the choice yourself, he would never have included any of the technical subjects. Billy didn't feel he had been given a choice. He was ushered in to see the careers officer, a man he had never met and hadn't seen since, and was asked a series of questions that decided his fate.

"Sit down. You are Billy Loy?"

The man didn't even wait for an answer. He wore the standard brown suit that all the male teachers seemed to wear, along with a white shirt and blue tie. His ginger moustache looked odd, as the rest of his shoulder-length hair was brown and his black specs filled his face, leaving his chin as the only part of his head exposed to the elements.

"It says here your test results suggest you should take seven O level subjects?" The man looked up from his clip board, looking Billy up and down with doubt in his eyes. "Well done. Okay, so what does your dad do for a living?"

"Nothing. He's dead."

"Okay, so what did he do before he died?" There wasn't a hint of sympathy in the man's voice or demeanour.

"Nothing."

"Nothing? He must have done something." The man was desperate to start ticking the boxes on the sheet of paper he was staring at.

"Not as far as I know." Billy tried not to sound like he was being cheeky or evasive. He had no idea what his dad did. He didn't think telling the story about his dad bringing a pig home once would cut the mustard.

"What does your mother do then? I assume you've got a mother?"

"She's a cleaner and sometimes works in the pub." At least Billy knew he was on firmer ground with this answer.

"Right, well you can't do that. Is there anything you would like to do when you leave school?" The man was beginning to lose patience.

Billy had honestly never thought about what he wanted to do when he left. Brian had recently left and started in the Rolls Royce factory as a labourer, but from what he had told Billy, it didn't sound like something he would like to do. As a boy, Billy had been obsessed with becoming an astronaut, but he now knew it was only in America you could do that, so he couldn't think of anything else he would really like to do.

"Not really."

The man muttered under his breath. "Jesus Christ. Okay, well you live here in East Kilbride and there's a lot of engineering shops here. A smart kid like you with seven O levels would be well suited to becoming an engineer, so I'll put you down for English, Arithmetic, Maths, Physics, Chemistry, Woodwork and Techie Drawing." The man ticked off the appropriate boxes as he listed the subjects.

"Can't I do Art?" Billy didn't want to contemplate life without art. "Or Speech and Drama?"

The man gave a snigger. "Nobody does Speech and Drama, son. Okay, we can drop Chemistry and you can do Art instead."

The man rubbed out one of his ticks and entered a new one. He looked up at Billy, surprised to see him still sitting there. "Okay, off you trot. Send the next one in when you leave."

And that was it. No explanation or discussion. When Billy got home and told Mary the subjects he was taking, she was confused.

"I'm surprised you're taking Woodwork. I thought you hated Woodwork?"

"I do."

"Why did you choose it then?" Mary laughed and shook her head.

"That's what the guy said I should take. Could I choose what I take?" Billy felt cheated.

"They're called options, Billy. You get the option to choose what you want to sit. You really need to start paying attention." Mary laughed and shook her head at Billy's naivety.

"But the guy said I had to take Woodwork and Techie Drawing to get a job..." Billy couldn't believe he had sold his life away.

"Well, he would know best, I suppose. Maybe you'll like it more when it's O level..."

The thing was, Billy didn't mind the subjects, it was the teachers who were the problem. Billy had the misfortune of having Mr Todd for both Woodwork and Techie Drawing, and for some reason he had taken a real dislike to Billy from day one. Brian had warned him about Toddy, as he was known by the pupils, because he had given him a hard time too, although Brian had only been allowed to sit a couple of O levels, so he hadn't taken any Techie subjects after second year. Billy had no idea what his problem was, but on the first day, Toddy had made his dislike very clear.

"Are you related to Brian Loy?"

"Yes, he's my brother."

Toddy had grabbed Billy by the arm and dragged him out of the classroom into the corridor. He pushed Billy up against the wall and crossed over to the classroom on the opposite side, entering with a brief knock on the door and returning with another teacher Billy would later learn was called Mr Booth. His nickname was Boozy because of the strong smell of alcohol everywhere he went.

"Look what we've got here Mr Booth, another one of the Loy clan." Toddy was rubbing his hands together with delight.

"Really? And are you a wee hardman like your degenerate brother?" Boozy leaned down so close that his nose was touching Billy's. The smell from his breath almost made Billy gag.

"No." Billy wasn't sure what degenerate meant but he got the impression it wasn't a good thing.

"You're a wee scumbag though, aren't you?" Toddy drove his point home with a punch to Billy's upper arm.

"Are you a scumbag?" Boozy followed suit, punching Billy on his other arm.

"No." Billy could hardly believe what was happening.

"Well, we're going to be watching your every move, ya little shit, and every time you put a foot wrong, we'll be there. And you'll be belted to within an inch of your life if you step out of line. Do you hear me?"

Toddy smashed his knee into Billy's thigh, giving him a dead leg, closely followed by Boozy doing the same thing to the other leg. Billy was determined not to show how much it hurt. He decided not to say anything in case it brought more punishment.

Toddy had been true to his word. He had been Billy's teacher every year so far, and his use of the belt was liberal to say the least. He belted everyone, but Billy seemed to get more than anyone else. It was part of the curriculum for the technical subjects. If Toddy thought someone wasn't paying attention, he would pick up a small block of wood that sat on his desk and launch it at the offending child's head. He rarely missed, which was hardly a surprise, the amount of practice he got. You then had to retrieve the block of wood for him and put it back on his desk, ready for the next boy who dared cause offence. The guy was a psycho and Billy was getting fed up with his abuse.

The PE teachers were worth avoiding, too. Although every boy attending Hunter was football-daft, the PE teachers were all rugby types, so football was never on the agenda unless it was snowing outside and the teachers couldn't be bothered going out in the cold. Only then would they toss a ball to the boys and send them out to play on their own. Everyone had to take a cold shower after any activity and it was usually then, when your whole body was freezing, that the teachers would come into the changing rooms and announce who hadn't given enough effort. The offenders would be belted on frozen fingers, making the pain all the greater, especially when it was being applied by huge men who played a lot of rugby in their spare time.

Most people enjoyed PE, especially when they got to play Pirates, a game set up in the gym with every monkey bar, climbing frame, rope and mat utilised. The object was to avoid capture by the two pirates, usually the two most sporty guys in the class, using all the apparatus available to get around the gym. If you touched the floor or were tagged by the pirates, you were out and had to sit at the side. Billy hated it. He would make sure he was always caught first, hanging around the first mat to make sure his capture was swift, so he could sit at the side and watch the others flail about. It was bloody dangerous, so Billy had no intention of putting himself in more peril than was necessary. He would often get the belt for lack of effort, but that was preferable for Billy. He had received the belt so much throughout his school life that it was no longer a deterrent.

Toddy was the only one who inflicted pain. The effort he put into belting Billy was even noticeable to the other boys.

"He fucking hates you, mate. Did you shag his maw or something?"

Billy had no idea why Toddy took such regular delight in beating him, but he was beginning to think forward to the time when he was leaving school and was considering finding out where the sadist bastard lived. He imagined turning up at his door the day after he had left and slapping the old fanny around a bit. He knew he would never do it, but daydreaming about it when he was supposed to be making the perfect dove joint helped the time pass a bit quicker.

CHAPTER THIRTEEN

A 10/21er

THE RED STAR – Blue Hill game reached half-time after fifty-five minutes. There was no timekeeping involved. Every street game was played until conclusion and every game was a 10/21er. This meant you played until one team had ten goals, whereupon it was half-time, and you could get a drink or go for a pee or whatever. The second half was played until one team got twenty-one goals or until fewer than five players were left in any one team because the rest had been called in for their dinner. On those occasions, the team with more goals at the time were declared the winners. The gravel pitch took its toll on knees, but nobody ever shirked a tackle or failed to dive if you were in goal. The biggest problem about playing on the waste ground at Runciman Place was that the goal on the left-hand side was in front of a sheer drop down a cliff to the dual carriageway running past the bus station. Any shot flying over the imaginary bar would end up on the road down to Blantyre. The rule was that whoever shot and missed would be the one to go and get the ball, which meant running down the red road to the stairs that led to the dual carriageway, then dodging the traffic to rescue the ball. By the time the person had climbed the stairs and come back up the red road, they weren't fit to play again. The team shooting towards the left-hand goal were generally losing at half-time because nobody wanted to shoot and miss and have to go and get the ball. So, at half-time, Blue Hill were winning 10-6.

Billy was standing at the side, talking to Danny Price. Danny was an old friend and although he played for Blue Hill, there was no competition between them. He did the milk too, working on Kojak's float.

"So, you just started last week?" Danny was puffing on an Embassy Regal, not caring if anyone saw him because this wasn't his street.

"Aye, I'm on Shagger's float. How long have you been doing it?"

"This is just my third week. I'm not really sure about it. What's it like on Shagger's float? Working with Kojak is a fucking nightmare. He's like fucking Hitler." Danny lowered his voice when he gave his opinion of his boss.

"Shagger's alright. You've got to do the job, mind, but you can have a laugh." Billy had heard Andy and Mark say they had a laugh, but he hadn't experienced it yet, so he had to take their word for it. He was too busy trying to keep up with Sandy and learn his run.

"Kojak just talks about fighting and being in The Woodie all the time. I got the job after Cheesy was sacked, but I think Kojak misses him. It's like Kojak was living his life through Cheesy, telling him what to do in fights and shit. A meeting of psycho minds, and now he's got me. I'm not in the fucking Woodie and he knows it." Danny took a kick at a tennis ball being used in place of the real ball for half-time entertainment as it passed and missed.

"Why did he sack Cheesy if he loved him so much?" Billy laughed at Danny missing the tennis ball. There was no point wasting energy when it was half-time.

"He caught him robbing houses apparently. You know, people cancelling their milk while they go away on holiday and shit is a green light for him to rob their houses. Kojak went mental apparently. The fucked-up thing is Cheesy blames me because I got his job. I can see it every time he walks past our house, he looks in the window and fucking scowls. Prick..." Danny ground his cigarette into the gravel pitch with his monkey boots.

Nobody wore football boots on the gravel. The guys who played for the organised teams would never waste their boots playing in a street game and the guys who only played at street level could never justify the expense of owning a pair to their parents. Everyone wore whatever shoes they had. Monkey boots were popular, but most played in their Clarks school shoes, much to the chagrin of many a mother.

"Are you going to the Genny's bridge on Saturday night?" Danny lit another cigarette, making the most of the half-time break.

"What's happening at the bridge?"

"We're having a cheese and wine party. A few of the bands and all the punks are going."

"Cheese and wine?" Billy laughed at the idea of punks passing round the cheese board.

"Aye! Obviously, you don't need to bring any cheese. As long as you've got wine, that's all that matters. And by wine, I mean Buckie or Old England or LD and shit." Danny laughed with Billy.

"Sounds good." Billy was chuffed to be asked.

"That Lisa and her pals are going..." Danny knew this would swing it.

"Really? Good. I need to talk to her about something." Billy thought this could be the opportunity to bring up her joining the band.

"We're going to get some acid." Danny wondered what the response would be.

"Acid? Like the hippy drug?" Billy didn't think punks liked hippies.

"Yeah, you hallucinate and stuff. It's fucking brilliant." It was easy to tell that Danny wasn't talking from experience.

"I'm not sure..." Billy liked a drink and he had smoked some pot at the First Priority gig in the Red Deer Centre, but this seemed a bit more dangerous.

"Well, I've ordered a dozen and it's first come first served, so if you want one, let me know early." Danny stubbed out his second cigarette.

"Where do you get them?" Billy was thinking about it.

"Kojak."

"Kojak? Kojak deals drugs?" Billy was genuinely shocked.

"Aye. Right, here's the wee man with the ball. Time for the second half." Danny walked over to greet the young lad who had taken his ball home with him at half-time so he could have a shit and not miss any of the game. The person who owned the ball had the power.

"Fuck, is it half-time already? What's the score?" Cheesy was walking on to the waste ground as though he owned it. He was wearing flared jeans and underneath the wide bottoms, he had Boofers, heavy platform shoes favoured by the toughest neds, on his feet. If he was planning on playing football, nobody was going to go near him when he was wearing those.

"You can't play if you're wearing Boofers..." One of the younger players for Red Star spoke out before he realised who he was speaking to.

"Shut it, ya wee prick." The boy had spoken out of turn, but Cheesy knew emotions could run high at street games so he was willing to let it go. "What's the score?"

"We're winning 10-6 but we're kicking that way in the second half." One of the younger Blue Hill boys was chuffed to be talking to someone as infamous as Cheesy.

"Ach, don't worry about that, lads. The star striker is here now..." Even half the Blue Hill guys rolled their eyes.

Nobody really liked Cheesy. He was a fucking grade-A nutter who didn't mind who he beat up. He was the undisputed leader of The Woodie, but he didn't save his aggression for the rival gangs. He would take on whoever crossed his path, and he did so with a level of violence nobody else was capable of matching. He would steal anything that wasn't nailed down, and the rumours were he had got a girl from the Murray pregnant. Nobody would have described him as good-looking, his gaunt face and skinny frame making him look taller than he was. His eyes were too close together, presenting a permanent scowl, but his persona and his reputation were enough to make him popular with the girls. An all-round bad boy who everyone feared, but nobody respected.

Cheesy didn't care if anybody liked him or not. He couldn't remember a time when anyone had liked him. He was adopted by his parents when he was two, although Cheesy had no recollection of it. He knew he was adopted for as long as he could remember. Both of his parents had always been very vocal about how they were stuck with him and how him arriving had ruined their lives. He wondered why they had adopted him in the first place, because there was certainly no love there. Both parents were heavy drinkers and the beatings Cheesy had endured over the years had made him immune from any fear for his personal safety. This lack of fear is what made him dangerous. When you were sacked from Kojak's float for being too mental, the alarm bells started ringing.

Billy had never had much to do with Cheesy. They lived on neighbouring streets and went to the same school, but Cheesy rarely went to school and his entire life was dedicated to The Woodie. Billy took no part in that, although he had been under a bit of pressure from his peers, including Cheesy, to join the ranks because his dad had been the main man of the same gang when he was Billy's age. Everyone seemed to think the Woodie gene would run deep, but neither Billy nor Brian had been tempted to follow in their dad's footsteps. Their mum had never said as much, but the boys had the feeling they would be letting her down if they had followed the same path. Billy didn't get it. He couldn't see why anyone would have loyalty to the area they lived to the point where they would defend the honour of the place with violence. Billy knew to defend himself and his family, but beyond that there didn't seem to be much point.

The game had restarted and Red Star quickly scored a couple of goals now that the fear of losing the ball with a wayward shot was taken away. Cheesy's first two touches were tackles that sent the victims high in the air. Now when he got the ball, nobody was going near him in fear of getting a size 8 Boofer in the face. Cheesy didn't run about. He stood near the Red Star goal, waiting for the ball to come his way, while trying to kick anyone who came near him. Danny was quite a good player, and he was beginning to see more of the ball, but every time he got it, Cheesy would start screaming for him to pass it to him.

"Here! Fucking pass it, ya spastic. I was clear there."

Danny did his best to ignore the abuse, but Billy could see it was bothering his friend.

"Just ignore him, Danny. He's not going to do anything." Billy spoke to Danny as he ran past him.

"I wish I had your confidence, mate. I tell you, because I got his job, he's just waiting for an excuse to have a go."

The game continued and Red Star finally made it 13-12 in their favour, the first time they had been ahead in the match. Danny took kick off and headed straight for the Red Star goal, determined to get the score back in their favour. He managed to dribble to within twenty yards of the goal when he could no longer ignore the screams coming from Cheesy.

"Pass to me now, ya cunt."

The venom in the final word was enough for Danny to know he didn't have an option. He played a perfectly weighted pass into the box for Cheesy to run on to. The goalie was already getting out of the way of the expected platform-shoed toe-bash so he couldn't miss. While the upside of wearing Boofers to a football game was getting to kick people very hard, the downside was when you eventually got to kick the ball, you were never going to be sure which direction it went. Cheesy ran on to the pass from Danny and with a flap of denim and a flash of Boofer, smashed the ball straight over the fence, sending it over the cliff and down to the dual carriageway. The usual ironic cheer went up whenever anyone kicked the ball down the cliff. Cigarettes came out of pockets to be smoked while the ball was retrieved. Some of the boys sat down where they stood, anticipating a lengthy wait. Everyone looked at Cheesy in anticipation of him going to get the ball.

"Come on, hurry up. You need to get it before it runs away down the hill." The lad who owned the ball was by the fence watching it bounce across the dual carriageway. Cheesy pretended not to hear.

"Come on Cheesy, go and get the ball." Danny couldn't believe Cheesy would do such a thing. Everyone knew the rules, they were written in stone.

"I'm not going to get it..." Cheesy was standing with his arms widespread, trying to look like an innocent man.

"Oh, come on!" Everyone was united in condemning Cheesy.

"No way! It was a shite pass from that prick." Cheesy pointed at Danny. "You go and get it."

"No fucking way!" Danny turned round to the other boys, looking for support.

"What do you mean?" Cheesy switched to aggression with ease. "Do you think because you're on Kojak's float it makes you a fucking tough guy all of a sudden? Go and get the fucking ball!" Cheesy was right up in Danny's face.

A murmur of excitement went round the pitch. Football was great, but a fight was much better entertainment. Danny stood his ground, but he could feel the confidence drain from him as he smelt Cheesy's bad breath in his face.

"Go and get the ball, Cheesy." Billy didn't raise his voice in any way.

"Stay out of this. It's got nothing to do with you." Cheesy didn't take his eyes off Danny.

"Aye, it has. It's my team's ball. Now go and get it." Billy's voice remained steady. Cheesy broke away from Danny and started walking towards Billy.

"What's your fucking problem? Do you think just because your old man was the leader aff for The Woodie a thousand years ago, you can go about acting like a hard man?" Cheesy used a confident tone that had made many back down from him in the past.

"There's only one person acting the hard man here and it's not me. Just calm down and go and get the ball. We're having a good game here, there's no need to spoil it..." Billy's calmness was bound to annoy Cheesy.

"Ah know what I'll spoil in a fucking minute, ya fucking twat!" Cheesy's rage boiled over as the spit spewed from his twisted mouth.

"What does that even mean?" Billy was openly laughing at Cheesy, and his confidence encouraged a few of the other boys to snigger. Cheesy lost it.

"Fucking Woodie!" With his war cry echoing round the houses, Cheesy launched himself at Billy. Billy timed his side-step perfectly and caught Cheesy square on the nose with a right hook, his knuckle bursting on the aggressor's face. Cheesy stumbled and fell to his knees but he was up and coming back for more in a split second. Billy hadn't expected such a swift response and was slow to defend himself. Cheesy caught him with a left and a right but neither punch did much damage apart from making his left ear ring. Cheesy's fury was unabated, but his balance was off. Billy slammed into him and both boys fell to the ground. They grappled and threw punches, but nobody was getting any purchase on their shots. The boys all crowded round the two on the ground and started the ritual chant when a fight was ongoing.

"Ow, ow, ow, ow..."

"Right, that's enough." The baying crowd started to part as Mrs Johnstone came wading in, pushing boys out of the way as she got to the centre of the action. "Stop it now!"

Billy and Cheesy stopped grappling and stood up. Billy still looked unruffled, but Cheesy was fuming. Mrs Johnstone stood between the boys, facing Billy with Cheesy behind her.

"I'm surprised at you, Billy Loy..."

"Billy didn't start it." Danny felt he had to stick up for his friend, considering he had saved him from a doing.

"Fucking shut it, you!" Cheesy hated Danny with a passion. Mrs Johnstone spun round to Cheesy, disgusted by his language.

"That's enough!" Her outrage was genuine.

"Aw fuck up, ya auld slag." Cheesy couldn't contain himself.

"Woah!" There was a general murmur of disapproval from the boys. You didn't question an adult and you certainly didn't swear at someone's mum.

"I don't know who you are, ya wee toerag, but you're not welcome round here. Do one before I go and get my husband."

Mrs Johnstone hoped this would be enough, because her husband wasn't in and even if he had been, he would never have come out to defend his wife. He would be more interested in watching the fight.

Cheesy looked around him and sensed that he was on his own for this one. It was best for him to leave and deal with everyone later, when there weren't any adults around. He pointed at Billy.

"You're dead." He turned to Danny, "You too. In fact, you're all fucking dead." Cheesy looked round at all the boys. Some physically shrank from his glare, but he couldn't help but notice defiance in some of the faces. He turned and stormed off.

"I'll be speaking to your mother about this, Billy." Mrs Johnstone walked back to her house, shaking her head as she went. The rest of the boys started to drift away. She turned to give them all one last withering look before she entered her house again, muttering to herself. "Fucking cheeky wee cunts..."

"Cheers, man. You've made an enemy there..." Danny was grateful to his friend.

"Ach, we've always been enemies. We just hadn't realised it yet." Billy laughed. "Do you fancy coming up to mine? I've got the new 999 album, it's fucking great."

Billy and Danny started walking over to the flats. All the other boys followed suit and headed off to see if they could get a drink from their respective houses.

"What about the game? Who's going to go and get the ball?" Nobody was listening to the young lad who owned the ball. The game was over, and his power was gone.

CHAPTER FOURTEEN

I Know What You Like

KOJAK DIDN'T LIKE drugs. To be more precise, he didn't like taking drugs. Buying them and selling them to the many losers who were his customers was another matter. One of the benefits of having been a well-known thug in East Kilbride was that other thugs knew who he was. It had been four years since he walked into a bar in Hamilton, meeting a girl he'd met the previous Saturday at The Olympia Ballroom, only to find himself in the company of Ben Greer, the main man from the Blantyre gang who had been the biggest threat to Kojak's Woodie career. The Blantyre mob were renowned for their violence and with Calderwood being the first area of East Kilbride you entered when you came up from Blantyre, skirmishes were regular. Kojak had faced Greer in a square go on a couple of occasions when they were teenagers but as each boy had become a man and their lives moved on from the youthful fights they both enjoyed, their paths hadn't crossed for some time. Kojak spotted Greer and his mates as soon as he walked in the bar. He thought about turning right round and walking out to avoid any hassle, but the girl he had come to meet had been nice, so he took the chance that Greer and his cronies might not recognise him, and he could meet the girl and leave to go somewhere else before anything happened. Kojak walked up to the bar and ordered a pint, trying not to draw any attention to himself. After a couple of minutes, Kojak was joined at the bar by one of Greer's mates.

"Are you Kojak?" Kojak turned and looked at the man. He was younger than both Kojak and Greer and he had a look in his eyes that Kojak recognised as danger.

"Who wants to know?" Kojak may have moved on from his gang membership days, but he was never going to back down from anyone if they wanted trouble. He held his pint glass tightly, ready to swing it into the young guy's face if he felt threatened.

"Mr Greer would like to have a word with you." Kojak looked past the guy at the bar to where Greer was sitting. He raised his glass to Kojak and smiled.

"Tell Mr Greer that I'm here to meet someone. I'm not looking for any trouble." Kojak felt his heart start to race.

"Aye, Karen won't make it tonight. You should come over and have a drink with Mr Greer instead." The young guy smiled at Kojak but there was no warmth in the gesture.

Hearing the girl's name made Kojak realise this hadn't been a chance encounter. Greer had probably used the girl to set Kojak up. There was no way he was getting out of the pub without having to confront the danger sitting in the far corner of the bar. Without showing any fear, Kojak hopped off his stool and walked over to where Greer was sitting. As Kojak approached the table, Greer stood up, but his actions weren't aggressive. He had a smile on his face. A purple scar ran from the side of his nose down to the corner of his mouth, making the smile a bit crooked, but it seemed genuine. His black suit looked expensive, and he exuded the confidence of a successful man.

"Kojak! How you doing, man?" Greer held his hand out to Kojak.

"I'm alright, Ben, how's yourself?" Kojak shook the man's hand, still gripping his pint glass in a way that would make it a weapon in a split second.

"Still driving the milk float?" Greer motioned for Kojak to sit down next to him.

"Aye." Kojak looked at the other men sitting at the table. He wasn't going to sit down until he was sure he wasn't walking into a trap. Greer looked at the other men and motioned for them to move away. The men immediately stood up and walked over to the far side of the bar.

"Come on, mate, sit down. I've not brought you here for trouble. I've got a business proposition for you." Greer was still smiling.

"You brought me here?" Kojak was finding it hard to believe that such espionage was possible for a common thug like Greer.

"Aye, sorry about that. Karen's a nice girl and if it's any consolation, I think she genuinely liked you, but I guessed you wouldn't have come if I had just sent you a message saying I wanted to talk to you..." Greer knew that Kojak's reaction to this news would determine how this was going to go. Kojak looked around the pub.

Greer's mates were standing at the bar, not even looking in his direction and the place was empty apart from them. He was interested to know what this was all about, but he wouldn't be dropping his guard just yet. He sat down facing Greer.

"Okay, I'm listening, but I have to tell you, Ben, I don't like being played..."

"I'm not playing you, mate, honest. Come on. We've all grown up since our street fighting days. I don't hold a grudge. I've got some business I can put your way. We'll both make money, and it won't take a great deal of effort to do it either." Greer sounded genuine.

"What's your business?" Kojak's reply showed Greer that he had successfully drawn his old adversary in.

Greer's business was drugs. He supplied most of Lanarkshire. There were a couple of families from Craigneuk who were trying to muscle in on his action, but he was confident they would be driven out of business if and when Greer decided. His main problem was he didn't have enough people he could trust to help him as his empire grew. The proposition to Kojak was for Greer to supply him with whatever he needed and together they would corner the East Kilbride market.

"I'm not sure there are any druggies in East Kilbride..." Kojak was out of his comfort zone, but the numbers Greer had been talking about made it impossible not to listen.

"Of course there are. I'm already supplying loads of them. Once you take over distribution you won't even need to look for them, they'll come to you. It's a goldmine, and it's guaranteed."

Kojak told Greer he would need 24 hours to think about it, but he already knew as he drove home that this was an opportunity he couldn't turn down. In the subsequent years, everything Greer had outlined had come to pass. Kojak now had a dealer in every area of East Kilbride, while he handled the Calderwood distribution himself. Greer had been right about the punters coming to Kojak. He didn't need to go looking for business at any time, although he had to put up with Greer often telling him he should be selling more than he was. Greer sold twice what Kojak did in Blantyre alone and it wasn't half the size of East Kilbride, but Kojak didn't rise to it. As far as he was concerned, Kojak didn't want to push his luck by getting too big too soon. Too many customers brought unwanted attention and Kojak knew the people of East Kilbride weren't as scummy as the people Greer sold to.

There were three types of customer Kojak dealt with. First were the potheads. They were your bread and butter, because they would be customers for life. You only had to buy what you needed once a month because the stoners were as regular as clockwork, all phoning with their orders within 48 hours of each other. Kojak would pick up what he needed from Greer on a Friday afternoon and be sold out by Sunday night. There was minimum risk, and the stock was only in Kojak's hands for one weekend a month. Although Kojak didn't really approve of any drugs, the stoners were all generally nice people who always paid on time, so he didn't mind them.

Next were the weekenders. Generally young people out for a good time on a Saturday night who were a bit more adventurous than a pint or two in the pub. They would buy pot to keep them calm in the week and at the weekend they would want speed or sulphate to mark the occasion of going out to wherever they went. They would be included in the monthly pot run but Kojak would have to be out every Friday night delivering the weekend element of their drug abuse. They could be unreliable, and Kojak had been forced to hand out a few slaps for late payment over the years, but most of them were okay. They were the stoners of the future, so it would pay in the long run for Kojak to keep them sweet.

The last set of customers were the worst ones. The junkies. They were unreliable, bad payers and they wanted you to be at their beck and call every minute of every day. Every one of them were smackheads and Kojak didn't trust any of them. The thing that surprised Kojak was most of them were women. And only a couple of them didn't pay for the drugs with money earned working the streets. Oggy pimped half the working girls in East Kilbride and Kojak was their dealer. It was weird they were both float drivers on the same route.

Being a float driver was the perfect cover. Police were never going to stop a milk float from going anywhere. Everyone got milk delivered so seeing the float driver going to the doors of customers and coming away with money wasn't unusual. In fact, it was downright ordinary. Kojak kept his daily stash in a box full of eggs, which he always kept in the cabin with him. Normal eggboxes would be mixed in with eggless boxes filled with whatever was being delivered. It was perfect. Kojak would nip down to Blantyre in the float before he started his shift and collect his order from Greer. He would then drive to a different location every day where his dealers for the rest of East Kilbride would be waiting for him. Each one would then head off with their share of the pickup to start selling in their respective areas. Kojak was strict with the dealers. They had to be on time, and they had to pay. He made it very clear that he wouldn't tolerate any turf wars between them. Each one had their specific area to service, and nobody deviated from the boundaries. If some would-be tough guy ever challenged one of them, or made threats to replace them, Kojak would gather all his guys together and deal with the problem before it got out of hand. Kojak liked that side of the job. It made him feel like he was the leader of the gang again, battering young hoodlums into submission. Obviously, he had to slap the junkies around quite a lot too when they tried to rip him off, but there was no fun in that. Kojak liked a fight, not slapping women around, although he did it as often as required. He couldn't show any weakness, or they would be all over him.

Kojak couldn't afford to get ripped off. Greer may have been his peer when they were in gangs as teenagers, but he was in a league of his own now. If Kojak went to him with a sob story about being ripped off, he wouldn't last a minute. At best he would be sacked, but more likely he would be made to disappear altogether. Greer had said to him when Kojak agreed to take the job on, that there would be no way out if he joined the group. Only a gracious retirement would be acceptable. Kojak was confident he would outlast Greer. The people Greer was dealing with were probably far more dangerous, so Kojak reckoned if he kept his nose clean until he had saved enough money to give it up, Greer would eventually come a cropper or go to jail and Kojak could get out. In the meantime, he tried to enjoy his job.

Shirley was one of Kojak's junkie regulars. She was also the mother of one of the boys on Oggy's float, Dick. And she was one of Oggy's girls, which made it a bit awkward. Kojak never let on to Oggy that he knew what he was up to and Oggy never mentioned Kojak's drug involvement, although he had no doubt Shirley told him whatever he wanted to know. Oggy would hit her for whatever reason and Kojak could understand why. He was going to be hitting her too if she didn't have his money today. Kojak walked into the flat and straight to the living room, where Shirley was lying on the sofa, quite obviously off her face on his product.

"Morning, Shirley." Kojak raised his voice enough to make sure Shirley would hear him. She woke up rheumy eyed and smiled. She was sporting a black eye.

"Morning, darling..." Kojak had no idea who Shirley thought she was talking to, but it wasn't him.

"Don't fucking 'darling' me, ya skank. Wake up." Kojak grabbed Shirley and slapped her hard on the face. Shirley shot up and started moaning.

"Fuck off. Stop hitting me. You've hit me enough."

Kojak went into the kitchen and filled the basin with cold water. He walked back into the living room and threw the contents over Shirley's head. This seemed to do the trick.

"Fuck off, Kojak! What are you doing that for?" As she took in her surroundings, Shirley began to remember the potential danger she was in.

"I need you awake enough to give me my money. Where did you get the black eye? Oggy?"

It wouldn't stop him from giving her a slap, but Kojak actually quite liked Shirley. She had obviously been quite pretty before life had trodden her into the ground.

"He thinks I'm too fat." Shirley touched her swollen eye gently.

"You're not fat..." Oggy was a wanker.

"Aw thanks, Kojak..." Shirley smiled.

"You're a fucking mess, but you're not fat. Get me my money."

Kojak didn't want Shirley to think he was on her side in any way. Shirley looked hurt but knew not to say anything else. She got up and went through to the bedroom, shouting to Kojak.

"Have you got a couple of wraps for me?"

"Shirley, if you've got my money you can have as many wraps as you want."

Kojak looked around the room and wondered when it had last been cleaned. Shirley came back into the living room with her purse in hand.

"How much do I owe you?" Shirley knew fine what she owed,

but she always liked to hear it before she showed how much she had to spend.

"You owe me twenty quid and if you want another two wraps on top of that, you give me forty."

Kojak hated how junkies always pretended not to know how much things cost. Shirley searched her purse for a few seconds and looked up with a petted lip.

"I've only got forty quid."

"Well, that's lucky, then." Kojak sounded a bit disappointed.

"Yeah, but there's no food in the house and I promised Dick I would get some shopping today. Can I give you thirty just now and I'll give you the rest tomorrow when you come round?" Shirley continued to search her purse as she spoke in the hope some notes may be hiding in the lining.

"I couldn't give a fuck if you've got food or not. If you don't have enough money, you should get out there and earn some more." Kojak towered over Shirley.

"You sound just like Oggy when you say that." Shirley sounded hurt.

Kojak slapped Shirley hard in the face, knocking her over onto the sofa.

"Don't fucking dare compare me to that slimy pimp cunt!" Kojak was raging at Shirley.

"I'm sorry, you're nothing like him. I'm really sorry. Please don't hit me." Shirley was lying on the sofa, her arms protecting her head from any further blows. Kojak hated himself for a second. "How about I give you thirty and we take ourselves into the bedroom? I know how to make it up to you. I know what you like." Shirley sat up and rubbed Kojak's leg, putting on her best puppy eyes, even if one of them was shining black. Kojak's lack of response gave her encouragement. "Come on baby. You're so tense. Let's get rid of all that tension." Shirley brushed her hand over Kojak's balls. Kojak took a step back, but grabbed Shirley by the arm and pulled her up off the sofa.

"Fine, but I want the full amount tomorrow night."

Shirley smiled and led Kojak by the hand into the bedroom.

CHAPTER FIFTEEN

The Ex-Gadabout

HUGH WAS AT a bit of a loose end. If he was honest with himself, he was at a loose end quite often these days. Driving the milk float made it difficult to have a social life. The early starts made it impossible to go out and have a bevvy on any night other than a Saturday, and this didn't fit in with his old friends. For them, Friday night was boys' night, while Saturdays were for wives and girlfriends. For a while, Hugh would try to go out on the Friday with his mates, but it was difficult to watch everyone sinking pints and having fun while he was watching the clock and drinking orange juice. Eventually his mates stopped asking if he was coming out with them, and Hugh could understand it. His own father used to say, 'Never trust a man who doesn't drink when he's on a night out. He'll be waiting to dip your pockets once you get pished.' Hugh wasn't dipping anyone's pockets, but he certainly wasn't adding to the fun, and he couldn't say he enjoyed himself.

What Hugh needed now was someone to share his life with, a proper relationship with a partner who he could look after and be looked after. He was a good-looking guy, he had a good job, and he had his own flat. Some people would consider him a catch. The problem was his reputation. When he started at the dairy, he had been a young chancer, a Jack-the-lad, and he had relished the nickname bestowed on him. What young lad wouldn't be proud to be called 'Shagger' in recognition of his prowess with the ladies, but Hugh wasn't a young lad anymore. In truth, Hugh had never been much of a ladies' man. When he started working, he had two girlfriends on the go at the same time and he enjoyed telling tales of how he played one off against the other, but the truth was since then he hadn't had a proper girlfriend at all. He had tried to live up to his reputation, having one-night stands and even getting amorous with some of the lonely female customers on his milk round, but it was all for show. Hugh was the lonely one now.

Going to The Salmon Leap for a pint each afternoon after he finished at the dairy was now his social life. He shared it with pensioners, the unemployed and alcoholics. The highlight was always when Brenda was in having a drink. Brenda was older than Hugh, but she was good fun. She worked odd hours like Hugh, so having a glass of wine in the afternoon was sometimes her only option. The fact she was a prostitute was neither here nor there for Hugh. People did what they had to do to make money, and Brenda never tried to hide what she was. She wasn't ashamed of it and Hugh admired her for how she composed herself, despite getting a bit of hassle from some small-minded people. Brenda was easy to talk to, and Hugh was grateful he could spend time with her without having to pay. Not that he would ever try it on with her. Brenda was a friend.

Hugh walked into the pub and scanned the snug before deciding to spend his time in the bar. The snug was empty, and even though Hugh disliked a lot of the old guys who hung around during the day, it was better than sitting on your own. A couple of the punters nodded to him as he walked in, but Hugh's heart leapt when he saw Brenda sitting alone at the bar. He ignored the others and walked over to join her.

"Alright, Brenda?"

"There he is! How's it hanging, Hugh?" Brenda's smile instantly cheered Hugh's demeanour.

"Can I get you a drink? White wine?" Hugh noticed Brenda's glass was almost empty, so he hoped she would agree as it would mean she hung around.

"Aye, why not? I'm not working tonight, so I can push the boat out a bit."

Brenda liked Hugh. He had a reputation as a bit of a ladies' man, but Brenda knew that wasn't how he was. If anything, she couldn't remember ever seeing him with a woman.

"It's alright for some. I don't remember the last time I had a day off, apart from a Sunday..." Hugh was looking for a member of staff to serve him, but nobody was around. "Hello!"

"Patience, my dear. They're short-staffed today. Mary's working the bar and the snug on her own." Brenda drained the last of her wine and shifted on her stool to face Hugh.

"Mary?" Hugh knew all the staff, but he couldn't place the name.

"Aye, Mary Loy? She only does the odd shift when they're short. She cleans the place..."

"Aw fuck, her boy joined my float last week."

Hugh hated interacting with the parents of the boys who worked on his float. They all wanted to ask him questions and hassle him about some complaint or other. It wouldn't be the first time he had sacked a boy just because their mum was a pain in the arse.

"And why would that be a problem? Is he no good?" Brenda always knew when Hugh was blustering about nothing.

"No, he's fine, I suppose..."

Hugh thought about it and realised he actually quite liked Billy. He seemed smarter than the other boys. Not book smart, none of the milk boys were that, but he didn't seem interested in the usual crap the boys talked about. He liked music and so did Hugh, although Billy's love of punk was a mystery to someone who thought Supertramp were the best thing since sliced bread. When Hugh had tried to slag the boy off for his taste in music, Billy had come out the next morning with a mix tape and a small cassette player to let him hear some of the stuff he liked. It was mostly shit, but Hugh admired him for his enthusiasm.

"Yes love, what can I get you?" Mary walked over to Hugh and Brenda.

"Can I have a pint of heavy and a large white wine please?" Hugh smiled at Mary. He could see a likeness to Billy, around the eyes and the easy smile.

"A large one? I hope you're not trying to get me drunk, Hugh!" Brenda's laugh filled the bar, making some of the old guys look up grumpily from their newspapers.

"Ach, you're off tonight. Let your hair down..." Hugh enjoyed making Brenda laugh.

Mary started pulling his pint.

"You not working tonight, Brenda?" Mary knew Brenda well, and she wasn't one of those who disapproved of her lifestyle.

"Nah. I'm at a bit of a crossroads if I'm honest. For the first time in my life, I'm bored of my job. This is the second night this week I've decided to give it a miss. It's too fucking cold. Maybe I'm getting too old for it..." Brenda accepted a fresh glass of wine from Mary and took a large mouthful.

"Nonsense. Too old? You look younger than some of the girls half your age." Mary wasn't telling any lies. Brenda was older than she was, but she looked much younger.

"Aye, give it a rest, Brenda. Stop fishing for compliments." Hugh paid for the drinks and sat on the stool next to Brenda. Mary brought over a cup of tea and settled next to them.

"I'm not kidding. I'm finding it harder and harder to drag myself out there every night. It's fine in the summer, but the cold nights are beginning to get to me." Brenda's knees had started to hurt when it was cold.

"Time for a career change?" Mary looked surprised.

"Maybe. I can't believe I'm thinking about it, but I am. Maybe you could give me a job, Hugh?" Brenda was keen to change the subject.

"Trust me, you wouldn't want to do my job either. It's just as cold." Hugh and Brenda laughed.

"What is it you do?" Mary had seen Hugh around, but she didn't know anything about him.

"Have you two never met? This is Hugh, he drives the milk float your Billy is working on." Brenda raised her eyes at Hugh, knowing he didn't want this conversation.

"You're Shagger?" Mary blushed after she said it. Hugh felt his own face go red too.

"It's just Hugh..." Hugh couldn't pretend he wasn't embarrassed.

"Sorry, I just blurted that out. I had no idea I was going to say that."

Both Mary and Hugh took a drink to hide their embarrassment. Brenda was pissing herself laughing.

"Why do they call you that anyway? I don't remember ever seeing you with a girlfriend, or is that it, you don't like to be tied down so you can run around town sowing your wild oats without a care in the world?" Brenda was taking the piss and usually Hugh wouldn't mind, but it didn't feel right in front of Mary.

"Ach, you know what it's like. I was a bit of a gadabout when I started working at the dairy and they love giving out nicknames, so I got stuck with that. Some of the guys think it's cool but it's a pain in the arse to be honest. I'm almost thirty and I live on my own, so Shagger hardly seems appropriate, but what chance have I got? Can you imagine me saying to Oggy and the other drivers that I didn't want to be called Shagger anymore? They would call me it even more, or worse, come up with something even worse." Hugh hoped he was being jokey, but it was hard to keep the truth out of his voice.

"Wow, a tart who's fed up with sex and a shagger who's not getting his hole. You pick the days to work in here, Mary. Maybe you should go over and help old Tommy pick the winner of the 3.30 at Kempton, you might have more fun." Brenda was joking, but the way she rubbed Hugh's back let him know that she was sympathetic to his trouble.

"I feel really embarrassed now. I'm sorry Hugh, I shouldn't have said that." Mary's blush wasn't going away.

"No, don't be daft. It's my own fault. I liked the nickname when I was younger, so I let it go. I can't complain now that it doesn't suit me anymore." Hugh wished they would stop talking about it.

Everyone paused and took a drink.

"So, how's he doing?" Mary felt it was her job to change the subject.

"Who?" Hugh had forgotten what they were talking about.

"Billy. How's he doing in the job?"

"Aye, good. He's a good lad, a good grafter. It's early days, like. A lot of them don't last more than a month, because it's hard work, but Billy seems to be made of the right stuff." Hugh hoped he didn't sound like a twat.

"Good. He seems to be enjoying it, although I'm guessing when I say that. Like any teenage boy he tells me nothing about anything." Mary smiled when she spoke about her son.

"It's probably for the best. If he's like every other teenage boy, he won't have anything interesting to tell you anyway. It's all music, football and fighting." Hugh laughed at his own joke, then realised who Mary was. "Not fighting or football with Billy, though, I was just talking in general. It's all about the music with Billy." Thankfully, Mary was laughing.

"You don't have to hide anything from me, Hugh, I know they all have their moments at that age." They both laughed again. A punter came in and stood at the other end of the bar, waiting to be served. Mary got up and walked over. Brenda leaned in close to Hugh.

"Mary's single, you know."

"Is she?" Hugh was surprised.

"Aye, and she's a really nice lassie." Brenda gave Hugh a knowing smile.

Hugh laughed. "And she's Tommy Loy's wife..."

"Fuck off. He's been dead for ten years or something. She's a widow." Brenda was enjoying making Hugh feel uneasy.

"Okay, but she's Tommy Loy's widow..." Hugh wasn't rising to the bait.

"What? Do you think his ghost is going to come back and kick your head in for asking his widow out for a date?" Brenda never ceased to be amazed at how stupid some men could be.

"I wouldn't put it past him..." Hugh took a large mouthful of his pint.

"Do you actually remember Tommy? He was just a daft laddie. All the stories you hear about him have been embellished beyond belief." Brenda knew she was playing it down, but she enjoyed playing matchmaker.

"I remember he was a psycho. Come on, Brenda, Mary is not going to be interested in someone like me. She's more likely to be interested in Kojak or Oggy or any one of the other psychos who come in here." Hugh wasn't going to get embroiled in Brenda's shenanigans.

"You're a fucking idiot sometimes, do you know that?"

Mary had gone off to check if anyone had come into the snug after serving the customer.

"Wah! What the fuck?"

Mary's scream from the snug did little more than raise the heads of the older patrons but Hugh and Brenda were off their chairs immediately and rushed through to see what was wrong. A strong smell of shit hit them as they ran into the small bar. Mary was standing with her hands over her mouth as she stared at one of the tables in the middle of the floor. A huge, steaming pile of excrement sat in the middle of the table.

"What the fuck?" Hugh couldn't believe what he was seeing. "Is that a dog shit?"

"It would have to be a fucking clever dog to have opened the door and got up on the table on its own. That's human shit." Brenda gagged.

"What sick fuck would do that?" Mary was beginning to cry.

Hugh left the two women standing and ran through to the main bar. He grabbed the man who had recently come in and been served by Mary.

"Have you just done a shit on a table in the snug?"

The whole bar looked up from the racing pages this time.

"Fuck off! What are you talking about?" The old guy looked at Hugh as though he was mental. Hugh turned to the rest of the old guys in the bar.

"Someone's just done a shit on a table in the snug!" Hugh couldn't keep the incredulity out of his voice. "Mary's in fucking tears through there and I'm not leaving until someone tells me who it was." Hugh was surprising himself at his level of determination.

The old guys all looked round at each other then back to Hugh. Davie Todd, a seventy-something retired career criminal, decided to speak for the group.

"You'd better watch who you're accusing here, son." Davie Todd hadn't been in a fight in thirty years, but he still had a menace about him.

"He's just walked in and nobody else is in there." Hugh was determined he wasn't backing down. He still had a hold of the old guy's lapels.

"If nobody's in there it could have been done any time." Davie Todd would never back down either.

"There's still fucking steam coming off it. It's fresh." Hugh turned back to the old guy.

"Two young fellas were leaving when I walked in." The old guy was showing no signs of being intimidated by Hugh, but his patience was wearing thin.

"Who were they?" Hugh's confidence was beginning to wane.

"I don't fucking know. Young people all look the same to me these days with their earrings and long hair." The old guy's comment drew nods of agreement from the other aged punters. Hugh let go of the old guy roughly and walked back through to the snug. Brenda was sitting at the bar with her arm around Mary, who was nursing a large brandy.

"Did anyone see anything?"

"The old guy who came in a few minutes ago said there were two youngsters leaving as he came in. It couldn't have been him. He would never have been able to get his arse up that high..." Hugh managed to suppress a snigger when he thought of the old guy trying to manoeuvre himself over the table. The smell helped keep the smile from his lips.

"Who would do such a thing?" Mary dabbed her eyes with a hanky. "And why? Why would anyone do such a thing?"

Hugh looked around, trying to decide what to do next. The smell of shit was beginning to make his eyes water too. He walked over to the table, took a deep breath and lifted the whole thing straight out of the door into the street. A woman passing the pub with a baby in a pram looked at him with shock in her eyes.

"It's not mine." Hugh couldn't think what else to say.

Hugh went back into the snug.

"I've left it out there. Leave it there. The cleaner can deal with it later." Hugh felt he had solved the immediate problem.

"I'm the cleaner." Mary started crying again, burying her head in Brenda's chest. Brenda looked at Mary, then pleadingly back to Hugh.

"See if there's a bucket in the back..."

Hugh mouthed the word fuck and went into the back to see what he could find. Twenty minutes later Hugh came back into the snug to find it empty. He went into the bar where Mary was sitting at a table with a couple of the old guys comforting her. Brenda was behind the bar, making sure everyone had a drink so Mary could compose herself. Hugh walked over to Mary.

"I've cleaned it the best I can, Mary, but I've left the table outside to get a bit of air about it. If you want my opinion, I would burn the fucker rather than bring it back in but it's up to you." Hugh had done all he was willing to do.

"Hey, watch your language in front of the lady." Davie Todd was old school, which meant his moral rules were all over the fucking place as far as Hugh was concerned, but rather than saying anything else he walked over to Brenda at the bar.

"Well done." Brenda was sincere. "Do you want a drink?" She held up a large whisky and Hugh nodded, still struggling to come to terms with what had just happened. Hugh drank the whole thing in one mouthful.

"I will get that." Hugh looked round to see Davie Todd standing behind him. "You did right by the lassie but the next time you come in here and throw your weight around, you'll get hurt. Okay?"

"He's sorry about that, Davie. It was just the shock..." Brenda accepted the money from Davie. Hugh looked back to Brenda with raised eyebrows, but she shooshed him with her eyes. Hugh shook his head. He stood up and put his jacket on.

"I think I've had enough for today. I'll see you, Brenda."

Hugh was out of the door seconds when Mary came running out after him.

"Hugh? I wanted to say thanks. Can I buy you a drink?" Mary's eyes were red from crying, but she still looked attractive. Hugh looked past her to the table sitting in the street. You would never know what had happened to it half an hour ago.

"Thanks Mary, but I think I've had enough for today." Hugh gave a small wave and turned to walk away.

"Let me cook you some dinner, then." Mary seemed determined.

Hugh stopped in his tracks and turned round again.

"You don't have to do that..." Hugh's mind searched for a way to get out of it, but Mary was nice. Maybe he didn't want to get out of it. They hadn't met in the best of circumstances, but there was something about her.

"I know. I want to." Mary smiled and sealed the deal.

"That would be great." Hugh returned the smile and for the first time in a long time, it was genuine.

"Good, I'll see you later. You know where I live. Around six?"

"Okay. Thanks."

Mary and Hugh smiled at each other for a comfortable time before he turned and walked away. It was a date.

CHAPTER SIXTEEN

You Don't Own Me

OGGY WAS TIRED. Not just physically tired, he was tired of everything. The life of a float driver was a tough one and the hours he worked were beginning to get in the way of his social life. Friday nights out were impossible when he had to be up at 3am the next day and Sundays, his one day off, were spent sleeping and doing the paperwork that went with being in charge. The boys were good at doing their rounds, mostly, but when it came to collecting the money, some of them were useless. He knew most of them were honest, so stealing from him wasn't the problem. The problem was half of them couldn't count. Spending a Sunday afternoon going over the individual books the boys used when collecting the money on a Friday was giving him a headache because not one of them ever added up properly. On top of that, Sunday was one of the days he had to check in with the girls he ran. Dealing with them would do nothing to help ease the pressure building in his temple.

Oggy spent his money wisely. He had a nice, three-bedroom house that was too big for him, but the money he brought in from handling the girls meant he was able to put a big deposit down on it and having the steady job with the dairy had enabled him to get a mortgage for the rest without any problem. The house would be fully paid off by the time he was forty and he didn't know anyone else who could say that. He had a nice car, and he had a nice suit hanging in the wardrobe if he should ever need it. He had watched his mates marry and produce a houseful of kids, but that wasn't the way he wanted to go. He liked looking after himself and not having to worry about anyone else. If his plan went the way he thought it would, he could give up the dairy job at fifty, sell the house and go travelling. He had treated himself to a fortnight in Yugoslavia a couple of years ago, and he reckoned he could live there for a fraction of the cost here. He was different from the other clowns working at the dairy. He had a future.

The bus station seemed quiet when he drove in and parked at the front. Only two of his girls were standing around the entrance, smoking cigarettes and looking decidedly uninterested in anything that was going on around them. He rubbed his eyes to stave off the growing pain that was in danger of growing to migraine status. He took a large breath and got out to face whatever trials he knew would be waiting for him.

"Where is everyone?" Oggy wasn't one for pleasant greetings.

The two girls hadn't seemed to notice Oggy approach. They both seemed far off in their own worlds. Both of them were obviously out of their face on smack or whatever it was they used to make their pathetic lives bearable. They looked at each other as though they were only noticing for the first time that they weren't alone.

"Ah've no idea. Maybe round the back?" The girl spoke so slowly, Oggy was ready to walk away long before she was finished talking.

Oggy drew the pair of them a dirty look and walked round the back of the station where most of the girls earned their money. A punter was walking towards him having finished his business with Frances, one of the single mums who was so far avoiding falling into the drugs void most of the others had gone down. The guy, a middle-aged, ugly fucker who looked like he was either on his way home from or going to church, avoided eye contact with Oggy as he sloped off back to his dull life after his weekly bit of excitement. Oggy stared at the punter as he walked past, not willing to let him feel comfortable with his shame. Frances was putting her knickers back on and tidying herself for the next punter when Oggy approached.

"Where the fuck is everyone?" Oggy didn't want to waste any more of his time.

"Hello to you too." Frances wasn't one of the worst ones, but Oggy was in no mood for backchat.

"Don't piss me around, Frances, I'm not in the mood."

"I don't know where everyone is. I've been here an hour and the only other people I've seen are the two zombies round the corner." Frances wasn't in the mood either.

"Is Brenda not here?" Oggy took another look around in case he was missing something.

"I've not seen Brenda for a while." Frances knew she was telling Oggy something he wouldn't want to hear. The girls who worked for him were slowly falling apart, mainly because of the drugs. The shelf life of someone in this line of work was never long in the best of circumstances. Brenda was an enigma having lasted as long as she had, but there was going to be a time when even she had had enough.

"What do you mean?" Oggy's patience was growing thinner by the second.

"I mean a lot of the girls haven't been around since Friday night." Frances was pissed off that she was the one having to field all the questions.

"Why? What happened on Friday night?" Oggy didn't like it if something had happened, and nobody had told him about it.

"Nothing as far as I know." Frances shrugged her shoulders.

"You're saying some of the girls have been missing since Friday and nobody told me anything about it?" Oggy had a bad feeling. "Talk me through what happened on Friday."

"Absolutely nothing happened. Usual punters, usual shite." Frances was beginning to see this could end up being her fault if she didn't play her cards right.

"So why are none of them here now?" Oggy was beginning to raise his voice.

"I don't fucking know, Oggy! Why don't you ask your mate Kojak? He was here doling out his poison as usual. Look at the nick of those two round the front. I swear they're all getting worse every time he shows his face." Frances could raise her voice too.

"Brenda doesn't take that shit." Oggy was sure Brenda wouldn't take anything, but there was a hint of panic in his voice.

"No, she doesn't. I think Brenda's just had enough of it all." Frances shrugged her shoulders.

"Don't be ridiculous. Brenda wouldn't miss a Saturday night, or a Sunday for that matter. If I find out something has happened to any of the girls and you haven't told me about it, there will be hell to pay." Oggy's patience was gone.

"What am I? You're fucking right-hand man all of a sudden?" Frances had taken enough.

Oggy took one step towards Frances and swung his boot into her groin. The woman crumpled to the ground, the wind knocked out of her. Oggy thought about following up with further blows but decided against it. He realised he was taking his frustrations out on the wrong person.

"Get back to work. And don't ever call that baldy prick Kojak my mate again." Frances groaned an incomprehensible reply as Oggy stormed off.

As Oggy drove towards Brenda's house, he could feel his eyes begin to blur, a sure sign that a migraine would be laying him low if he didn't get some painkillers down soon. He could do without having to deal with this just now, but he would never forgive himself if something was wrong with Brenda and he hadn't done anything to help. He would drop in to see her, blag some painkillers, then go and see Linda. Linda was a junkie, but Oggy had a soft spot for her. She was the only one of the girls he ever slept with. Maybe that would help his migraine. He had read somewhere that sex was good for a migraine and Linda was always receptive to his advances. She was young and had only been on the streets for a few months, so her body was still in good shape. As he parked the car outside Brenda's, he noticed her curtains twitch, so he knew she was definitely in. He had a key for all the girls' houses, but he never used the one he had for Brenda's house. She had never given him a moment's trouble since he first met her, so she had never had to hide from him, unlike the others who regularly tried to dodge paying him for his services. As he walked up the path, Brenda's front door opened, and she walked into the living room without saying anything or greeting him with her usual smile. Oggy followed her into the living room.

"Alright, Brenda? Is everything okay? I missed you down at the bus station." Oggy could sense something wasn't right.

"I'm fine." Brenda looked tired.

"The girls said they hadn't seen you for a few days. I was worried." Oggy looked around to see if there was anything obvious he was missing that would give him a clue to what was wrong.

"Were you? I haven't been down for a while." Oggy noticed that Brenda couldn't look him in the eye.

"Are you ill? Quite a few of the girls were missing. If there's some kind of bug going round, maybe you should see the doc."

Oggy was fishing. He could feel something was wrong, but he got the impression Brenda wasn't keen on saying what it was.

"No, I'm not ill, I'm just tired." Brenda was being over-defensive.

"That's not like you, Brenda. Is something going on that I should know about?" Oggy could clearly see that something wasn't right.

"I think I'm done, Oggy. I've had enough. I don't want to do it anymore." Brenda finally looked at Oggy.

A stabbing pain behind the eyes reminded Oggy that he needed some pain relief. He looked around Brenda's living room, not a cushion out of place and spotless.

"Do you have some Paracetamol? I've got a blinding headache." Brenda nodded and walked off into the kitchen. "I suppose we all need a break some time, Brenda. Why don't you take a few days off to recharge the batteries?"

Brenda came back in and tossed a packet of tablets to Oggy.

"No, a break won't do it this time. I'm done. I've been offered a job." There was defiance in Brenda's voice that Oggy had never heard before.

"A job?" Oggy laughed. "What job could you do?"

"Barmaid. I helped out the other day in The Salmon Leap and the manager offered me a job. I said yes." Brenda shrugged her shoulders.

"Just like that? You weren't going to discuss it with me?" Oggy felt his ire begin to rise again.

"I didn't think there was anything to discuss, Oggy. I'm my own woman, you know that." Brenda was trying to convince herself as much as Oggy.

Oggy took two pills from the packet and looked around. "Water?"

Brenda rolled her eyes and walked back into the kitchen. Oggy heard the tap running.

"You may be your own woman in spirit, Brenda, but you're one of my girls. I've always treated you well, given you a free rein, but this isn't a job you just quit. You know that." Oggy tried to dry swallow one of the pills but had to spit it out again before he gagged.

Brenda came back in with a glass of water. "I'm forty years old on my next birthday. I always swore I would give it up before I hit that milestone. There's only so much the body can take, you know."

The pain in Oggy's head surged again. "Don't I know it," he said almost to himself.

Oggy took the pills and washed them down with the water. It was weird how much better the water tasted in East Kilbride than it did in Hamilton. Oggy supposed the place had to have one thing going in its favour.

"It's not the right time, Brenda. I need you out there. Fuck knows what kind of shit the others would get up to if you weren't there to keep them on the straight and narrow. Maybe in a few months things will have calmed down a bit and we can look at reducing your workload. I can do without the hassle right now, okay?"

"It's not your call, Oggy. I've decided. I've had enough. There's too much hassle now. Most of the girls are on heroin and the punters use them like punchbags. It's not the same anymore. I'm done." Brenda tried to sound confident, but there was a waver in her voice.

"You're done when I decide you're done!" Oggy's temper rose to a roar, which he resented due to the pain in his head as much as anything else.

"You don't own me, Oggy." Brenda almost sneered at Oggy, doing nothing to help his temper. Oggy threw the glass of water at Brenda's head, narrowly missing her. It smashed against the wall behind her.

"That's where you're wrong, Brenda, I do fucking own you and all the other slappers who take up so much of my time." Oggy was raging now. Brenda went to walk past him towards the door.

"It's time you left." Brenda was defiant but frightened.

Oggy punched Brenda on the side of the head, knocking her into her coffee table. She looked up at him with a look of shock on her face that Oggy had never seen before.

"I'm sorry Brenda. I shouldn't have..." Oggy regretted his actions immediately.

"Get out!" Brenda screamed at Oggy. She looked hurt, not from the blow to the head, but from the action itself.

Oggy went to speak, but realised he didn't have anything to say. He took one last look around the living room, hoping for inspiration and found none. He turned on his heels and left quickly. When he got to the car, he banged his head on the steering wheel, letting his frustration get the better of him. He should never have hit Brenda. She may have been a hooker, but she was a lady and didn't deserve to be treated like that. He was out of order, and he knew it. Oggy slammed the car into gear and sped off, the wheels burning rubber as he went.

Oggy drove to Linda's on automatic pilot. He jogged up to her flat and opened the door without knocking. Before he was halfway down the hall, Oggy knew there was something wrong. The stench filled his nostrils and there was an atmosphere that stank of danger. Oggy nudged the living room door open with his foot and there was Linda lying on her sofa, the needle still sticking in her arm. She was grey in colour and the pained expression on her face would haunt Oggy for days. He had never seen a dead body before, but there was no doubt about it. She was gone.

CHAPTER SEVENTEEN

Having a Shit

CHEESY WAS BORED. He could never understand why his pals weren't out and about as much as he was. Playing football wasn't his thing, mainly because he wasn't very good at it. It was fun to go and kick a few of the fuckers about the pitch but all the twats who took it seriously were beyond him. Other than fighting and robbing, Cheesy had no hobbies. He had enjoyed working on the milk but that prick Kojak had put an end to that. Cheesy couldn't understand why he had been sacked. Of course, he used the milk round to scope out houses that were going to be empty so he could rob them, who wouldn't? Kojak probably did the same kind of thing when he was the same age, so why would he object to Cheesy doing it?

The Calderwood Square was where Cheesy felt most at home. It was his domain, and nobody fucked with him when he was there. The other gangs in East Kilbride wouldn't dare come anywhere near, whereas Cheesy often led raids to the equivalent precincts in The Murray and The Westwood. The feeling of having chased the rival gang away from their territory was a real high, but nobody ever came to try it here. The Woodie were the top dogs and nobody else came close. The Calderwood Square consisted of about 25 shops, including a hardware store, two butchers, a supermarket, an off sale, two bakeries, a newsagent, a chemist and The Salmon Leap pub. Cheesy had robbed every one of the shops at some point. The library doorway provided shelter when it rained, the chippy provided food when he was hungry, and the café provided cigarettes and juice whenever he was flush with money. The low wall at the front of the café was where The Woodie sat, challenging anyone who went by to even look at them the wrong way. The three phone boxes in front of the chippy were the toilets, even though there were public toilets at the back of the news kiosk. The official toilets were rarely open because it was such fun smashing the shit out of them when they were.

Cheesy was the undisputed leader of the gang. Nobody was daft enough to challenge him because they knew they would have to go to the ends of the earth to avoid his wrath if they ever did. Billy Loy was playing on Cheesy's mind because he had had the nerve to stand up to him. Cheesy had no doubt he could beat Billy in a square go, but the mere fact he had stood up to him and caught him with a lucky punch was a direct challenge. If that old boot hadn't come out and stopped the fight, Billy would be finished. The problem was, Billy's dad had been a Woodie legend back in the day. He had been killed by the Blantyre boys while defending the square and that gave him a status that Cheesy could only dream of. It meant Billy was almost untouchable, even though he had never done anything to gain the respect his father had earned. Billy didn't run with The Woodie so Cheesy didn't see why he should be given any respect at all.

Respect was everything to Cheesy. He knew all his peers feared him and that was important, but he also had a hunch that nobody would be too sad if he took a kicking from someone. He wasn't welcome in any of his friends' houses, whereas Billy Loy would get a piece at anyone's door just because his dad was a local hero. It wasn't fair. The only person Cheesy could truly rely on was Nicky Brown, his best mate since primary school, but even Nicky's parents had recently stopped allowing him into their house after Nicky had been caught shoplifting in Corson's Store down next to the primary school. They had blamed Cheesy, but that wasn't fair. Cheesy hadn't been caught, so why should he take the blame?

None of the lads were sitting on the wall when Cheesy got to the square. It pissed him off when nobody was there. What else could they possibly be doing rather than sitting defending their territory and waiting for Cheesy to turn up and decide what they were all going to get up to that night? Cheesy went into the chippy.

"Hello Malcolm, how're you doing, son?"

"Fine thanks, Mrs Locetti."

Margot Locetti was probably the only person in the world who still called Cheesy Malcolm. He couldn't remember the last time either of his parents had used the name they had given him. Despite the Italian surname, Margot hailed from Greenock, but she had married into the family and embraced the culture that came with it. She knew Cheesy was a little shit but if being nice to him stopped any of the toerags who hung around outside her shop from trashing the place, it was a small price to pay. Every now and then she would need to call the police if her customers were being terrorised, but the stupid wee fuckers never clocked on that it was her making the call. She worked here six nights a week and would do almost anything for a quiet life.

"A roll and chips?" There was hardly any point in asking. It was all the boy ever ordered.

Cheesy perused the menu board, but he had been thinking about what he was going to have all day. "No, can I have a haggis supper today?"

"Wow, somebody's flush. Have you won the pools or something?" Margot said it with enough of a smile that wouldn't cause offence, but she doubted if he would notice even if she did intend it.

Cheesy smiled, but he was never going to explain that he had the money courtesy of the till of the Salmon Leap's snug bar. Him and Nicky had spotted that nobody was in there the other day and had lifted the £3.48 float money along with a huge bottle of vodka. As usual, the thrill of stealing had moved his bowels and he had enough time to take a dump on one of the tables before anyone came in. He saw it as his calling card, doing the same thing in the many houses and shops he had emptied over the years. If the cops could ever trace you by smell, he would be fucked but that was never going to happen. Nicky would keep watch while he did it, but he never joined in for that side of the job.

"None of your pals out tonight?" Margot tried to keep the boy sweet. She had heard enough stories and seen him in action outside the shop often enough to know that he was evil.

"Doesn't look like it. Have you seen any of them around?"

"No, not tonight. Maybe you should take your supper down the road. They're probably all down at your place looking for you." Subtlety wasn't something she had to waste on Cheesy.

"I doubt it."

Nobody came to Cheesy's house, not even Nicky. His parents made it very clear that they didn't want anyone poking around their business and if he ever brought anyone home, they were made to feel unwelcome. Cheesy didn't feel welcome, so nobody else would either.

Cheesy sat on the wall outside long enough to eat his dinner then decided to go and see where everyone was. He would pick up the vodka from his house and then go in for Nicky. Nicky always knew where everyone was and what they were getting up to.

He could hear his parents as soon as he walked into the house. Music was blaring and they were singing along heartily to the Unionist LP that was seldom off the Dansette record player, songs about King Billy and guarding Derry's walls. Cheesy crept past the living room and up the stairs to his bedroom. He closed the bedroom door behind him and went to the chest of drawers below his window. The three drawers had little in them, but the bottom drawer was where he always hid anything he didn't want his parents to know about. It wasn't as if his mother was ever in there putting clean clothes away. He lifted the old school shirts that probably didn't fit him anymore and began to panic. The vodka wasn't where he left it. He pulled the drawer out fully and emptied it onto his bed. It definitely wasn't there. He sat on the bed, searching his brain to remember if he had planked it somewhere different. A loud whoop came from downstairs as his parents started singing about the sash their father wore. Cheesy felt the anger rise. He ran downstairs and burst into the living room. His mum was dancing with her arms outstretched while his dad sat on the sofa with a big smile on his face, clapping along to the music. Cheesy's bottle of vodka sat in the middle of the coffee table, three-quarters of it already gone.

"That's my fucking vodka!" Cheesy went to lift the bottle.

"Leave it where it fucking is." His dad's smile disappeared and there was the usual threat in his voice.

"How did you find it?" Cheesy couldn't believe what was happening.

"We hired Sherlock Holmes. How the fuck do you think we found it? It was in your drawer." Cheesy's mum always spoke to him like he was a piece of dirt on her shoe.

"It's mine. You had no right…"

"Yours? And where did you get it?" Cheesy's mum decided to go down the moral route. "You're only fourteen, you don't get to have vodka."

"I'm fucking fifteen!" Cheesy felt just as outraged that they couldn't even get his age right.

Cheesy's dad jumped to his feet. "Don't you talk to your mother like that."

"Aw shut up, ya auld prick. I was having that tonight." It had been some time since Cheesy would back down when his father showed aggression towards him.

"Ya fucking cheeky wee cunt." Cheesy's dad grabbed him by the arm and swung him against the wall. Cheesy bounced back and headbutted his dad below the eye, sending him crashing onto the coffee table. Before his dad could take in what was happening, Cheesy was on him, raining punches into his face. He didn't hear his mum screaming as he raised himself up and started kicking his prostate father in the head. Cheesy felt a sudden clatter on the back of his head as glass from the bottle his mum struck him with showered the room when it smashed. He stopped kicking his dad and turned to her, punching her once in the face with all his might. She fell to the ground, landing next to her husband on the floor, both of them bleeding from their injuries.

"Get out!" His mum was screaming as she held her unconscious husband's head in her lap. Cheesy kicked his dad in the stomach and punched his mum on the side of the head before he took a step back, the red mist beginning to lift.

"Leave! And don't come back. You're not welcome here anymore." His mum was sobbing now.

"Don't worry, I won't be back." Cheesy stormed out of the living room and back to his bedroom. He grabbed his school bag and emptied it onto his bed, refilling it with the few clothes lying around his room. He ran down to the kitchen and grabbed the only sharp knife in the house then went back into the living room. The fear he saw in his mum's eyes when he walked back in with the blade in his hand was enough to let him know he had won. He put the knife in his bag and left, the living room looking like someone had gone berserk with blood everywhere.

Cheesy went to the Braes swing park to decide what he was going to do next. He often went there when he had to think about anything. Sitting on a swing, you could look down to the lights of Glasgow shining in the Clyde valley. It helped him realise there was life outside of East Kilbride. The lump on the back of his head was pounding. He wondered if anyone would believe him that it was his own mother who had hit him with a bottle. None of the adults he had come across in his life had believed him when he talked of the beatings he had received at the hands of his parents, not the thrashings with the buckle end of a belt or the punches, kicks and even burns he had been subjected to. It didn't take him long to realise there was no point telling anyone about them because it was beyond the realms of adults' imaginations. It was easier to brand him as the problem, and after a while he decided it must be true. Other kids he knew got the odd smack from their parents but none of them were held under water in the bath until they passed out, which had happened to him on one occasion. He was out of the house now and it was time for him to step up and take charge of his own destiny.

"Cheesy!" Nicky entered the swing park and cheerily greeted his mate. "Where have you been? I went up to the square, but nobody had seen you."

"I've been here." Cheesy was subdued.

"So I see. Are you up for a bevvy? We could tan that vodka..." Nicky was slow to pick up on Cheesy's mood.

"No, we can't. My mum and dad nicked it." Cheesy was still staring down at the Glasgow lights.

"Aw fuck's sake, man. I've been looking forward to that all day."

"Tell me about it." Cheesy rubbed the lump on his head.

"Is that blood on your hands?" Nicky was instantly wary. He knew how dangerous his friend could be and how easily he could fly off the handle. It didn't matter if you were his best friend or his worst enemy, it was always best to tread carefully.

"Aye. Don't worry, it's not mine." Cheesy tried to force a smile.

"What happened?" Nicky wasn't sure he wanted to know, but his curiosity would always get the better of him.

Cheesy told Nicky about his fight with his parents and how he was now out of the house for good.

"Wow, what are you going to do?" Nicky hoped any future plan wouldn't include him.

"Well, that's what I've been thinking about here. I've got a plan. I'll find somewhere to squat short term. I'll get some money together, get a flat and get on with things on my own." Cheesy said it all with little conviction.

"Right." Nicky didn't sound too convinced. "You make it sound easy."

"Oh, it won't be easy mate, but it's what I have to do. I'll need to borrow your tent for a while. I'll camp down the glen for a few nights until I find a place to squat." The tent was the only part of the plan he was sure about.

Nicky sat on the swing next to Cheesy and joined him in looking at the lights of Glasgow.

"Where will you get money? Are you going to get a job?" Nicky thought it sounded unlike Cheesy to be planning a career.

"I'll go on the rob. As I say, I've got a plan. I'll need your help for the first bit though. I'm going to steal Kojak's eggs." Cheesy looked at his friend to see what the reaction would be.

"Are you fucking mental? Kojak will kill you if he catches you." Nicky was already thinking of a way out.

"Yeah, well, we won't get caught. I'll rob a few of the boys doing their accounts too. Easy money..." The last thing Cheesy needed was somebody checking him with reality.

"It sounds dodgy. If Kojak doesn't get you, the polis are going to be after you." Nicky was searching for reasons to stop Cheesy going down a destructive path.

"Fuck the polis and fuck Kojak. If that baldy cunt comes after me, I'll do him. He's fucking old and he's gone soft, telling me I can't rob houses because he delivers milk to them. What's that all about?" Cheesy was beginning to convince himself.

Nicky didn't doubt Cheesy had thought about this, but he wasn't as confident he could pull it off. "I don't know, mate; it all sounds a bit iffy..."

Cheesy didn't have time for his friend's doubts.

"I've no choice, Nicky. All I ask is you give me the tent tonight and then help me nick the eggs tomorrow. After that I'll deal with the rest." Cheesy gave Nicky a reassuring smile. He knew his mate wasn't as tough as he was.

Nicky resigned himself to go along with the plan for now. He changed the subject before he got roped into anything else. "What are we going to do for a bevvy tonight? It's Friday, man, and now your parents have spunked our vodka. I've not got any money."

"Me neither. We'll have to find some wee wanks having a carry out and confiscate it from them." Cheesy wiggled his eyebrows the way he always did when he was suggesting getting up to no good.

Nicky thought about it. "I hear they punk wanks are having a party down at the General's Bridge tonight. We could go there and take booze from them?"

"Is Billy Loy going?" Cheesy was interested.

"I assume so." Nicky instantly wondered if he had opened a new can of worms. Cheesy jumped off the swing and clapped his hands, full of vigour now he had sorted his future.

"Excellent! Let's go rally the troops."

CHAPTER EIGHTEEN

Technical Doing

BARRY TODD HAD fallen out of love with teaching. If he was honest, he had never really been in love with it in the first place, but when the chance to get out of the steel works and move into education had come along, he had jumped at it. The physical work had been tough and that feeling of never quite being fully clean, the dirt ingrained in his hands and fingernails, had been a pain. Barry had missed serving in the war by a matter of months, but his national service had been tough, the feeling then being that the next conflict wouldn't be far away, therefore the next generation of soldiers should be ready and able when it came round. It provided a solid foundation for Barry's life as an engineer, teaching him skills and a work ethic that had seen him excel as an apprentice and be heralded as a reliable journeyman as a turner/fitter. He had a romantic notion that moving into teaching would give him an opportunity to pass on his knowledge and help develop the next generation of brilliant engineers. The reality hadn't lived up to its billing and these days he found it harder to drag himself into Hunter High, never mind give the job any effort.

The latest nail in his education coffin had been the sacking of his best friend at the school, Harry Booth. Harry liked a drink, everyone knew that. Even the kids affectionately called him Boozy, but it didn't stop him from being a great teacher. The problem was, the new generation of teachers coming through didn't have a clue how a school like Hunter High worked. They had all been to teacher training college and had their heads filled with liberal ideals about it being every child's right to a fair and proper education, with the teacher there as a conduit to make sure every child had the opportunity to reach their full potential, blah, blah, blah. It was all bollocks. The kids at this school were all scumbags and their parents were scumbags before them, and all they had in front of them was working in a factory or a building site. The school's job was to inject a bit of discipline into their miserable lives and make sure they were at least fit for the menial dead-end jobs they had in front of them. Doing away with the National Service that had shaped Barry's character so well had been the biggest mistake ever made. The kids were running wild and the new generation of teachers coming through were doing nothing but encourage it, because they didn't have the same character-building experience Barry had had. Some of them were even talking about banning the belt, for fuck's sake! God help them if that ever happened.

One of the liberal pricks, who had only been in the door for six months, went to the Education Board and complained about Harry, saying he was drunk every day and exaggerating how little time he spent in the classroom. They didn't even have the decency to go to the headmaster first, who would definitely have told them to fuck off before having a quiet word in Harry's ear. Harry was suspended while an investigation went into full swing and three weeks later Barry got word that Harry wouldn't be coming back. He was sacked, pension gone and everything. A fucking disgrace. Barry had been talking to an old pal recently who told him his engineering works would welcome him into the workforce with open arms and he had been sorely tempted. It was an open offer, so Barry was weighing up his options. The thought of going back to manual work was daunting, but it had to be better than dealing with fuckwit kids with no futures. At least it was Friday today, and the last class was his favourite of them all.

The last two periods would give Barry another opportunity to heap misery on the little shit that was Billy Loy. Annoyingly, the boy was quite bright and if he continued the way he was going, there was a good chance he would pass his exams at the end of the year. His prelim marks had been in the top ten for his year. If Barry was going to leave Hunter High, the last thing he wanted to achieve was the ruination of the boy's chances of a future.

Barry had known Billy's father, Tommy. Actually, he didn't know him so much as know *of* him. Tommy had lent Barry's dad some money and then charged exorbitant interest rates, threatening both him and his wife with violence and increasing the amounts due every week when they couldn't pay. Barry had no idea it was going on. His dad's stupid pride had stopped him asking Barry for the money he needed, and his mum's loyalty to her husband stopped her from telling her son when things were getting out of hand. Barry found out what had been going on when his dad ended up in hospital from a beating delivered by Tommy. Barry erupted when his mum finally gave in and told him the full story. He stormed off to find Tommy fucking Loy, but everywhere he went, he was warned off by people telling him how much of a hoodlum Tommy was and how he would just end up in hospital alongside his dad if he was stupid enough to try anything. Barry had let his anger subside, but he was determined to be there the next time Tommy came calling for a payment. He would pay the loan shark off and make it clear that if he came anywhere near again, Barry wouldn't hesitate in going to the police.

One week later, the news broke that Tommy Loy had been murdered in some gangland hit and Barry celebrated. Nobody else ever came looking for the money, but Barry's dad never got over the beating and the trauma he had been through. The physical scars healed but the psychological damage could never be repaired. Barry's dad took his own life six months later.

When Brian Loy had started at the school and Barry heard who his father was, he had made it his life's ambition to get some retribution for his dad. Unfortunately, Brian had been educationally challenged so he only took O Level subjects for the first two years, and he hadn't landed in any of Barry's classes. Billy had been in Barry's woodwork and drawing classes since first year. The problem was, the wee fucker was a hard nut to crack. No matter how much abuse Barry inflicted on the boy, he had never been able to draw so much as a tear from his big blue eyes. Barry gave every ounce of strength he had to each lash of the belt, but not once had Billy even flinched. It didn't stop Barry from trying at every opportunity he got. This afternoon he would go all out and make sure the wee shit was bawling his eyes out. Maybe then Barry could call time on his education misadventure and get back to the real world of a proper working life.

Billy was looking forward to the party at the Genny's. All he had to do was get through double Techie Drawing, rush home to get his dinner, do his milk accounts run and then he could get round to Danny's for the acid experiment. He was nervous about taking the acid, but nothing ventured, nothing gained. His immediate concern was getting through Toddy's class without getting his usual belting. The man really was a psycho, and it wasn't just Billy's imagination that he was picked on more than most. At least Boozy was out of the picture now. The rumour was he had been sacked for drinking in the storeroom, which surprised nobody, so Toddy had lost his tormenting buddy. Billy swore if Toddy tried to beat him up again without witnesses being there, he would knock the old prick out. He was a big man, but Billy didn't think Toddy would be so sure of himself if his partner in crime wasn't there to back him up. Within ten minutes of entering the class, Billy's hopes of an incident free afternoon were dashed. Toddy was handing out the homework the boys had handed in the week before, giving his usual barbed comments as he went round the class.

"Rubbish."

"If you let your dad do your homework again, Smith, I'm going belt you into next week."

"This beggars belief, Simpson. A monkey with a packet of crayons could do better than that."

"Where's your homework, Loy?" Toddy stopped behind Billy.

"What?" Billy had been expecting a negative comment about the work he had handed in. Toddy slapped Billy on the back of the head.

"Are you deaf as well as stupid, boy? Where's your homework?"

Billy turned round in his chair to face Toddy. "I handed it in last week like everyone else." He managed to speak through gritted teeth.

"Where is it then?" Toddy showed he could talk through gritted teeth just as well as Billy.

"I don't know. You must have lost it."

Some of the boys sniggered, drawing a threatening look from Toddy which silenced them all again.

"Well, you can stay behind after class and help me and my belt find it, okay?" Toddy shouted the last bit of the sentence into Billy's face. Billy turned back round in his chair, not wanting to show how annoyed he was at the injustice being thrust upon him for the umpteenth time.

Billy stayed in his seat when the bell rang for home time, a couple of his mates clapping him on the shoulder as they left in the only show of support open to them. Billy had fumed for the whole class. Toddy was taking the piss. Once everyone had left and Toddy had gone through the pretence of tidying up in silence, he went to the drawer of his desk and brought out his belt. He walked to the side of the classroom where he had more room to wield his strap, also making it less likely that anyone passing by outside would see what was happening. He gestured to Billy to stand in front of him. Billy remained on his seat.

"I handed my homework in." Billy struggled to keep his voice steady.

Toddy looked at Billy with fire in his eyes. "Get your arse up here and take your punishment like a man."

Billy stood up, throwing his seat back violently as he did. He walked over to Toddy and held his hands up, the right one on top of the left. Toddy let fly with the belt, but his aim was off a bit, catching Billy across his thumb. Billy hoped he managed to stop himself from wincing, but getting caught on the thumb was always more painful than a direct hit.

"Missed. Again." Toddy knew he hadn't missed. After a while, he was beginning to sweat and had lost count of how many lashes he had administered, when Billy lowered his hands and put them behind his back. "Again!"

"That's twelve. You can't give me any more than that. It's the law." Billy still hadn't shown a flicker of discomfort.

"The law?" Toddy laughed. "What would a little hoodlum like you know about the law? I missed you with half of them anyway. Again!" Toddy's blood was boiling. The little prick was going to crack soon, he could sense it.

"You've gone too far!" Billy raised his voice for the first time.

"Again!" Toddy was almost frothing at the mouth, his face red from his exertion and his frustration. Billy slowly raised his hands again. Toddy jumped as high as he could and brought the belt swinging down with all his might, hitting Billy halfway up his arm. The force of the blow sent Billy's hands down as low as they could go without his legs buckling. Toddy paused to check the response on the boy's face but there was nothing. "I missed! Again!"

Billy raised his hands again slowly, but there was a look of determination on his face that Toddy would have done well in noticing. Toddy took another jump and swung the belt, but this time Billy separated his hands slightly, timing it perfectly to catch the end of the belt as it struck. In one action he ripped the belt out of Toddy's hand and swung the handle end round, smashing the teacher on the right cheek. Toddy was off balance and went spinning into the desks, knocking over some chairs. Before he could recover, Billy had covered the ground between them and was swinging the belt at his head. Toddy was cowering under a flurry of blows, the thick belt catching him again and again on the face and head. Billy followed each blow of the belt in his right hand with a left hook with his fist, the frustration he had been feeling for months pouring out of him. It was only exhaustion that made him stop, Toddy now lying on the ground, tears running out of his eyes. Billy leant down and stared into his teacher's face.

"We're done. You try that again and I'll fucking kill you."

Billy left the classroom, leaving Barry sobbing on the floor. He waited to make sure the thug wasn't coming back before he got up and dusted himself down. He could feel red welts from the belt burning on his face as the tears flowed. He took a last look around the room.

"Fuck that."

As he left, Toddy already knew he wouldn't be back. The kids could all rot in hell as far as he was concerned. He would call his mate who had offered him a real job and he would start on Monday.

CHAPTER NINETEEN

Huh?

"WHAT DO YOU do with it?"

"Put it on your tongue and swallow it."

Billy and Danny were standing looking down at two tiny squares of paper that Danny had taken out of an envelope and placed on the table. Each square had a skull and crossbones on it.

"Does it hurt?"

"What?" Danny looked at Billy as though he was daft.

"Well, some acids burn you, don't they?" Billy didn't think his question was daft enough to elicit Danny's patronising response.

"Of course not." Danny didn't seem too sure now. "Will we do it at the same time?"

"Okay, let's go."

The boys picked up the tabs, counted to three and popped them on their tongues. After they had swallowed, they looked at each other, studying to see any kind of adverse reaction. They sat down on Danny's bed and waited. After five minutes, Billy broke the silence.

"Feel anything yet?"

"Nothing."

After another five minutes of silence, it was Danny's turn to speak.

"I don't feel anything."

"Me neither. Fuck, we've been sold duds." There was almost relief in Billy's voice.

"Fuck it, at least we've got our wine. We can still get pished and have a laugh." Danny was keen to forget it was him who had bought the tabs, especially if they had been ripped off.

"Aye, maybe the wine will help it come on." Billy sounded hopeful it wouldn't be the case.

"Come on, will we head down the Genny's?" Danny was keen to

get out of his house in case his parents could notice what the boys were up to.

"Aye, let's go." Billy was just as desperate to leave.

"Will I get some cheese?" Danny didn't know if there was anything other than Dairylea triangles in the house.

"Don't be daft." Billy laughed.

The General's Bridge wasn't a bridge. It was a bridge, but it wasn't where the party was being held. The real General's Bridge was a good bit further down Stoneymeadow Road, near Crossbaskets. The party was being held on top of one of the old viaduct walls which had supported the Caledonian railway line built in the late 1800s, linking Busby, East Kilbride and Blantyre, terminating at the now derelict Calderglen station. The railway line had been dismantled between the 1940s and 1960s when the new line had opened to support the new town springing from the old village and its surrounding farms. The abandoned viaduct walls were now overgrown with grass and weeds and provided a playground for the children of Calderwood. None of them knew the history of the area so the viaduct was mistakenly christened The General's Bridge, or the Genny's as it was commonly known.

To reach the Genny's you walked through the tunnel below the dual carriageway running down to Blantyre and Hamilton. The heavily graffitied underpass was solely designed for pedestrians to reach the bus stop where you caught the 201 bus, servicing the workers heading to the various industrial jobs Lanarkshire had to offer. Behind the bus stop there was a fence and nothing else as far as the commuters were concerned.

For the children, when you climbed over the fence behind the bus stop there was the playground of Calderglen wood and the abandoned viaducts. During the day there were rope swings, mock battlefields, cross-country bike tracks and all manner of adventures brought to life by youthful minds. When it snowed, the steep hill down to Stoneymeadow Road became a sledge run unsurpassed anywhere else in the town. Many young bones were broken, and teeth smashed out by misadventure, but it was thrilling, and the adults didn't seem to know of its existence, which made it even more exciting.

By night it was the domain of the teenagers. For the same reasons as the younger kids during the day, it was a refuge where they could get up to whatever they wanted without any adults coming down to spoil their fun. It was remote enough that noise was never going to be a problem and dark enough to ensure that even if any stray adult, or more importantly the police, did wander down, the teenagers could hide or disperse without any fear of being identified. They knew the place like the back of their hand whereas adults would be in danger of breaking an ankle in the various rabbit holes or falling from the viaduct onto the road below. It was the perfect spot for a party.

Neither Billy nor Danny was feeling any effect from dropping the acid tabs when they climbed the fence at the back of the bus stop. The bus stop had been smashed up because the plastic windows were missing. They could immediately hear the sound of drunken merriment and as they crested the hill, they saw what was causing all the hilarity. A group of boys were sitting on one of the bus stop windows, using it as a sledge to hurtle down the slope towards a pile of snow at the bottom which had been modelled into a ramp. Most of the boys had already fallen off before the window hit the ramp and took off. The two lads still on board took off in separate directions as the window flew into the air, coming to a thumping halt just before the small burn which ran alongside the road at the bottom of the viaduct. The crowd on top of the viaduct all cheered as the window continued its journey through the wire fence and onto Stoneymeadow Road. Thankfully, very few cars used the old road now that the dual carriageway had made it redundant to everyone bar the patrons of East Kilbride private golf course, who still had to go that way to get to the club house.

"That looks fucking dangerous." Billy had stopped in his tracks.

"Yeah. Fancy a go?" Danny looked excited at the prospect.

"Maybe later. Let's get pished." Billy held up his bottle of Old England and clinked it with Danny's bottle of Buckfast. They smiled at each other and started towards the viaduct.

An hour later there must have been thirty people on top of the viaduct wall, a small fire going strong to help keep everyone warm in the freezing winter night. Billy had been sitting looking at his hand for the past ten minutes, fascinated at how his fingers trailed in the light from the fire. He looked round the people sitting close to him. A group were playing chew the dowt. As a non-smoker, it was never a game Billy had taken part in, but tonight it was fascinating him. Cigarettes were always thin on the ground for the teenagers so sharing was a big part of life. In this game, a cigarette was passed round, each person getting one drag before passing it to the next participant. The aim of the game was to take your drag without letting the ash fall off the end. Whoever let the ash fall first, had to chew the stub end of the cigarette for a count of twenty seconds, something that Billy imagined was disgusting beyond words. This round was going well. The ash remained intact and there could only have been a few drags remaining when it was passed to the singer of Teenage Vice, whose name Billy couldn't remember. The precarious ash was bent at an angle Billy couldn't believe and the tension was incredible. The singer put the cigarette to his lips while he lay flat on his back, hoping his position would help the fight against gravity, but just as he began to suck, the ash toppled onto his face, much to the delight of everyone watching. Billy had been holding his breath so long watching the game that he had to gulp in cold air to reinflate his lungs before he passed out. He shook his head and rubbed his eyes to bring himself back to reality.

Every second person had a crisp bag held up to their mouth, inhaling in and out like someone having a Golden Wonder panic attack. The smell of glue and Zoff hung heavy in the air. Zoff was a substance designed for removing stubborn sticking plasters, available in any chemist, but on top of the Genny's it was a cheap alternative to glue that gave a buzz without the acne most solvent abusers experienced. To Billy, the glue sniffers were breathing in unison and the sound of the crisp bags expanding and deflating was becoming louder by the second. There was also a guy sat in the corner with ginger spiky hair who was beginning to look more like David Bowie every time Billy looked at him.

Billy felt someone kicking him on the foot and it was only then he realised that Lisa was standing right in front of him. He had no idea how long she had been there.

"You wanted to talk to me?"

Lisa looked spectacular. She was dressed in black from head to toe and her hair was spiked out all round her head, making it hard for Billy to calculate where her head stopped, and the clear night sky started. Her make-up was just like Siouxsie Sioux from The Banshees. Billy wasn't sure but he may have drooled.

"Huh?"

"Danny said you wanted to talk to me about something. Have you been sniffing glue?" Lisa could tell something wasn't right, but she wasn't sure what.

"No." Billy was indignant. Lisa shrugged and started to walk away until Billy remembered that he did want to talk to her. "I mean no, I haven't been sniffing glue. I do want to talk to you though. I've written this song. It's a duet for Suzi Quatro and David Bowie over there," Billy nodded at the ginger guy in the corner, "but until I can get it to them, I'm going to use it for my own band. We're called Handclap. You won't have heard of us yet but we're going to be huge. I think it would really suit your voice and I suppose I could pass for a poor man's Bowie so I was thinking we could do it until I can track Suzi down." Billy stopped talking abruptly, wondering who he was talking to before he remembered it was Lisa. He looked up to make sure she was still there.

"You've never heard my voice."

"Huh?"

"You said the song would really suit my voice, but you've never heard my voice." Lisa had noticed how weird Danny had been acting earlier but Billy seemed to be on another planet.

"I have."

"When?"

"Just there." Billy wondered if Lisa was on something. Maybe she was so drunk she didn't realise she was talking.

"I mean you've never heard me sing." Lisa rolled her eyes.

Billy thought about this for a while until he forgot what he was supposed to be thinking about.

"Huh?"

"Are you on acid?" The penny was beginning to drop for Lisa.

"Yes!" Billy remembered now. "But I don't think it's working."

"Cool. So, you want me to join your band?" Lisa would never be taking acid, but she liked the fact Billy did. He was cute in a drugged-up, trampy kind of way.

"Yes! How did you guess?" Billy held his hands out in astonishment, as though Lisa had read his mind.

"You just said. Look, never mind, when do you practise?" Lisa wasn't going to spend too much time on this conversation when the chances of Billy remembering it were so slim.

"Tuesday nights at the Long Calderwood youth club?" Billy couldn't be sure, but he thought that sounded familiar.

"Okay, I'll come on Tuesday and see what you're like and let you know." Lisa turned and started to walk away.

"Would you like to sit?" Billy didn't want Lisa to leave.

"Nah. Engrossing as it is to listen to you talk shite, I have to get up the road." Lisa gave him a smile and walked off into the darkness.

"Okay. Bye." Billy lay down on the grass, no longer capable of holding his incredibly heavy head upright.

"Alright, Billy?"

The new voice made Billy sit bolt upright again. It was only then that he noticed Dick sitting next to him.

"Dick? What are you doing here?" Billy recognised Dick, but he surprised himself by knowing his name.

"I always come here. This is where me and my mates hang about." Dick was smiling his familiar smile. Billy looked really confused.

"You've got mates?" He couldn't keep the deep-felt surprise out of his voice.

Dick started laughing. "Aye, half of the guys here are my mates. You're not the only punk in town, you know."

Billy looked around. It was true he hadn't a clue who half of the people were, but not in a million years would he have guessed they were Dick's mates.

"You like punk? I had no idea..." Billy wondered if he had any idea about anything. If Billy was honest, he didn't know very much about Dick at all. He knew he worked on Oggy's float, and nobody seemed to like him, but he couldn't remember ever talking to him before. Billy couldn't remember if Dick had said anything in reply, so he took the chance and spoke again. "Wow. That's great. So, who are your mates?" Billy still wasn't convinced any of the people were really there with Dick. Maybe the acid was beginning to kick in and he hadn't noticed.

"That big guy there is my cousin Benny, then there's Sid, Stooge, Col, Tam and a whole bunch of others. They're the Blantyre punks." Dick was pointing to a load of shapes sitting round the fire.

"Blantyre?" Billy went rigid.

"Aye." Dick kept on smiling.

"Fuck's sake," Billy tried to get up but his legs were way behind his brain and refused to respond. He just toppled over, his head landing on Dick's lap. "I need to get out of here." His mouth was behind his brain in the response stakes too.

"Why?" Dick was laughing now.

"You don't understand, these guys killed my dad." Billy tried to get up again, but Dick held his arm.

"Don't be daft, they didn't kill your dad. The guy who killed your dad is in the jail." Dick's voice was soothing.

Billy put his hands over his face and rubbed his eyes, hoping that this would clear his mind, or even better, transport him somewhere far away from what was happening.

"Your dad was killed by a guy called Sammy Graham. He got eighteen years, and he killed another guy in prison two years ago, so he's not going to be out until he's an old fella. You don't need to worry about him. And it wasn't a gang fight either. Sammy killed your dad because he was a grass and he'd been shagging Sammy's wee sister. She was a Tim, and your dad was a Hun. There was a big Rangers/Celtic thing. Anyway, Sammy's wee sister had a wean and your dad wouldn't admit it was his because he was married to your maw by that time. Sammy eventually found out who the dad was and lured Tommy to a bogus meeting one night and killed him. All that stuff about your dad taking on the Tyre gang single-handed is a lot of shite made up by The Woodie of the day to stop any scandal. It was easier to make your dad into a hero than it was to accept the leader of their gang had gone to the polis and been shagging a Tim." Dick laughed at the stupidity of it all.

Dick's smile hadn't faltered once in all the time he was talking. Billy stayed still for what seemed like an age, not taking his hands away from his face. Eventually he slowly removed his hands one finger at a time, hoping Dick would have gone by the time he opened his eyes. He looked round to see Dick still sitting there, smiling at Billy as though nothing had been said.

"Did your maw never tell you the truth about all of this?" Dick offered Billy a cigarette.

"No!" Billy couldn't take it all in. "Who told you all of this?"

"My maw." Dick was so casual.

"And how the fuck does she know all of this?" Billy was struggling to follow.

"Ah, that's the interesting bit." Dick was laughing again.

"That's the interesting bit? How?" Billy was getting frustrated.

"Because she is Sammy's wee sister." Dick made a kind of 'ta-DAH!' gesture with his hands.

Billy's legs were ahead of his brain this time. He was up and running before he realised what he was doing. He bound down the hill from the top of the viaduct and started sprinting back up towards the fence and the dual carriageway. He couldn't see a thing in front of him. About twenty yards up the hill he ran straight into a bush and toppled head over heels into the middle of it. Everything was deathly quiet. Billy decided to stay where he was until he could work out if he had injured himself or not. His mind was spinning around and crashing into confusion until he became aware of people standing right next to him. He couldn't see anyone, but he could sense danger and stayed as still as he could.

"Right, let's go and kick fuck out of these pricks. Grab as much booze as you can and be careful nobody falls off the bridge." Billy recognised Cheesy's voice. "And remember, if Billy Loy's there, leave him. He's fucking mine."

Billy held his breath as he heard numerous voices grunt in agreement. In the moment's silence, he feared they had spotted him lying in the bush right next to them and were waiting for him to breathe again before pouncing on him and kicking him around the place. Then the silence was broken.

"Fucking Woodie!" The gang standing next to him all started running towards the viaduct, their battle cries filling the air. Billy wondered if now would be a good time to make his escape, but he waited to see what would happen because he couldn't trust his body to run in the right direction. The Woodie battle cry had barely faded when a response came whooshing down from the top of the viaduct.

"Tyre! Fucking come ahead!" The familiar battle cry of the Blantyre gang sounded angrier than The Woodie one.

Two seconds later the sound of retreating Woodie boys came whizzing past Billy.

"Run! It's the fucking Tyre up there, not the punks!"

Thankfully nobody made the same mistake Billy had and came

tumbling into the bush beside him. The last thing he heard was Cheesy shouting at his retreating comrades as he chased after them.

"Get fucking back here, ya poofs. Stand your ground, ya useless cunts."

Cheesy was still shouting after his gang members but his voice was disappearing into the distance as they all ran away. As Billy crept out of the bush to head home, he could hear the people on top of the viaduct laughing uproariously. Billy wondered if any of what had happened was real or if the acid was finally kicking in.

CHAPTER TWENTY

He Loves a Chip

BUNNET DIDN'T MIND the cold. You couldn't live in East Kilbride and be bothered by the cold. The town was at the top of a hill no matter which direction you looked and sometimes it was easy to believe the myth that it had its own climate. When it snowed, it snowed. As Bunnet preached to the boys he employed, and their mothers who fussed over them, three layers of clothing and a pair of sturdy shoes were all you needed to survive.

Friday was the only night Bunnet let himself stray from his strict in bed by eight regime and even then, he never strayed past nine-thirty. A couple of pints in The Salmon Leap, a game of darts and a fish supper on the way home was his way of letting his hair down. How some of the younger drivers could drink the amount they did and still manage to do the job the next day was beyond him. Tonight, Kojak had been in the bar, and he was legless by the time Bunnet left. He always seemed to have plenty of money to throw around, buying drinks for all and sundry, but Bunnet knew that all the people who surrounded him and benefitted from the splashing of the cash had not one ounce of respect for him. They took his drink and laughed at his jokes, but when he was gone nobody missed him.

Bunnet liked The Salmon Leap. His flat was probably slightly nearer The Matelot, the other pub in Calderwood, but the people who went there weren't as friendly. In fact, Bunnet would go as far as to say the people in The Matelot were weird. It was one of those places where everyone went quiet if a stranger walked in, as though they all had something to hide. The Salmon Leap was boisterous and busy, and the regulars were a welcoming bunch. It was the only pub he knew of that had both a Rangers and a Celtic supporters bus run from it. It could still get a bit lively at times, especially on Old Firm days, but there wasn't a pub in East Kilbride that didn't have its problems where violence was involved. It was part of the drinking culture.

The walk home was always brisk. Bunnet didn't like eating his fish supper until he got home, so he would power walk down the road, even when the snow was thick like it was tonight. The streets were always quiet by 8.30. Bunnet had no idea where all the kids went at night. During the day you would see kids everywhere, playing football, having fun inventing games nobody was sure about or climbing trees and making the most of the many swing parks available. By seven there were still some seen hanging around in groups, especially outside the chippy where the local neds would get their fun by being obnoxious to anyone who happened to come by but tonight, even they were nowhere to be seen. Bunnet guessed that the snow had driven most of them inside. Up ahead he could see a young woman with a pushchair struggling through the snow, heading in the same direction as he was but at only half the pace. As he got nearer, he realised it was the young girl who had moved into the flats next to his with her baby.

Bunnet lived in what were classed as 'cottage flats'. There were only four in a block, all one bedroom, but they were surrounded by rows of three-storey houses designed to house the mega-families every town had. One of the houses next to him had nine children in it. The very idea of living with nine children made Bunnet shudder. He liked kids, but nine was ridiculous. He found it strange that the council would house a young mother and her baby in a one-bedroom flat, but housing was at a premium in the town. Houses were being built at an incredible rate, even though the factories seemed to be closing right, left and centre. You would think the demand for houses would go down if the jobs were disappearing, but Bunnet guessed the council knew better than him and they would be working hard to bring more jobs to satisfy the demand of the growing tenant numbers. More houses meant more customers for the dairy, so who was Bunnet to complain? Everyone still needed milk whether they had a job or not.

Bunnet was keen to let the young woman know that her neighbours were there to help her if she needed it. Community was important. He had seen Oggy going in and out of her place a few times, making him wonder if perhaps the child was something to do with him. Bunnet hoped not. Oggy didn't strike him as father material and just the other day he had spotted him grab the young girl roughly by the arm and point angrily in her face as she was going into her flat. Bunnet knew what went on behind closed doors between a man and his wife was none of his business but when it happened in the middle of the street, right outside his flat, it gave him the right to at least make sure she was okay. He quickened his step and caught up with her just as a teddy bear was launched from the pushchair by the crying child. The mother hadn't noticed, so Bunnet picked it up and jogged the final few yards.

"Here you go, love. You've left somebody behind." The woman physically flinched as she spun round to face Bunnet. Her face was white as a sheet and her eyes were bright red from crying. "I'm sorry, I didn't mean to give you a fright. That's the problem with snow, it deadens the sound of footsteps..." Bunnet smiled, hoping this would show the girl that he meant her no harm. "You won't get far without this." Bunnet held up the teddy bear. "It sounds like the bairn needs it..."

The girl took the bear from Bunnet and gave it back to the baby. She avoided eye contact and immediately started to walk again. The pushchair got stuck in the snow and nearly toppled over. She let out a small yelp and the tears started to flow again.

"Hey, hey. It's hard pushing that thing in the snow. Don't let it upset you. Here, let me give you a hand." Bunnet put his hand on the handle of the pushchair.

"Get your fucking hands off my baby. What do you think you're doing?" The girl looked like Bunnet had tried to dip her purse or something.

Bunnet held his hands up. "It's okay, I just want to help. I'm your neighbour. My name's Ken."

"What?" The girl looked at Bunnet for the first time. Bunnet was holding out his hand to shake hers.

"My name's Ken, although most people call me Bunnet, for obvious reasons." Bunnet pointed at his ever-present cap. "I live at number 95 in the block next to you. I've seen you in the street a couple of times. I'm just on my way home from having a pint so I'm going the same way as you. I can push the bairn for a bit to give you a break if you like?"

The girl looked at the pram then back to Bunnet. "Maggie."

"Maggie! Is that you or the bairn?" Bunnet was relieved she seemed to be relaxing a bit.

Maggie laughed. "It's me. I don't think he would be too pleased at being called Maggie."

Bunnet laughed too. "Sorry, I never know with babies whether it's a boy or a girl. I never had any myself..." Bunnet suddenly felt sad about that, but quickly caught himself and bent down to the child. "So, what's your name, young man?"

"This is Adam." Bunnet could hear Maggie's pride in her voice.

"Pleased to meet you, Adam." Bunnet shook the baby's hand. Adam had stopped crying and looked fascinated at the strange man bending over him. "Here Maggie, let me push him for a while. Your arms must be aching pushing through all this snow."

Maggie stepped aside and let Bunnet take charge of the pushchair. She lit a cigarette and walked along beside him. Bunnet thought she seemed nervous, but the poor girl was probably just at the end of her tether, bringing up a baby on her own.

"You've not lived here long, Maggie. How are you finding it?" Bunnet guessed he would need to start the conversation. Maggie was only interested in her cigarette.

"It's okay." Maggie's voice still shook a little, as though it wouldn't take too much for the tears to return.

"It's not a bad place to bring up a kid. The swing park is right next to us so this wee one will be flying around there before you know it. And there's loads of other kids around so he'll have a gang of mates in no time."

"Aye." Maggie didn't sound too sure.

"And what about you, Maggie? Do you work?" Bunnet knew she probably didn't, but he had never been very good at small talk.

"Not really." Maggie wasn't giving anything away.

"Aye, it must be tough trying to fit a job in when you're running after this one all the time. It's like a full-time job, I would imagine."

Maggie didn't answer and Bunnet didn't push it. If the lassie wanted a bit of quiet to have her cigarette, it was understandable. They walked in silence until they reached the flats.

"Well, this is me here, Maggie. Will you manage the rest of the way on your own? I can help you into the flat if you want..."

"No!" Maggie was insistent, but then softened. "Thanks, Ken. I appreciate it."

"No problem at all, hen. I'll get in and heat this up, see if it will defrost me a bit." Bunnet pulled his fish supper out of his pocket. The smell of salt and vinegar cut through the cold air.

Maggie laughed. "That's what it was. I could smell that all the way and wondered where it was coming from. It smells brilliant."

Bunnet laughed too. "Aye it's my Friday treat, a fish supper."

"Lovely. Enjoy." Maggie looked down again as she started to walk away.

"Have you eaten yet, Maggie?" Bunnet had a feeling.

Maggie stopped and turned round. "I'm sorry?"

"I get a fish supper every Friday but after a couple of pints, I never finish it. I always end up throwing half of it away if you fancy coming in and sharing it with me." This was a lie. Bunnet loved his fish supper and picked every last greasy bit of it off the paper wrapper, but the girl looked like she hadn't eaten for a week. Maggie hesitated before answering.

"Och no, I couldn't..." She was convincing nobody.

"Don't be daft. Honestly, it'll just go in the bin. Come on, we're neighbours now. Neighbours look after each other round here..." Bunnet smiled the smile he used for winning over new customers for the milk round.

"Well if you're sure... I've not had a chance to eat anything yet..." Maggie was fighting her instincts but the smell of salt and vinegar was driving her crazy.

"Of course. Come on. I think I've even got a biscuit or something for young Adam if you think he'd like it." Bunnet hoped that would close the deal.

"Oh, I'm sure he would. He loves a chip too..." Maggie smiled at Adam, who was watching the adults talk like he knew what they were saying.

"That decides it then. Let's go eat."

Bunnet let Maggie and Adam into the flat. He went into the kitchen to put the fish supper in the oven for ten minutes. The extra time taken pushing the pram had left it stone cold in his pocket. Maggie took Adam into the toilet to change his nappy. By the time she came out Bunnet was bringing two plates through with the split fish supper and a wee side plate with a handful of chips and a piece of shortbread on it for Adam. Maggie looked a lot more relaxed. She had obviously washed her face while she was in there.

"I don't have a table, so it'll just have to be on our laps if that's okay." There had never been room for a dining table and Bunnet would have felt stupid sitting at it on his own.

"Oh, it smells great, Ken. Thanks so much." Maggie looked round the living room. "Your flat is so nice. Much nicer than mine…"

"Well, I've been here a long time. You've just moved in. I'm sure you'll have yours even nicer than this once you get on your feet." Bunnet was delighted with the compliment. He did his best to keep the place nice.

Maggie handed the small plate to Adam and set about devouring her own. She almost inhaled the food, while Adam immediately went for the shortbread, sucking the sugar off with a smile on his face. Before Bunnet had eaten half of his, Maggie was scooping up the last of the grease on her plate with the last chip.

"Aw man, that was delicious. Thanks Ken, I can't remember the last time we had a chippy tea." Maggie lit another cigarette and sat back in the chair.

"Any time, Maggie." Bunnet was pleased he had offered to share his food. The girl was obviously struggling, and he liked helping people.

"So, what is it you do, Ken?" Maggie was beginning to relax in his company.

"Actually, I'm in the same game as your pal Angus." Bunnet watched to see what the reaction would be to the mention of Oggy's name.

"Who?" Maggie was looking round for an ashtray. When she couldn't find one, she flicked her ash on her empty plate.

"Angus. You probably call him Oggy…" Maggie immediately froze.

"You're the same as Oggy?" Fear had crept into her eyes.

"We work for different dairies, but we work the same area. I've seen him coming out of yours a few times." Bunnet wasn't going to mention that he had seen Oggy being rough with her. "We're rivals, really. He drives for Wisemans and I'm with Hamiltons, but we work the same route."

"Dairies?" Maggie looked confused.

"Aye, you know, milk floats. He delivers for Wisemans, and I deliver for Hamiltons."

Maggie thought about it for a while. "That'll be why he's around all the time..."

"Did he not tell you that's what he did?" Bunnet gave a small chuckle of disbelief.

"I had no idea. I thought he made his money from the girls and that was all." Maggie was speaking without thinking.

"The girls?" Bunnet thought he might be getting somewhere. Maggie sat up and started to tuck Adam back into the pushchair, as though she had said enough already and thought it best to leave. "What girls?"

Maggie thought hard and then sat back in her chair again, a look of resignation on her face. "Look Ken, I hate to burst your bubble about your mate, but Oggy is a pimp. He runs all the girls around here and if I'm honest he's not a very nice man. I would appreciate if you didn't tell him I said that, but he's not being very nice to me just now so I don't see why I should stick up for him..."

Ken couldn't believe it. "He's a pimp?"

"Sorry, I should go. I need to get Adam to bed." Adam looked up at the sound of his name, sugar all over his face now.

"And you work for him?" Bunnet couldn't keep the disappointment out of his voice.

"How do you think I got the flat?" Maggie was tired of being judged and having to explain herself to people.

"But how did he get the flat? These are council flats..." Bunnet had so many questions running through his head, he couldn't think where to begin.

"I've no idea and I don't care. All I know is I don't have to work the streets and I don't have to go back to live with my oh-so-judgemental parents. He's got flats all over the place and as long as I make money for him, I get to live there rent-free." Maggie looked at how disappointed Bunnet was and felt sorry for him. "I really appreciate the food, Ken, I really do, and I'm sorry I'm the one to let you know the truth about your mate, but I'm not going to apologise for doing what I have to do for my son. I can't get a proper job and I'm never going to get a flat from the council. I do what I do to survive."

Maggie stood up and pushed Adam out of the flat, leaving

Bunnet staring into space, unable to process what he had just heard. Maggie was long gone before he replied.

"I can assure you he's not my mate."

CHAPTER TWENTY-ONE

Acid Hangover

HUGH NAVIGATED THE float up Geddes Hill carefully. The thick snow levelled the roads, so the bottles of milk didn't rattle so much in their crates, the hum of the electric motor the only sound breaking the clean, crisp air.

Saturdays were the toughest day of the week, but they could also be the most fun. The boys were encouraged to bring a mate out with them to help deliver the double run. There was no delivery on a Sunday, so people would double up on a Saturday to avoid going without. This meant there were fewer bottles on board and more two-pint cartons, which made carrying each load a nightmare. Cartons didn't fit the crates as well, so everything was bulkier and more difficult to carry. Bringing your mate out with you meant less hassle for the boys and created a party atmosphere, with eight boys crammed onto the float instead of the usual four. It meant more work for the drivers, too. The float was heavier and more difficult to manoeuvre, and you always had to be on the lookout for inexperienced boys falling off or trying to jump on and off at the wrong moments. It was down to the boys themselves to pay their mates, so the drivers didn't lose out financially. During the summer months it was easy to encourage a mate to come out and help, but when the snow was this heavy and the biting cold found its way into your bones in no time at all, it was sometimes a harder sell. A lot of boys left the job in the winter, so every morning each driver had bated breath until everyone was picked up, present and correct.

Billy was sitting outside the flat waiting to be collected, his head in his hands as though he was still half-asleep. Even as Hugh pulled to a stop right in front of him, Billy still didn't move.

"Billy!"

Hugh's shout snapped Billy into automatic pilot. He rubbed his eyes and walked over to the float, staggering slightly as he moved. He hadn't been in the flat. The acid had only started to wear off slightly about half an hour ago and he hadn't managed to climb the stairs to rest before it was time to work. He wasn't sure how long it had taken him to get from the Genny's to his current position, but it had felt like a lifetime. He had spent a long time in the underground car park at the high flats, only a hundred metres from the underpass leading to where everyone continued their night out, after he had left. Paranoia had kicked in and he was wary in case Cheesy and his cronies were still lurking around, waiting to pick off revellers as they headed home.

Billy had never felt so confused. Had he spoke to Lisa? Where was Danny? Had he really seen David Bowie on top of the viaduct and what the fuck had he ever done to make Cheesy hate him so much? He couldn't even be sure any of it had really happened. It had been so dark that he couldn't be sure it had been The Woodie standing next to him while he hid in his bush. And the whole Dick thing? Surely that couldn't have really happened. Surely his mum would have mentioned it if his dad had been involved with Dick's mum. Billy knew his dad was a bit of a Jack-the-lad, but he couldn't contemplate the idea that he would have treated Mary so badly. The only thing that was clear in his mind was the certainty he would never be going near acid again. The hours spent in the underground car park had been terrifying, although he remembered laughing a lot too. At one point he had poked his head out to see if the coast was clear, only for one of the streetlights to bend down in front of him and give him a friendly wink. That had reassured Billy that the acid was working and he wasn't just going insane. He had fretted a lot about what he had done to Toddy, crying at one point at the thought of not getting to take his exams. It seemed to all have happened at once, yet he wasn't sure any of it had happened at all.

Now that he was coming down from his trip, he had a headache and the thought of doing a Saturday shift was the last thing he wanted to contemplate. He had imagined the milk float being stuck in the snow and it was so clear a vision that he thought it was true. Now the float was in front of him, and he had nowhere to hide. Billy climbed into the cab and lay down on the shelf where the boys usually sat.

"Are you okay?" The concern in Hugh's voice was genuine. The boy looked haunted.

"Not really." Billy closed his eyes, hoping that would make everything go away.

"Is it a hangover or are you unwell?"

Hugh wasn't about to force the boy to work if he was ill, but if it was a hangover, he would have no sympathy. If it was any other boy he probably wouldn't ask, but he had been seeing Mary quite a bit recently, although neither Billy nor his brother knew anything about that yet. If he had to give Billy some special treatment over the other boys to gain some favour with his mother, then that's what he was willing to do. Things were going well, and he liked Mary a lot, so it would be a small price to pay.

"I don't know if it counts as a hangover. I dropped an acid tab last night and I feel a bit weird." Billy still had his eyes shut so he couldn't see the look on Hugh's face.

"You what?" Hugh was genuinely shocked.

"I took acid. It was okay at first but then I freaked out a bit and I've been feeling weird ever since. It's wearing off a bit now, but I won't be in any rush to take it again." Billy kept his eyes closed.

Hugh couldn't believe the matter-of-fact way Billy was dropping this bombshell. He didn't consider himself to be a prude, he had smoked a bit of hash in his younger days, but acid was something else. That's what rockstars took, not fifteen-year-old milk boys.

"Where the fuck did you get acid from?"

"Danny bought it off Kojak. Everybody takes it…"

Billy opened one eye, sensing that what he was saying was causing a reaction in Hugh that he didn't expect. Hugh was a bit of an arsehole, but he was okay usually. Billy had forgotten he was an adult.

"Kojak sold you acid?" Hugh couldn't believe what he was hearing. He knew Kojak was dodgy, but he would never sell drugs to kids.

"Yeah. He sells anything you want. Pot, acid, mushrooms, speed…" Billy trailed off and closed his eyes again. If Hugh was going to be a prick about it, there was nothing Billy could do about it now.

"Kojak does?" Hugh was convinced Billy was winding him up.

"Everything okay?" Mary's voice gave Hugh the fright of his life.

He looked up and saw her standing in the balcony at the front of the flat, clutching her dressing gown tightly around her to keep out the cold. Hugh gathered himself and waved up to her.

"Aye, we're just heading off."

"Is he there? I didn't hear him going out." Mary was squinting to try and get sight of Billy.

"Aye, he's here. Tired, but he's here." Hugh waved again and set off down the hill. He drove down the hill until he was out of sight from Mary and stopped again.

"What the fuck, Billy? Acid? You can't be fucking around with that kind of shite."

Hugh was at a loss at what to say. He didn't want to come across all fatherly in case he gave everything away. Mary had made it clear she was going to tell the boys about seeing him when the time was right. She was making sure there was something there worth telling them before she committed herself, and Hugh understood that completely. He had felt the same, although he had already reached the conclusion that there was something good between the two of them, but he didn't want to get over-keen in case it scared her away. He had no idea how to play it. The best he could do was treat the boy the same as he did the others. The thing was, none of the others were taking acid. At least he didn't think they were.

"It's no big deal, Shug, fuck's sake. Everyone takes it. And I won't be taking it again, it's too heavy." Billy was getting comfortable, lying on the cabin shelf.

Hugh didn't know what to say. "Are you fit enough to do your run? Have you got a mate coming out with you to help?"

"Nah. I'm sure I'll be alright once I get going. I just need to get my head down for a bit while you pick everyone else up."

Billy curled up tighter against the cold and looked like he was asleep instantly. Hugh set off again, not really knowing what to do for the best. Should he tell Mary? If he did it would probably spoil any chance he had of gaining Billy's trust for the future, but if she found out about it and discovered he knew and didn't tell her, it could end their relationship before it got started. He decided to carry on as normal and think later what the best course of action could be. He couldn't handle this and do a Saturday shift at the same time.

"Do you remember my dad, Shug?" Billy's voice sounded

dreamy, and he still had his eyes shut. Hugh panicked and stopped the float again. Billy had never spoken about his dad before with him. Why was he doing it now? Hugh had a bad feeling about this.

"Yeah. He was older than me, I didn't really know him, but I remember him. Sort of." Hugh would have to play it by ear and hope he didn't fuck this up. One wrong word and he could ruin everything with Mary.

"Do you remember when he died?"

Hugh was glad Billy had his eyes shut. He wouldn't see the blind panic his questions were causing. "I remember when it happened. Tragic." Hugh hoped this would be enough.

"Why was he killed? Do you know?"

"It was a fight, I think. Something to do with a feud with some bad guys from Blantyre. The Blantyre guys were all mental in those days..." The truth was, Hugh didn't know any more than that, so he wasn't keeping anything to himself.

"Was he like you, my dad?"

"What do you mean, like me?" Hugh was convinced Billy knew he was seeing his mother now and was about to expose him. "I'm not a fighter, Billy..."

"You know, a shagger about town. Do you think he was cheating on my mum?"

"Listen, I don't know what you've heard about me but I'm not like that. I don't shag around. The guys at the dairy call me Shagger to wind me up. I'm not like that at all..." Hugh was sounding too defensive, too panicky. If he wasn't careful, he was going to give himself away. Billy gave a little chuckle.

"Aye, okay." He clearly didn't believe Hugh. "But was my dad like that?"

Hugh took a second before he answered. "I've no idea, mate. Where are you getting all this?" Hugh worried that calling him mate was too familiar.

"It was just something someone said last night. At least I think someone said it. Fuck knows. Maybe I just imagined it. I'm never taking acid again." Billy was starting to drift off into sleep.

"Just get your head down, Billy. I'll get the other boys to cover your run this morning. You sleep it off and everything will be okay after that."

Hugh waited until he was sure Billy was asleep before setting off again. He shook his head and fretted about how this was going to play out.

CHAPTER TWENTY-TWO

Roundabouts and Shakespeare

CALDERGLEN WAS DESCRIBED by East Kilbride Development Corporation as a 'pleasure ground' for the people to enjoy. It was a deep valley created by the water of The Rotten Calder and ran around the eastern side of the town. Calder House had been established in the 15th century, its 300 acres taking in what was now Calderwood, but only underground ruins of the stately manor remained. If you didn't know the history, you would never be able to imagine the splendour of the estate, with only one wall of the old train station built specifically for the mansion still visible amongst the overgrown trees and bushes. At the top end of the glen, Torrance House stood, another stately home built in the 17th century. It was no longer stately and was used as the clubhouse for the municipal Torrance House golf course, which stretched out towards Strathaven.

During the summer, The Glen, as it was commonly known, became a place for families to stroll and fishermen to try in vain to land something they could be proud of. The pool at the bottom of Horseshoe Falls was a popular swimming spot, the more adventurous climbing to the top of the thirty-foot falls to jump in. It had become a rite of passage for the locals to be able to say they had jumped the falls and survived. In winter nobody went near the place. It was dark and cold and a long way from when it was inhabited by the great and the good. The only resident now was shivering in a tent and wondering what was going wrong in his life.

Cheesy hadn't slept a wink. It wasn't just the cold that kept him awake. He kept hearing noises coming from the woods and he couldn't stop imagining it was The Tyre coming through to get their revenge on him for disturbing their party at the Genny's. He couldn't believe the rest of his gang had shat themselves so quickly when they realised it wasn't the punks having a good time on top of the viaduct. Running away like that was embarrassing, and Cheesy would make sure each and every one of them paid a price for their cowardice. He had already given Nicky a doing for putting them in such a precarious situation, suggesting it was the punks who used the place as their own, although that was backfiring on him now as he had alienated his partner in the crime he intended committing today by beating him up. Stealing the eggs from Kojak was going to be more difficult now, but not impossible.

The plan was foolproof. Cheesy knew Kojak's milk round better than Kojak did, having worked on the float for years before the baldy wank sacked him. The ideal spot to hit the float was when Kojak and that fanny who took Cheesy's job went in to deliver the milk for Sadlers Wells Court, one of the high flats that separated Calderwood and the slightly newer Long Calderwood estates. It took two of them to do the flat, one delivering the milk to the odd numbered floors while the other did the evens. Two lifts serviced the flat, each person using a different lift to make the deliveries. In all, it took around fifteen minutes to deliver to all fourteen floors, and for that whole time, the milk float sat unmanned outside, the other boys off delivering to the surrounding streets. Cheesy would hide at the lockups until Kojak entered the flat, grab the huge egg box and make his escape down through the field at the bottom and across the dual carriageway into the woods that led down to where last night's humiliation had taken place. At that time on a Saturday morning there would be nobody around to see him commit the robbery, and by the time Kojak came out and noticed the eggs were gone, Cheesy would be far away and out of sight.

Cheesy hadn't told Nicky about the eggs being a cover for Kojak's drug stash. He would never have agreed to help if he had known just how severe any repercussions would be, but Cheesy could handle Kojak. If it came to it, he would do the cunt. Kojak was getting soft. It was time for new blood to take over, and Cheesy was ready for the challenge.

Bunnet prided himself in the fact that he had never had an accident while driving the milk float in all the years he had been doing it. Okay, it was unlikely he was going to crash into any other traffic because there wasn't any around for most of the time he was on the road, but weather conditions could make it very tricky, even when the roads were empty. Concentration was key, especially when the snow was this heavy on the ground. The problem was, Bunnet was finding it hard to concentrate this morning. The back end of the float had already spun out while he was going round the Whirlies Roundabout, the heavy load of a Saturday shift making it difficult to control the skid he had experienced. Roundabouts. East Kilbride was full of roundabouts. It was as if the town planners had all been non-drivers and when they had come to a junction, no matter how busy that junction would be, the answer was to throw a bloody roundabout at it. Clueless. You could get dizzy driving from one end of the town to the other.

Bunnet's concentration was drifting because he couldn't stop thinking about Maggie. The revelations about Oggy she had delivered the night before were shocking enough, but Bunnet had run into her again this morning when he was leaving the flat to start his run. She was going into her flat as he was leaving his.

"Maggie?" Bunnet was surprised to see her out and about at this time, especially without Adam. "Is everything okay?"

Maggie looked exhausted. Her face was gaunt and the only way Bunnet could describe the look in her eyes was haunted. She didn't look happy to see Bunnet.

"Fuck's sake, are you fucking stalking me or something? Every time I turn round, you're there."

Bunnet was hurt by her reaction. "I'm just going to start my shift." He was defensive but he didn't know why he felt that way.

"Aye, well, I've just finished mine so if you don't mind, I'm knackered." Maggie walked away from Bunnet, not looking him in the eye as she left.

"Where's Adam?" Bunnet had to ask.

Maggie stopped and walked back to Bunnet, this time staring him down with a look of tired aggression. "What, are you a fucking social worker now? Adam's fine. He's fast asleep indoors just like I want to be. Keep your fucking nose out of my business, alright?"

"Have you been out sleeping with men, and you've left Adam at home on his own?" Bunnet already knew the answer, but his disbelief demanded he ask the question. Maggie let out an ironic laugh.

"Sleeping with men? What century do you live in? I don't sleep with men; I fuck them as quickly as I can. I suck their sorry cocks while I pretend to enjoy it. None of them are men, they're all sad fucks who can't get it at home, so they come to me, and I sell it to them. Is that what you want to hear? Now fuck off and leave me alone. You don't get to judge me for the price of a fucking fish supper..."

Maggie started to cry and stormed into the flat. Bunnet was rooted to the spot as he watched her go. How could a young girl's life be so cruel? She could only be a teenager herself and already Maggie was looking as weary as some of the old dears Bunnet delivered milk to who had been through a war and come out the other side with less than they had before it. It was almost 1980. Things shouldn't be like this.

As Bunnet made sure the crates on the float were still secure after his skid, he knew he would have to put Maggie to the back of his mind until after his shift. He had a duty of care to the boys he was about to pick up and he couldn't afford to let his mind be anywhere other than on the road when the weather was this bad. He decided he would ask around to see exactly what was going on. Maybe Hugh would be able to shed some light. He worked with Oggy, so if anybody knew anything about what he got up to it would be him. Bunnet quite liked Hugh, despite the ridiculous lothario image he radiated. Surely he wasn't involved in this kind of thing, although Bunnet wasn't sure what he could believe now. In the meantime, he had too many roundabouts to deal with.

Oggy was late loading his float. Today was the first time he had slept in since he started driving. Sleep hadn't been coming easy since he found Linda lying dead in her flat and it wasn't getting any easier because as far as he knew, nobody had noticed that she wasn't around anymore. When sleep did come, it was full of visions of Linda decomposing on her sofa. How could nobody have reported her missing? How could anyone's life be so worthless? Obviously, Oggy couldn't tell anyone he had found her dead; too many questions would be asked about his relationship with her. They would want to know how she came to be living in a flat rented out to a person who didn't exist. Oggy's contact in the Development Corporation who gave him flats in return for cash and his hole whenever he wanted it would crumble under questioning, he was sure of that. Everything would lead back to Oggy, and it wasn't fair. Fucking Kojak was to blame for all of this. It was him who sold the drugs to the girls. And it was the drugs that killed Linda. Oggy was watching all the girls on smack going downhill rapidly. Christ knows what that baldy cunt was cutting his gear with, but whatever it was, it was becoming deadly. Oggy could feel the time drawing near when he would have to either cut and run or deal with Kojak once and for all. There was no way he was taking the blame for something he wasn't responsible for.

Kojak was fuming. The boys on his float were going to be the death of him. The useless wee prick who had taken over from Cheesy hadn't turned up this morning and neither had Nicky. Now he only had three boys to do a Saturday shift and one of them was a mate out for a jolly who didn't have a clue what he was doing. He had already fallen jumping off the float and smashed eight pints before they had completed half the round. All of this meant Kojak was going to be late for his meeting with Greer, and that never went down well. He had to finish the run, deliver his weekly hash to the potheads and shoot down to Blantyre to pick up next week's supplies from Greer. The only good thing was how well the acid had sold this week. He hoped asking for double the usual amount of acid for this week would sweeten Greer's mood and let him off lightly for being late. Now he had to deliver to Sadlers Wells Court on his own and that wasn't easy. It was hard enough doing it with help, the only part of the run where Kojak worked up a sweat. Doing it on his own meant he would have to go up in one lift and come back down in the other, which would double the time it usually took.

The East Kilbride town planners had obviously been partaking in some acid of their own when they had been naming the streets of Long Calderwood. It had started off fine in Calderwood, using the names of councillors and dignitaries who had been important when the new town was created. Geddes Hill, Runciman Place, Baillie Drive, all tributes to faceless men long forgotten in 1979, but acceptable as reasonable street names. Then they built Long Calderwood, and the acid must have kicked in. They decided Shakespeare, Walter Scott and J M Barrie should be the major influence for this area. The high flats became Shaftesbury Court or Globe Court, leading down to streets like Hamlet, Falstaff or Orlando. Then it got even more ridiculous. Thrums, Tewkesbury and Edmund Keane. Who the fuck named a street Edmund Keane, and when it was suggested, why wasn't there an outcry? Now Kojak was sweating buckets in Sadlers Wells Court, swearing that if he ever met the town planner responsible, he would kick his cunt in.

Cheesy hid behind the lockups and watched as Kojak struggled to drag the ten full crates of milk needed to deliver to Sadlers Wells Court into the flat. He was having to do it on his own, which made Cheesy uneasy at first, but it must have meant that Danny hadn't shown up this morning, making Kojak's decision to get rid of Cheesy even more irrational. It would serve him right for being a wanker.

Cheesy waited five minutes to make sure nobody else was going to turn up to help and when he was sure Kojak was working solo, he made his move. The egg box was huge, but it was only three-quarters full, so it was easy to lift down from the float and make a swift getaway. Five minutes after lifting them, Cheesy was in the woods on the other side of the dual carriageway, dreaming of the massive fry-up he could have if he only had a house to go to. The disappointment of not getting to eat any of his haul was forgotten when he found what he was really looking for near the bottom. Seven half dozen boxes stuffed to the brim with hash. Cheesy stifled a whoop of delight. Things were looking up.

Kojak had spent half an hour in Sadlers Wells Court. His mood wasn't helped when Mrs Glavin on the 9th floor came out while he was delivering to the flats round the other side and took the lift down to the ground, meaning the milk for the floors below went with her and Kojak could do nothing but wait for it to come back up to him. When the doors opened on the 9th floor again, Mrs Glavin got the fright of her life at the sight of a sweating Kojak standing angrily in front of her.

"Oh my God! Drew! What the hell are you doing?" Mrs Glavin clutched her chest and swayed as though she would faint. For one second Kojak hoped she would, and he could leave her and get on with it. She tightened her dressing gown around her chest, in case the sight of her in her nightie, headscarf and slippers would be too much for Kojak to resist.

"I'm delivering the milk, Mrs Glavin. What are you doing up at this time?" Kojak managed to smile through gritted teeth.

"I thought I heard somebody in the close, so I went down to check it out. It was probably just you. You're awful loud this morning." Mrs Glavin checked every time there was a noise in the close out of civic duty, not because she was a nosy cow, like that Mrs Cuthbert at number 78 had suggested.

"Aye, well, two of the boys didn't turn up this morning so I'm rushing a bit." Kojak stepped past Mrs Glavin into the lift. "I thought you might have guessed it was me when you saw the crates of milk in the lift." It was difficult not to use a tone.

"Och, it's a bit early for me to be thinking, son. Would you like a cup of tea?" Even a sweaty milkman would be company.

Kojak pressed the button to take him down to the next floor. "No thanks, Mrs Glavin. As I say, I'm in a bit of a rush today."

"You'll rush yourself into an early grave..."

Kojak hadn't heard the end of Mrs Glavin's advice. The door closed and he was off.

The cold, fresh air was a welcome relief when he left the tower block. How people could live in those things was beyond him. The view was great, but Kojak always felt it was like coming out of prison when he finally walked out the door. It was claustrophobic and always had a stale smell. He jumped into the float and turned into the lockups to do a three-point turn. There were only a dozen lockups at most, which always struck Kojak as pointless. How did you decide which twelve households got to lock their car up securely? It was as though they were designed to cause arguments. Suddenly, something felt wrong. Kojak felt panic rise in his chest, but he was confused as to why. Then it struck him.

"Where the fuck's the eggs?"

Kojak jumped out of the cab and ran back into the flat, hoping forlornly that he had maybe moved them there without remembering. He checked under the float and ran down to the end of the lockups, his mind racing as to what could have happened but there was nothing to be seen. The pot! Over 250 quid's worth of pot gone. He'd have to tell Greer what had happened and hope he would give him time to pay back what was lost and he would have to ask for more to satisfy his potheads, who would already be chewing their knuckles waiting on him to deliver. Whoever had done this was going to be in big trouble, if he survived the meeting with Greer. Who the fuck would be so stupid to steal from him? It couldn't have been anyone who knew him, because they would know he would hunt whoever it was down and do some real damage to them when he caught them. As he thought about going back in and asking Mrs Glavin if she had seen anyone running off with a huge box of eggs, he heard the familiar sound of a milk float heading down Tewkesbury Road just below him. It was Oggy, heading down the road as though nothing had happened, on his way to deliver milk to the people of Bolingbroke, Waverley and Ivanhoe. Kojak swore again if he ever found the town planner who had come up with those street names, he would kick his cunt in.

CHAPTER TWENTY-THREE

Guess Who's Coming To Dinner?

EVERYWHERE STANK OF cigarette smoke. Smoking was the national pastime for everyone in Scotland, closely followed by drinking, football and hating yourself. Nobody even noticed the stench because there was virtually nowhere you could go to escape it, so on the odd occasion you walked into clean air, it felt weird. Mary was aware of the yellow staining on the walls of the pub, the library and even the dentist's waiting room, but no amount of cleaning was going to shift it. She was proud that her home was the exception. Mary had never smoked because she didn't like it – not the taste, not the smell and certainly not the racking cough that seemed to be the soundtrack to most people's lives. She had an aunt, Lilian Dean, who had started smoking aged 79 because she missed the smell when her twenty-a-day husband had died of lung problems. Everyone had found the story touching, but Mary thought Lilian was insane.

Mary was proud that neither of her boys smoked either. From an early age she had warned of the dangers and the astronomic cost smoking would burden them with. She told stories of houses burning down, lungs exploding, teeth falling out, massive debts, all in the name of smoking, and she wasn't sorry that she had made most of the stories up in the hope it would put them off for life. It had worked so far, although she knew that the peer pressure young Brian would be under now that he was working on a factory floor would be fierce. Whatever happened, both boys knew that she wouldn't approve of them embracing the habit and under no circumstances would she allow it to happen in her home. The flat was painted in bright colours, with no yellow walls in sight.

It was important that Hugh didn't smoke either. Kissing

someone who smoked was like licking an ashtray and Mary was enjoying kissing Hugh. Tommy had been her first love, so her experience of men was limited to a certain extent. She had taken time to analyse what had gone wrong in their relationship and was satisfied that none of it had been her fault. The picture she painted of their dad for the boys was nothing like what it had been in reality. The truth was, Tommy had left the family home at least six months before he died, and Mary hadn't been sorry to see him go. His death had softened the memory, but she could remember the lonely nights, wondering where he was or who he was with. The legend his murder had created was something everyone else celebrated. Mary remembered the beatings, the fear and the loneliness before she had gathered the strength to chuck him out of the family home and change the locks.

Hugh was different. He was sweet and he treated Mary like an equal. They hadn't slept together yet, but Mary wanted it to happen. She just had to make sure it was the right thing to do for the whole family, because it was a commitment she wasn't going to take lightly. Hugh seemed happy to wait and hadn't put any pressure on her at all, but Mary wasn't going to let her physical desires get in the way of bringing her kids up. How she felt about Hugh came second to how the boys would react to him. She hadn't told either of them she was seeing anyone yet because she wanted to be sure in her own mind that it was serious before she took the next step. Billy seemed to like Hugh as a boss, but Mary knew it would be different to consider him as anything more than that. She had worked hard to give the boys a picture of their dad as someone who loved them and cared for them, but now she worried she had let the legend become something that was impossible to replace with someone else.

Brian wouldn't be a problem. Working at Rolls Royce had been the best thing to happen to him. He had always been a bit daft, a little bit too carefree as a child. Mary worried she had mollie-coddled him too much when his dad died. Billy had been six when it happened and it had seemed to wash over him without too much damage being done, but Brian was eight and had memories of his dad playing football with him and buying him presents, the kind of memories an eight-year-old boy would hold onto, but recently he had said something that made Mary see she had probably underestimated how much he actually remembered. He was talking about someone at work who was going through a divorce. The man moaned about his wife and how she was treating him badly in the separation.

"He's got some cheek. He would come in every Monday and brag about what he got up to at the weekend, boozing and shagging, and how he would give his wife a slap if she got out of line, and now he's moaning that she's bringing all this stuff up in the divorce settlement. It's a miracle his wife put up with him for as long as she did. She should have taken a leaf out of your book and kicked him out long before now."

Mary hadn't said anything. She had given him a big hug, which he reciprocated for the first time since he had become a teenager. She hadn't realised he remembered the bad times and she could tell by the sincerity of the hug that he was proud of how his mum had dealt with it all. For the first time, Mary realised her boy was growing up and she was proud of how he was turning out.

Billy was the worry. He rarely spoke about his dad and Mary wondered if she had let the legend become too real for him. He would be leaving school and venturing out into the real world in no time and Mary worried he would begin to hear stories about his dad that didn't fit with what he had heard in his childhood. She hoped that having someone like Hugh beside her, a stable male influence, would help Billy deal with any disappointment reality would throw at him. She was ready to take the next step in her new relationship with Hugh and hoped Billy's reaction would be positive.

"What are you up to tonight?" Mary hoped to keep the conversation light. Billy was sitting eating his cornflakes, reading the *NME* which had recently replaced his copy of *The Beano*.

"Nothing. Band stuff."

Mary was used to her sons not giving much information as to their whereabouts of an evening.

"Well, make sure you're here for dinner. I've got a friend coming round and I want you both here." Mary was nervous.

"Whatever." Billy didn't look up from his paper. "Is the guy who killed dad in jail?"

Mary stopped dusting the fireplace and turned round to Billy. She had a sudden fear that her son was reading her mind.

"I would imagine so, why?"

"What was he called? Can you remember?"

Mary's mind was racing. Why would Billy be asking about this now? For a second, she wondered if Hugh had let anything slip to Billy, even though Mary had made him promise he wouldn't until she was ready.

"Ehm, Sammy something. Sammy Graham, I think it was. What's brought all this up?" Mary was trying to sound casual, as though it was something they spoke about all the time, but there was a shiver in her voice that she hoped Billy wouldn't notice.

"I was just wondering." Billy didn't look up from his paper.

Mary continued cleaning, her heart pounding in her chest. She thought she was ready to tell Billy the truth about his dad, but him bringing it up had sent her into a panic.

"Who's coming to dinner?" Billy changed the subject with ease.

"Hugh."

"Hugh who?"

"Hugh! McDonald!" Mary didn't think they knew anyone else called Hugh. Billy finally looked up from his *NME*.

"My boss Hugh?" Billy looked like the mere suggestion was ridiculous.

"Yes, your boss Hugh!" Mary felt her face go red. "We've been seeing each other a bit. in the pub and that..."

"Shagger? You've been seeing Shagger?" There was a mixture of anger and disappointment in Billy's voice.

"Oh Billy, don't call him that. You know it's just a nickname the other drivers gave him. I thought you liked Hugh?" Mary didn't like being defensive, but it was important.

Billy stood up and walked out of the living room. As he reached the door, he turned and looked at Mary. "Shagger? Will you never learn?"

Mary heard the front door close as Billy stormed out. She didn't know whether to run out after him or not. Brian walked in from the kitchen with a bowl of cornflakes in his hand.

"That went well..." Brian gave his mum a reassuring smile.

"What does he mean, will I never learn?" Mary was genuinely at a loss.

"I'm guessing he's beginning to hear some true stories about our beloved father. You must have known it was going to happen."

Mary looked like she had been punched in the stomach, the air knocked out of her. "So, Shagger is coming for tea?"

Mary ran to the toilet and cried for the second time in a matter of weeks.

CHAPTER TWENTY-FOUR

You Represent Me

KOJAK HADN'T SLEPT, which was really annoying because Saturday night was the only night he didn't need to set his big alarm clock on the other side of the bedroom for a ridiculous hour and get up the next day to switch it off. If the clock wasn't on the other side of the room, he knew he would never get up to face the milk run. He hated that clock. His mind wouldn't slow down enough to let sleep come. He had gone through every person he had known over the years who was brave enough to steal from him and the only ones he could come up with were either in jail or they were the people in Blantyre who had made it clear he would have to do something about being robbed or they would do something to him.

He was two hours behind by the time he finished his round on Saturday and had taken the chance to visit a few of his potheads to see if anyone else had approached them with a deal, thinking that might lead him to who the culprit was, but nobody had been near any of them and all he got was a lot of whining because he didn't have their weekly stash for them. Not one of the lazy fuckers had shown the slightest consideration for the predicament he was in. He ended up being three hours late for his meeting with Greer in The Parkville in Blantyre. Before he even sat down, Kojak could tell Greer was in a bad mood.

"I'm looking forward to hearing why I've been sitting here all morning instead of getting ready to head over to Paradise, Kojak. I'm sure it's good, but it had better be very fucking good."

Kojak hated the way Celtic supporters called the smelly dump that was Parkhead, Paradise. Greer knew Kojak was a Rangers man and he took great delight in reminding him that Greer's team had won the league eleven times to Rangers' three over the last fifteen years. On the three occasions Rangers had won, Kojak had never had the nerve to bring it up. Now even Aberdeen and Dundee United were doing more to challenge Celtic's dominance than Rangers were. Kojak didn't go to the games, but he read the papers and there was no getting away from the fact that Rangers were shite.

"I've had a nightmare. Two of my boys didn't show up this morning, so the milk round took much longer than usual and then some wide cunt robbed the float while I was in delivering to one of the high flats..." Kojak wasn't looking for sympathy, but he couldn't help thinking it sounded like he was.

"Not my problem." Greer was mopping up the last of a runny fried egg with a bread roll.

"No, but whoever it was thought they were stealing some eggs from me, when they actually made off with my full stash of pot." Kojak waited for this to sink in. "So, I'll need a double batch of pot this week until I find out who it was that robbed me. I'm sure as soon as they realise what they've got, they'll come running to me with their tails between their legs..."

"You lost my pot." Greer looked like someone had shat in his shoes.

"No, someone stole it!" Kojak found it hard to accept that he must kow-tow to Greer now.

Greer slammed his fist on the table he was sitting at, making the plates of grease that had been breakfast jump in the air.

"You let someone steal from me?" Greer shouted and bared his teeth.

"No! They stole from me, and I didn't fucking let them. Trust me, when I find the fucker, they'll be drinking soup through a straw for months." Kojak had raised his voice too, but not as loud as Greer had.

Greer looked round at the gormless numbnuts he always had sitting with him while he was doing his deals. Every one of them looked at the floor rather than meet his gaze.

"You represent me, Kojak. If they steal from you, they steal from me, and I can't have that. Are you saying I need to come up to that cesspit and do your job for you?"

Greer looked like he would love the opportunity to put Kojak in his place. He called Kojak's town a cesspit, but Blantyre was an even bigger dump, and he knew it.

"Of course not. I'll deal with it." Kojak tried to keep his cool. It was hard for him to hear someone talk to him like this, but he knew he could never match the force Greer could muster if it came to a war. A straight square go between the two of them would be no problem for Kojak, but Greer had an army behind him while Kojak had nobody to stand beside him if the need arose. His days as the leader of a large pack were long gone. His peers had all moved on to jobs and wives and some semblance of respectability. Drugs were something none of his so-called friends wanted anything to do with, so he was on his own. "And you won't be out of pocket. I'll square you up if it's gone for good."

Greer let out an ironic roar of laughter. "You'll square me up? You think I fucking care about a few hundred quid? This isn't about money, ya fucking baldy twat! This is about my reputation. Do you know what happened to the last person who stole gear from me?"

Kojak wasn't sure if Greer was expecting a response, so he chose to say nothing.

"Tell him…" Greer motioned to the gorilla sitting to his right, waving his arm towards Kojak as though it was below him to talk any more. The gorilla looked like a rabbit caught in the headlights. It was obvious talking out loud wasn't what he was generally asked to do. He didn't know what was expected of him.

"I don't know, boss." The gorilla looked around at the other goons, looking for some kind of answer. Greer picked up one of the breakfast plates and smashed it off the gorilla's head, spreading porcelain and bacon fat all over the floor. The gorilla fell to the floor holding his head, although Kojak doubted the blow had been hard enough to warrant that kind of response. He guessed the gorilla had been in this situation before and it was easier to feign injury than take any further punishment.

"Why am I surrounded by fuckwits?" Greer was raging, his eyes popping out of his reddened face. Kojak wondered if he had been sampling his own wares along with his full English. "The last cunt to steal from me fell in The Clyde and never came back up."

Greer looked round the table until he got mumbled responses of agreement from his entourage, but Kojak could tell none of them knew what he was talking about.

"Don't worry, whoever did this will pay for it. You don't need to do a thing." Kojak just wanted to get out of there and get on with his day.

"So says the man who can't even control a bunch of schoolboys well enough to finish his fucking milk round on time! You've got until next week, Kojak, I'm not joking. If you don't sort this out, I'll come up and show you exactly how to deal with staff problems. Got it?" Greer spat out the last sentence while staring at his employees sitting round him. They all nodded emphatically. "Take him out to the van and sort out his gear. I've got a game to go to."

Greer dismissed Kojak with a wave of his hand.

Kojak spent the rest of Saturday going round his potheads, giving them their gear and warning every one of them that if anyone approached them selling stuff, they had better let him know, no matter how cheap the person was selling it for. He even hinted there would be a reward of sorts for anyone who gave him information leading to the thief.

He was sure none of the potheads would have done it. For one thing, it had happened too early in the morning and none of them had the bottle to go against someone like Kojak. He kept coming back to the sight of Oggy's float disappearing down the road when he had come out of the high-rise. He was sure Oggy would know he supplied some of his girls with smack, but how would he know about the eggs? It was possible Oggy had taken the eggs as some kind of prank and didn't realise what was in there, but why would he want to fuck with him like that? They didn't know each other all that well, but Oggy had to know Kojak wasn't a prank kind of guy. Playing a prank on Kojak was like challenging him to a square go and surely Oggy knew enough that he wouldn't want that. He was from Hamilton or some other scummy part of Lanarkshire, but he would know from his years working in East Kilbride that Kojak wasn't to be messed with.

Now, on the Sunday morning without sleep, Kojak had convinced himself that Oggy was the culprit, and it was all part of an elaborate plan to take over his business and drive him out of East Kilbride. He wouldn't be surprised if Greer had put him up to it, two Lanarkshire cunts sticking together to take Kojak's crown in East Kilbride. He knew he would need to confront him, and he knew exactly how he could do it. That wee tart, Maggie, was working for Oggy now and Kojak was due to pay her a visit today to deliver her next fix. He would find out from her when Oggy was next due to pay her a visit and make sure he was there waiting for him. One way or another, the smarmy cunt was getting a slap.

CHAPTER TWENTY-FIVE

Concorde Farted

BILLY DIDN'T KNOW what to think. He could remember snippets of his dad, like the trike he had got him for his birthday or being carried on his shoulders while walking along the front in Rothesay one summer, but the biggest memory he had was when Billy had said he liked Celtic instead of Rangers, without really knowing what that meant. He had heard a kid in the street saying Celtic were much better than Rangers, so he thought it made sense to support them if that was the case. The fury his dad had shown at his revelation was still very clear in his mind. If Mary hadn't stood in front of him, protecting him, Billy had no doubt that his dad would have hit him. When Billy closed his eyes, he could still see the hatred. All the stories he had heard since his dad died seemed to cloud the image of that day, making Billy doubt his memory, but the realisation that his dad had been trouble and worse, that he treated Mary badly, brought the vision of that anger he had experienced into focus.

An old guy had stopped Billy in the street once and told him how much of a hero his dad was. The guy was steaming drunk, so Billy had taken what he said with a pinch of salt, but now it seemed to be more likely that the sentiment was true.

"Your dad was fucking superman, wee man. He started The Woodie; did you know that? He never took any shit from anyone and every one of The Woodie boys would have crawled over broken glass for him. No cunt could match him in a square go, he was a fucking superstar. And I'll tell ye, there wisnae a lassie in the whole of East Kilbride who widnae drop her knickers for him either. A fucking superstar."

Billy had gone home and told Mary what the man had said, proud at how much the man had thought of his father. Mary had been quick to play it down.

"I don't think you can believe anything a drunk man says to you in the street, son. He was just your dad. He loved you very much and that's the only thing you need to know."

Billy had been ten or eleven then, so he accepted his mum's explanation and moved on with his life without question. Now he was fifteen and he was hearing the same things. What was that old saying? There's no smoke without fire? Billy could feel himself choke with the amount of smoke coming his way now.

And now he had the revelation that his mum was seeing Hugh! Yet another guy who was god's gift to women, if you believed the rumours surrounding him. To be fair, Billy quite liked Hugh and he had no doubt his boss would never be involved in fighting or robbing and the like, but he still didn't want his mum to get hurt by someone. It was hard to understand why Mary would feel the need to have a man in her life when she was so old. She must have been pushing forty, for Christ's sake! The idea of the two of them having sex made Billy shudder.

The Calderwood Community Centre could only have been five or six years old, but it already looked tired, and a bit run-down. Billy remembered when it was being built. On the way home from primary school, the foundation trenches had been the perfect setting for games of Japs and Commandos, kids from all around gathering to battle each other by throwing stones and clumps of mud to defend their allotted territory. Billy remembered it all coming to an end when one boy was hit in the eye with a speeding piece of shrapnel, meaning he had to wear a patch for months after it. Now the building was used for jumble sales and political meetings, keeping the battleground alive, only now it was pensioners and labour councillors in danger of losing an eye.

Recently, the council had started having discos on a Wednesday night, hoping to bring the youth of the area together and combat the rising trouble the gang culture was breeding. While it was a commendable attempt, nobody had realised that only the local youths would attend, meaning only one of the gangs would be represented, meaning trouble was unlikely. It didn't stop the people who lived in the immediate vicinity complaining about the noise, but for now it was being championed as a success, so any complaints fell on deaf ears. Tonight was the first time the hall had been turned over to the youth on a Sunday, and Billy doubted anyone at the council knew exactly what was being planned. The number of local punk bands was increasing every week, but there was nowhere for most of them to play, so this was a trial run for a potential series of Sunday night gigs.

The Sinister Turkeys were headlining the gig, but up to seven bands had managed to secure a spot on the supporting bill. Handclap were due to play first, and Billy had never looked forward to something as much in his life. Being the first band on meant the only chance they had to get a sound check was turning up at lunchtime, while nobody else was around. The hall seemed much bigger than it did when it was full of teenagers strutting their stuff to The Bee Gees or Boney M on a Wednesday night. Billy felt his nerves begin to jangle, but as soon as Lisa walked in, looking every inch the rock star, the tension left him. The plan was for Lisa to learn the songs during the sound check and perform them at night, which wasn't as ridiculous as it sounded as, due to time constraints, the band were only being allowed to play three songs. Even if she had to sing using a piece of paper to read the lyrics, nobody would mind. The punk rock, do-it-yourself attitude was strong, and the audience would be full of the other bands and their hangers-on who would all be in the same predicament. The thing Handclap had in their favour was that none of the other bands had Lisa standing out front.

"Wow, you look great." Billy jumped down from the stage where Andy and Rab were busy setting up the gear to welcome Lisa. Lisa smiled, fully aware of how good she looked and becoming more confident by the day about how the way she looked affected the boys who were swarming around her on a regular basis. "Are you ready to learn the songs?"

"Yeah, let me hear them." Lisa was nervous but she would never let it show. Phoney self-confidence was something she had mastered to cover the many times she felt out of her depth.

"I've written the lyrics out for you. Let's go!" Billy leapt back up onto the stage enthusiastically.

"I'll watch you from here first. That'll let me get a feel for your songs. You sing them and I'll work out how I can put my own stamp on them." Lisa turned away, pretending to study the lyrics before Billy could say anything.

Andy and Rab glanced at each other. They didn't share Billy's enthusiasm for having Lisa in the band. They thought she was a bit of a poseur who had jumped on the punk bandwagon to get attention rather than embracing the music, but it was Billy's band, so they went along with it for now. The boys rattled through the songs, each one a variation on the three chords they knew how to play. Seven minutes later it was over. Lisa clapped enthusiastically at the end and the boys all smiled at each other proudly.

"Right, jump up and we'll go through them again with you singing." Billy's confidence was on fire.

"No, you play them again and I'll read the lyrics while you're playing. It'll let me get it straight in my head." Lisa came to the front of the stage and continued to study the sheets of paper Billy had prepared for her.

"Okay." Billy sounded less enthusiastic, but he counted the boys in, and they set off again, playing even faster than the first time.

"Cool." Lisa had walked to the back of the hall while the boys played, studying the lyrics intently as they powered through the set.

"Right, your turn. Come on." Rab didn't have the patience Billy had.

"Right, that's you. Off!" The singer from Teenage Vice had come in while the boys were playing and was climbing on to the stage.

"What?" Billy had no idea anyone else would be around at this time, so he was surprised to see the older boy climbing onto the stage.

"Your time's up. There's too many bands on tonight and we've all got to get a soundcheck in. You've had two. That's it." The Vice man was already unplugging Billy's bass from the amp and getting a guitar out of its case.

"Who put you in charge?" Rab stood up from the drum kit to challenge the older boy.

"My dad hired the hall, and the amps and drum kit belong to Teenage Vice, so I guess that answers your question." Billy and the others all looked at each other. "So, if you want to play at all tonight, I'd get off the fucking stage and fuck off. You're on at seven sharp so be here no later than five to." The singer gave the boys a look, surprised that they were still standing there. "Off you pop."

"Come on guys, forget it. We'll blow them off the stage later when we play." Lisa spoke confidently. The Teenage Vice singer looked round, noticing Lisa for the first time. He looked at her with a smile and then turned away laughing to himself.

"Whatever. Come back at seven."

There was only one thing left to do in preparation for the gig. Lisa went home to prepare herself while the boys bought a carry out and headed into the woods across from The Salmon Leap to gain the Dutch courage they would need to perform in front of people for the first time. Andy and Rab began to voice their concerns after a few cans of Colt 45 had been sunk.

"Are you sure she can sing?"

"Are you joking? She looks fucking brilliant. You heard her, we'll blow them all off the stage!" Billy couldn't believe the other guys had doubts.

"Aye we heard her, but we only heard her talking. She hasnae sung a note yet."

"We're a punk band! Anyway, she's right into Blondie so she's going to sound brilliant." Billy's certainty sounded shaky.

"My maw's right into Perry Como but she clears the room when she opens her fucking mouth. Why don't you just sing tonight, Billy? We can get her in for a few rehearsals after and if she's any good, we can use her for the next gig..." Rab thought being reasonable would help Billy see sense.

"We can't! Listen guys, I didn't want to say, but the rumour is there's going to be a guy from Stiff Records here tonight. If we play our cards right this could get us a deal!" Billy's enthusiasm exploded, but Andy and Rab looked at each other and burst out laughing. "What are you laughing at?"

"We started the rumour to see if anyone was daft enough to believe it. As if Stiff Records have any idea there's a gig happening in a community centre in East Kilbride. They've never heard of fucking East Kilbride."

Billy's face was burning as his bandmates bent over with laughter. He slowly began to see the joke and ended up laughing as much as they were. "Ya dirty fuckers."

Twenty-four cans of Colt 45 later, Billy and his bandmates staggered into the community centre ready to rock the place to its core. By 6.45 the place was packed. Punks from all over East Kilbride had turned up along with a lot of curious local kids and a smattering of anxious parents who stood uneasily at the back of the hall. Ten minutes later the Teenage Vice guy came over to them.

"Right, you're on."

"Our singer's not here yet." Billy wasn't feeling as nervous now that the beer had taken hold, but he could still feel his legs tremble.

"I couldn't give a fuck. Either get your arses up there now or you're not playing."

Billy led his bandmates onto the stage and started plugging their gear in. Just as Billy decided to go ahead without Lisa, the doors opened and there she was. The whole place turned to look at her and the place fell silent. Standing next to her with his arm around her waist was Cheesy. Billy's heart sank.

"What the fuck is he doing here?"

Cheesy led Lisa to the side of the stage and helped her on, never taking his eyes from Billy nor the stupid grin off his face. The crowd started to applaud politely as Lisa walked to the front of the stage and took her place at the microphone. Billy walked over and whispered to her.

"Why's Cheesy here?"

"I'm going out with him. He's here for me." Lisa smiled at Cheesy, and he gave her a juvenile double thumbs-up in return.

Billy couldn't hide his shock, but before he could say anything else, Lisa took up the mic and shouted out to the crowd.

"Good evening, everyone. We're Lisa and The Handclap. One, two, three, four..."

There was a moment of silence before the rest of the band realised she was counting them in, which meant they all came in at different times. The shambolic noise was only made worse when Lisa started singing. The sound coming from her was unrecognisable. Someone later said it sounded like the squeak of a balloon slowly deflating while Concorde farted. Whatever it was, it wasn't anything like how the band had sounded in the soundcheck. They all finished the first song at different times, stumbling to a halt with a final shriek from Lisa. There was a single beat before the entire audience responded with uproarious laughter. Some of them were openly pointing at Lisa with tears of laughter running down their faces. She spun round to Billy, raging at him.

"You fucking cunt! How could you do this to me?"

Lisa handed the mic to Billy and stormed off the stage and into the arms of a scowling Cheesy. The crowd cheered at her departure, making her cry. Cheesy bounded onto the stage, running towards Billy with murder in his eyes. Before he could reach him, Billy swung the microphone through the air, smashing it into Cheesy's face. His two front teeth flew out in a spray of blood and the crowd cheered again. Lisa picked Cheesy up from the stage and half-carried him off.

"You're fucking dead!" Cheesy was screaming abuse at nobody in particular as Lisa led him out the door. Billy picked the mic back up and shouted a count to his bandmates. They responded with perfect timing, and they set off playing the next two songs of their set. By the end, the crowd were cheering and pogoing all over the place.

"We're just called Handclap, by the way!" Billy walked off stage to be congratulated by the crowd. Two minutes later, the fire alarm went off. Someone had set fire to the coats in the cloakroom and the entire hall had to be evacuated.

CHAPTER TWENTY-SIX

Fucking Stobo

GREER HAD PHONED Kojak twice since the meeting on Saturday, both times ranting and raving about what he was going to do if nothing was done about the missing drugs. Kojak was convinced Greer was putting more cocaine up his own nose than he was selling, and it was only a matter of time before he made a critical mistake. Kojak only had to make sure he kept things ticking over until that day came and he could enjoy watching the manky fucker's fall from grace. Maybe he could take over the whole operation, although Kojak was sure there would be no limit to the number of Blantyre psychos waiting in the wings to step in when their boss was finally nailed by the cops or, more likely, he was found dead somewhere with either a bullet in his head or a syringe in his arm. It seemed to be the natural life cycle of a drugs kingpin. Not Kojak, though. He stayed clear of the product himself and continued to maintain his profile as a local milkman with violent tendencies when required.

The identity of the person who robbed him was still bugging Kojak, and Greer's sniping was driving him to despair. There was no doubt he would have to do something about it, but he had sent out enough warnings to the users he dealt with to convince him that the gear had been stolen by some opportunist lowlife who had stolen the eggs without knowing what was really in the boxes. Whoever it was could still have no idea what they were sitting on because none of it had found its way onto the street. He had even put the word out to his regular egg customers to give him a shout if anybody appeared at their door offering them a cheap half dozen, but nobody had come forward so far. That left him with Oggy. The paranoia his lack of sleep on Saturday had brought on had subsided now he had time to think about it rationally. It was still a strong possibility that the big-nosed prick had stolen the eggs, but it would have been a harmless prank, not an attempt to take over Kojak's business. Float drivers were renowned for playing tricks on each other, letting down tyres or gluing crates to floats and the like, but nobody had ever had the nerve to do that kind of thing to Kojak. He liked a laugh like the next guy, but everyone knew once the laughing stopped, you would get a slap if you tried it on with him. As he walked up to Maggie's flat, he was convinced that was how things would play out. He would confront Oggy, have a laugh, get his eggs back and slap the ugly cunt around a bit. If Greer asked, and he undoubtedly would, Kojak could tell him it was sorted, and everyone could move on.

Kojak quite liked Maggie. She was a junkie scumbag and a dirty wee whore, but she was nice. She could only be eighteen at the most, but she was already looking twice that age due to the smack. Kojak wondered what had happened first in her short life. Had she been a junkie who got pregnant while on the game or had the birth of her sprog out of wedlock driven her out of the family home and into the downward spiral she was now in? Kojak couldn't give a fuck either way, but he sensed Maggie had been a good kid at one point who was seriously down on her luck. She opened the door of the flat before Kojak had the chance to knock. The dark rings round her eyes seemed to be thicker, making her face seem more skeletal than usual. She was in a right old state.

"Where the fuck have you been? I've been waiting for hours..." Maggie turned and walked down the hall.

"And good morning to you too, Maggie."

Kojak followed her into the living room and wrinkled his nose at the smell. The boy was sat in a playpen, blissfully unaware of the squalor he was living in. The room was a mess, and the coffee table was covered in drug regalia. Two used needles lay on the floor, within easy reach of the toddler if he had the energy to climb out of his baby jail cell.

"You shouldn't have tidied up on account of me." Kojak treated all his customers with contempt. The drug trade was a closed shop, so he had no need to keep any of them sweet. If they wanted their fix, they had to deal with him, no matter how much they hated him. Putting up with Kojak looking down his nose at them and showering them with sarcasm was the least of their worries.

"You're late." Maggie was shaking.

Kojak didn't follow any timetable, but everywhere he went, people accused him of being late, even when it was milk he was delivering to the door. Maggie was in her purse, counting out coins to make sure she had enough to buy what she needed. Kojak ignored her and looked into the kitchen that adjoined the living room. Compared to the living room it was spotless, probably because it was rarely used.

"Have you got any food in here?"

"We've already eaten." Maggie wasn't interested in anything other than doing her deal.

"Yeah, well, I haven't and I'm hungry. Be a love and knock me something up, will you? Toast will do." Kojak wasn't hungry, but he wanted an excuse to hang around.

"Are you fucking joking?" Maggie stopped counting her money and looked at Kojak with contempt.

Kojak gave Maggie a look that told her he was serious. "Toast. And put it on a plate. We're not all animals like you. Are we, wee man?" Kojak gave the boy a smile and he responded by holding up a toy car in the hope that the stranger might play with him. Maggie sat open-mouthed on the sofa until she realised Kojak wasn't going to give her what she needed until she had done what he asked. She jumped up and stormed into the kitchen.

"Fuck's sake!"

Kojak thought about sitting down but decided against it.

"When is Oggy due to come round next?" Kojak raised his voice enough for Maggie to hear him in the kitchen.

"What?" Maggie's patience was wearing thin.

"You heard. When is he due to pick up his immoral earnings?" All the girls who worked for Oggy would put up a pitiful pretence of ignorance, probably at his insistence, but Maggie knew any attempt at denial now would only delay her fix longer.

"Today. Soon. I don't know. He's worse than you at being on time." It was a hollow dig, but Maggie felt better for having made it.

Kojak thought about insisting she be more precise, but he realised Maggie probably didn't know if it was morning or dinner time, so it would be pointless. He would hang around for as long as it was tolerable. The boy in the playpen seemed happy playing with his cars, but Kojak wondered when he had last had a bath or when he had last tasted fresh air. Kojak was certain that as soon as the boy could walk, he would be outside running feral like so many of the kids these days. People like Maggie shouldn't be allowed to have kids.

"Here." Maggie came out of the kitchen and handed Kojak a plate with two slices of toast on it. A tiny blob of strawberry jam sat in the middle of each slice. The child hauled himself onto his feet at the sight of the food and looked at Kojak with big panda eyes.

"When did he last eat?" Maggie looked away and started to roll herself a cigarette. Kojak could tell she didn't know the answer. Kojak tossed a slice of the toast into the playpen. The boy lost his balance trying to catch it and fell onto his arse. The toast landed jam side down, but the boy had it in his hands immediately and started sucking the jam off. "How can you live like this?"

Before Maggie could answer, the front door opened, and someone started down the hall towards the living room. Kojak moved against the wall so that whoever was coming in wouldn't see him until they were fully in the room. He put his finger to his lips to warn Maggie not to give any warning that he was there. Oggy walked into the room without noticing Kojak was now standing behind him. Maggie sat motionless on the sofa, looking at Oggy with fear written all over her face.

"What's wrong?" Oggy knew instantly something wasn't right.

Maggie's eyes gave an involuntary twitch which was enough to make Oggy turn to look behind him. Before he had fully turned, Kojak swung the plate he was holding and smashed it against the side of Oggy's head. Kojak expected Oggy to fall to the floor like the goon Greer had hit with a similar plate the other day, but Oggy just looked confused for a second before swinging a right hook, catching Kojak on the side of his head. It all happened so quickly, neither man had time to think about what to do next. They both took a step away from each other and raised their fists in readiness for a flurry of blows that never came. Maggie was screaming and the child was crying, adding to the confusion.

"What the fuck are you doing?" Oggy seemed genuinely confused as to what had just happened.

"I've come for my eggs." Kojak looked just as confused at the way things were playing out. This wasn't how he had envisaged things.

"Eggs?" Oggy looked round at Maggie, hoping she might throw some light on what was happening, but she was still screaming in her own confusion. Oggy turned back to Kojak. "What fucking eggs? What are you talking about?"

"Somebody knicked the eggs off my float on Saturday." Kojak hoped this would be enough of an explanation to force an admission of guilt out of Oggy.

"And you think I did it? Are you fucking mental? Why would I knick your eggs?" Oggy's reaction was enough for Kojak to know he was barking up the wrong tree. The two men stood facing each other, fists raised, but neither knowing what to do next. Maggie was still screaming, and the boy was standing in his pen, bawling his eyes out at the state of his mother. At the same time, Kojak and Oggy turned their attention to Maggie and shouted in unison.

"Shut up!"

Maggie snapped out of her spell and stopped screaming. She stooped and picked up her son, cradling him against her chest, trying to soothe and quieten him. Oggy and Kojak turned to face each other again, lowering their fists now that things were calming down a bit.

"You've got a fucking cheek coming round here accusing me of shit after what you did to Linda." Oggy was the first to find his voice.

"Linda? Who's Linda?" It was Kojak's turn to not know what Oggy was talking about.

"Fucking Linda! One of my girls. She lives in the flats in Stobo..." Oggy was a bit embarrassed that he didn't know Linda's surname.

"Fucking Stobo..." Kojak allowed himself a second of imagining attacking the town planners again for coming up with stupid street names, "What about her?"

"She's dead! Overdosed on that shit you peddle..." Oggy blurted out his answer without thinking.

Kojak stopped. He racked his brain for the last time he had seen Linda. He hadn't seen her for a while, but he thought she was hiding from him because she owed him for the last fix.

"I haven't heard anything..."

"I don't think anyone's found her yet. I mean, what does that say about people these days? She's been dead over a week, and nobody's found her yet..." Oggy shook his head in disbelief.

"How do you know she's dead then?" Kojak was finding it hard to believe.

"Because I saw her lying there with the needle still in her arm. She was blue and the stink was incredible. She was fucking dead alright." Oggy struggled to stop his voice from cracking.

"Linda's dead? Why didn't you phone an ambulance? If you found her, why didn't you phone an ambulance?" Maggie's voice was trembling again, as though another bout of screaming was about to start.

"Fuck that." Oggy held his hands up in defence.

"It's not his job to mop up after some junkie. And fuck trying to blame me. I sell the shit; I don't force any of them to buy it. If they overdose it's got fuck all to do with me..." Kojak was in defence mode too. Maggie looked like she was ready to explode. She put Adam back in his pen and picked up her purse. She took out two notes and threw them at Oggy, then grabbed Kojak's hand and emptied the rest of the contents of the purse into it. Kojak took out a small bag of powder and handed it to her without a word.

"Now get the fuck out of here before I do something I regret." Kojak and Oggy looked at each other, both at a loss as to what to say. "Get out!" Maggie screamed at the two men and pushed then both in the chest. Without a word, Kojak and Oggy turned and left. By the time they had gone their separate ways outside, Maggie was cooking her fix, knowing that everything would be okay in a minute.

CHAPTER TWENTY-SEVEN

Our Problem

HUGH THANKED BRENDA for the drinks and headed back to the table where Mary was sitting, worrying about what they should do next. Not many people used the snug bar so they knew they could talk without fear of their business becoming local tittle-tattle. This was new territory for Hugh. Not only had he never been part of a serious relationship, the added ingredient of kids who were nothing to do with him meant he was walking blind on the eggshells Mary was scattering all over the place. Billy hadn't turned up for dinner after learning Hugh was coming round and Mary was fretting about it. Hugh didn't think it was as big a problem as Mary was making out, but he had the sense not to voice his opinion. He liked Billy and, as far as he could gather, the boy didn't have a problem with him. At dinner, Brian had spoken about the need to tell Billy the truth about his dad, a truth that Hugh had no idea about. Of course, he remembered the legendary Tommy Loy, but Hugh had never been a part of the gang scene as a kid so when Tommy was murdered, it barely registered with him. He had heard all the stories of Tommy's bravery, standing up to the Blantyre hoodlums single-handedly, his Robin Hood tendencies, being a harmless Jack-the-Lad character, but Hugh remembered him as a dangerous ned who was best avoided. He couldn't voice his opinions to Mary and certainly would never have let Billy know what he thought of his dad. All he could do now was listen to Mary and hope he didn't say the wrong thing.

"Do you remember my husband?" Mary had drunk half of her wine in one gulp before she started talking.

"Not really. I was aware of him, but I was only a teenager when he died. I've heard some stories over the years, but nothing bad. Everyone around here talks about him fondly as far as I know." Hugh hoped this would be enough of an appraisal to avoid him having to give further opinion. Mary laughed but tears weren't far away.

"Yeah, the stories. The all-round good guy with the heart of a lion, kind to old ladies and loyal to his friends. You're right, ask anyone in Calderwood and they'll tell you a fable about how much he helped everyone, how he would give you the shirt off his back if your need was greater than his, but it's all bollocks." Mary took another mouthful of wine to give her the courage to continue. "The truth is he was a bully. Not just to the gang of reprobates he gathered around himself, to everyone. He was a thief too. He robbed every shop and house in the area, but nobody would ever admit to knowing it was him who had stolen from them. They were too scared of him. His reputation allowed him a free rein to do whatever he wanted, and he knew nobody would ever stand up to him for fear of receiving a beating or worse." Mary spoke nervously, as though her words were a betrayal.

"Why did you marry him?" Hugh thought it was a natural question to ask but the look Mary gave him made him realise it may be best to just let her talk without giving any input. Mary relaxed a bit as she realised Hugh wasn't trying to wind her up.

"Oh, he was charming. We were childhood sweethearts. I knew he was a bit of a tearaway, but it was exciting at first. He started his gang, and all the local lads followed him everywhere. It was fun to be his girlfriend and receive the respect of all the other girls. Everyone was jealous of me. Then we left school and instead of getting a job and settling down, he turned to villainy on a full-time basis. I thought he would change and grow up like everyone else around us, but he couldn't let go. He was the leader of the gang. I don't think anyone else wanted him to change either. The others would still enjoy the odd night out with him, the odd scrap for old times' sake, but for Tommy it was a full-time job. And then I got pregnant." Hugh couldn't be sure, but he thought Mary winced.

"With Brian..."

Mary smiled. "Yeah. So, we got married. It's what you do, isn't it? We got married, got the flat and settled into it. At least I did. Thinking about it now, from the day we married, I probably saw less of him than I had when we were just boyfriend and girlfriend. He would justify not being around much by being the provider. There was always money, although I genuinely had no idea where he got it from. He certainly didn't have a regular job or anything. He would disappear for days, weeks at a time and come home with pocketfuls of cash and presents for the kids. Every now and then he would declare that we were going on holiday, weekends in Rothesay or Arbroath. We even went to Blackpool once, which was really exciting, but he ended up getting in a fight with some guys from Liverpool or somewhere and we had to leave in the middle of the night to avoid it escalating into something he couldn't handle. It was as though he was always running away from somebody or some situation he had created." Mary was reminiscing fondly, but there was an edge in her voice.

"Must have been tough..." Hugh had no idea what to say.

"It was. But I had the boys." Mary smiled warmly. "To the outside world I had everything. If I moaned about him not being there enough, he would tell me how lucky I was and how there were women queuing round the corner who would be more than happy to take my place if I didn't like it. I didn't have a job or any money of my own. I was stuck."

Mary drained her glass and looked up to the roof, hoping to find the strength to continue talking.

"You don't have to..." Hugh took Mary's hand and squeezed it gently.

"No, I want to." Mary took a deep breath before continuing. "And then one time when he had been gone for a couple of weeks without so much as a phone call, he came home like the prodigal son, and I snapped. I told him I had had enough, and he had to leave."

"Good for you." Hugh was proud of how Mary was confronting her past.

"No, not good for me. He kicked the shit out of me." Mary started crying.

"Jesus..." Hugh didn't know how to respond. Violence was alien to him. Mary sniffed back the tears and continued.

"After that, he would give me a slap for anything and everything. People would see the black eyes and the bruises, but they would all look the other way. I guess they thought I deserved it, or they were just glad it was me getting it and not them, I don't know."

"Couldn't you go to your parents, or the police even?" Hugh

couldn't imagine putting up with what Mary had been through. Mary laughed out loud, wiping away the tears.

"Are you joking? My parents would have blamed me! And if I went to the police, he would have killed me, I have no doubt about that. No, I just had to take it and hope each time he disappeared that he wouldn't come back. His mother knew it was going on, but I got the impression she had been through worse with her husband. She thought it was normal and would have given me a hard time if I complained. The boys were at school, and they idolised him. To them he was 'Super Dad', who showered them with sweets and toys while I was the wicked mum who made them do their homework and brush their teeth..." Mary filled up again.

"The boys adore you..." Hugh squeezed Mary's hand again.

Mary nodded and fought against the tears. "I know. I gave them all the love they needed." Mary dabbed her eyes with her hankie and gathered the strength to continue. "And then one day he came home, and he was in a foul mood. I don't even remember what I said to aggravate him, but he started laying into me. I honestly thought he was going to kill me. Halfway through, Brian came running in and jumped on his back, trying to protect me and Tommy turned on him. He picked my beautiful boy up and threw him against the wall like a rag doll. He lay on the floor, with blood coming from the back of his head and I started screaming. I think it gave Tommy a real fright because he stopped and just stood there with his mouth open. I screamed at him to get out and never come back. I screamed and screamed until he eventually left. Brian was fine, and I honestly thought he didn't remember it happening until now. That was the last time I saw Tommy. He was killed two months later."

Mary and Hugh sat in silence, holding hands across the table, neither knowing what to say next. Eventually Mary broke the silence.

"I never talked about it with the boys. Even in death, he held me in fear. I was frightened that if I told them what their dad was really like, they would resent me for it. They would hear all the stories about how great he was, how legendary he was. I couldn't compete with that." Mary's confidence in what she was saying was absolute, but her voice gave away the deep doubts she had.

"You don't have to compete with it! Brian obviously remembers more than you think, and Billy's a smart kid. He's not going to believe the word of strangers over you. He loves you very much. He wouldn't want you to suffer now, he would want to know the truth. I'm sure of it." Hugh couldn't see any other logic being an option.

"I don't want to spoil his memories of his dad…"

"Jesus, Mary, I understand that, but the boy is asking questions so he's obviously beginning to hear things about his dad that don't equate with the snippets he remembers. Don't you think it would be better for him to hear the truth from you rather than some random?" Hugh wasn't sure of his ground, but he was convinced it was the right thing to say.

"You're probably right, but where would I start?" Mary stood up and gathered her purse. "I need another drink. Same again?"

Without waiting for a response, she headed to the bar. Brenda came round from the other side of the bar and gave her a hug. Mary was crying again, and Hugh was happy that Brenda was there to offer a shoulder. His head was spinning from what Mary had said. The admiration he had for her had grown incredibly after hearing her story and he decided there and then that he wanted to be a major part of her life from now on. He wanted to give her a life she could enjoy.

"Have you got a minute?" Hugh hadn't noticed Bunnet come into the snug. He sat down before Hugh could tell him now wasn't a good time for a chat.

"Not really, mate."

"You need to make time, Hugh. This is serious." Bunnet looked around the snug to make sure nobody was listening, but apart from Mary and Brenda at the bar, the place was empty as usual. "I need to let you know some home truths about your partner."

Hugh racked his brain as to who his partner might be. "My partner?"

Bunnet looked at Hugh as though he was trying to hide something. "Angus, or Oggy, whatever you want to call him."

"Since when was Oggy my partner?" Hugh wondered what Bunnet was on about.

"Come on, you work together on the Calderwood run." Bunnet wasn't going to take any shit.

"We both do the Calderwood run, but I think calling him my

partner is a bit strong. I can't even say I like the guy very much, because I don't know him." Hugh had no idea where this was going.

"Whatever. Listen, I've found out delivering milk isn't the only thing he does." Bunnet had another look round the room to make sure nobody was listening. He leaned in close and spoke quietly. "He also runs a string of prostitutes."

Hugh leaned back in his chair, mainly to get away from the smell of Bunnet's hot breath. Hugh looked round the room this time, half expecting the guy from *Candid Camera* to jump out and tell him he was part of an elaborate hoax. He looked back at Bunnet and realised the older man was completely serious. He leaned back in to Bunnet and spoke in the same conspiratorial voice he had used.

"I know."

Bunnet looked amazed. "You know?"

Hugh leaned back in his chair and stopped the pretence that anything being said was a secret. "Of course I know. Everyone knows. The only surprising thing about this is that you don't know."

Bunnet looked genuinely shocked, as though Hugh had just admitted to knowing who shot JFK. Mary returned from the bar with a fresh pint for Hugh and a large glass of wine for herself. Hugh admired that if you didn't know she had been crying, you would never have guessed by looking at her.

"Alright, Bunnet?" Mary sat down at the table and noticed the shocked look on Bunnet's face. "Is everything okay?"

"Bunnet's just found out that Oggy helps the girls out and he seems to be outraged by it." Hugh gave Mary a look to show he hadn't invited Bunnet to join them.

Mary looked at Bunnet as though he was daft. "Really?"

Bunnet couldn't believe what he was hearing. "You knew about this, Mary?"

Mary laughed. "It's hardly a secret, Bunnet. He gives them a bit of protection, that's all. Keeps the nutters at bay and that..."

Bunnet sat back in disbelief. "I can't believe I'm hearing this."

"Ask Brenda. He looked after her for ages. Brenda!" Hugh waved at Brenda to come over and join them. There was nobody else in the bar, so she wasn't being pulled away from anything important. She walked over smiling. "Bunnet's just found out that Oggy's a pimp and he's amazed that everyone else already knows about it."

Everyone looked at Brenda expecting her to start laughing along with them, but her smile disappeared at the mention of Oggy's name.

"We're trying to tell him he looks after the girls, makes sure they're safe and that..." Mary sensed the change in Brenda's demeanour. "Is that not right?"

Brenda took her turn to look around the room to make sure nobody else was listening. She looked frightened. "That was the idea at first, yes."

"There's a young girl in the next block to me, Maggie she's called, really young with a baby. She's terrified of him and I saw him pushing her around in the street. It didn't look like he was looking after her..." Bunnet kept eye contact with Brenda until she looked away.

Brenda turned to walk back to the bar. Mary grabbed her by the arm. "Brenda? Are you okay? Is there more to Oggy than we know?" Brenda looked down at the ground, as though she didn't want to be there. Mary looked at her friend with compassion. "Brenda?"

Brenda decided to talk. "He did look after the girls. Now he seems to spend more time hitting them himself than protecting them. He's getting a bit out of control, to be honest."

"See! I knew it!" Bunnet was happy his concerns were justified. Mary shot him a glance to shut up.

"Did he hit you, Brenda?" Mary still held Brenda by the arm. Tears filled Brenda's eyes, but she fought to stop them rolling down her face.

"Once."

"See!" Bunnet couldn't contain himself.

"Shut up, Bunnet." Hugh urged Bunnet to read the situation and hide his delight about being right. Bunnet realised immediately that now probably wasn't the time to gloat.

"I'm sorry, Brenda." Bunnet turned to Hugh. "We need to do something about this."

"We need to do something about this? Why? It's nothing to do with me." Hugh couldn't believe what he was hearing.

"He's your partner!" Bunnet pointed his finger at Hugh accusingly.

"Fuck off, Bunnet, stop calling him my partner. I've got nothing to do with his business. The guy's a nutter..." Hugh could feel himself being dragged in. "And what about your partner? If you really want to appoint yourself the sheriff of Calderwood, maybe you should start a wee bit closer to home."

"Ach, come on. Drew's a daft young laddie, but he would never get mixed up in that kind of thing." Bunnet wasn't going to let Hugh change the subject that easily.

"A daft young laddie? Kojak is a grade A psychopath, and he might not be involved with the girls but what about the drugs?" Hugh couldn't believe Bunnet was so naïve.

Bunnet laughed. "What do you mean, drugs?"

"Fuck's sake, Bunnet, what planet do you live on? Kojak is the major drug dealer around here." Hugh wanted to bang Bunnet's head off the table.

"No. Don't be daft. I've known him since he was a wee boy. Who told you that?" Bunnet was having none of it.

"The boys. Where else do you think they get their pot and their acid or whatever? It's Kojak!" Hugh realised he was shouting now and lowered his voice. "He supplies all the boys."

"What?" Bunnet couldn't believe it.

"What?" Mary's eyes were wide open.

Hugh realised he was on shaky ground and started back pedalling as quickly as he could. "Not *all* the boys, obviously, but a lot of them."

"He's right. I didn't know about selling to the boys, obviously, but Kojak supplies all the girls with smack. Trust me, he's just as dangerous as Oggy, if not worse." Brenda could see that Hugh needed some backing.

"Jesus Christ." Bunnet looked like somebody had punched him in the stomach. He snapped himself out of his trauma and stood up. "We need to do something."

"There you go with this *we* again! It's terrible, but it's not my problem." Hugh was determined not to be dragged into Bunnet's madness.

"If he's selling drugs to children, it's all of our problem. And if Oggy's running round beating up women, it's all of our problem." Mary was challenging Hugh. "Nobody's asking you to stand up to them yourself, we all need to do it."

Hugh looked at Mary, Brenda and Bunnet in turn. They were all looking at him with expectancy in their eyes. He wished he hadn't got out of bed that morning.

CHAPTER TWENTY-EIGHT

Tears and Snotters

BILLY WONDERED IF the gig had been a success. The response of the crowd to Lisa had been humiliating, but the way the band had pulled it back together after Billy had smashed Cheesy in the face with the microphone had been exhilarating. And because none of the other bands had got to play after the fire, it meant Handclap's performance was the only thing anyone was talking about. That and the speculation of what Cheesy was going to do to Billy in response to losing some teeth. Billy wasn't worried about Cheesy. He was getting used to dealing with bullies.

The bedroom felt particularly cold. When Billy poked his head out from under the covers on his bed, his breath filled the air as if he was puffing on a Capstan full strength. He looked over and was surprised to see Brian awake for once.

"Morning."

Billy and Brian had always got along okay, but nobody would have described them as bosom buddies. They led different lives, with different friends, and now that Brian was working, there was no common bond like there had been when they were both attending Hunter High. Brian's taste in music was nothing like Billy's. He liked Elton John, while Billy liked Wreckless Eric, and their mutual disinterest in football was hardly something that brought them together.

"How did the gig go?" Brian stretched and yawned as he spoke.

Billy was surprised Brian knew anything about the gig. "I haven't decided yet."

Brian laughed. "You take your time over things, don't you, Billy boy? By the time you make a decision over something, whatever you're deciding about is long gone. You should live a little. Go with the flow a bit more..."

"Is that what your vast experience has taught you?" Billy wasn't in the mood for life lessons from someone he saw as a daydreamer. "Those two years you have over me really do amount to a lifetime's experience..."

"Those two years mean I remember a lot of shit you don't." Brian wasn't going to let his wee brother be cheeky to him.

"Like what?"

"Like our old man. How much do you actually remember about him? Not the crappy stories you've heard from mum, actual things you remember?" Brian turned to face Billy, making sure he kept the bedclothes covering him as much as he could.

Billy thought about it. "Not a lot, really. I remember him getting me a bike. A couple of holidays..."

"You don't remember him leaving?"

"When he was murdered, you mean?"

Brian laughed and shook his head. "He left long before he was murdered."

"What do you mean?" Billy furrowed his brow.

"Mum kicked him out long before..."

Billy sat up straight. "She what?"

"There you go again." Brian shook his head and smiled.

"What?" Billy was defensive. He didn't like Brian talking down to him.

"When it comes to Dad, you're always ready to blame Mum for some reason, as if it was her who killed him."

"Fuck off..."

"No, you fuck off. She took a lot of shit from him that you know nothing about and all you do is treat her like dirt." Brian was being serious now.

"That's not true." Billy stopped looking at Brian. He knew he took Mary for granted sometimes, but he never treated her badly and always tried his best. He was the one doing well at school, not Brian.

"Yes, it is. She's worked really hard to make a life for herself and now that she's finally ready to cut your apron strings and stop pandering to you, you're acting like a fucking baby. I know this guy Hugh isn't exactly Superman, but she likes him. You acting like a wee prick about it will probably stop her seeing him, because she'll do anything to protect you. Just like she has your whole life, making up stories about the old man so you don't get upset about what he was really like. It's time to grow up, Billy..."

Brian turned away from Billy, not expecting to get through to him. Billy took his time, thinking about what Brian had said before he replied.

"So, what was he really like, if you know so much?" Billy wondered if Brian had any answers, but he doubted it.

"I don't pretend that I know everything either, I doubt she even knows everything, but I know he used to kick fuck out of her on a regular basis..."

Billy threw off his bedclothes and jumped out of bed to confront Brian. "No way!"

Brian didn't react to Billy's aggression. There was no way he was exposing himself to the cold.

"Ask her yourself. I saw him do it. He fucked me off a wall once when I tried to stop him." Brian was tired of beating around the bush. Maybe it was his job to tell his brother the truth if his mum wasn't willing to do it.

Billy turned and ran out of the bedroom.

Mary was in the kitchen. The twin tub washing machine was making a hell of a racket recently, but it still got the clothes clean and that was the important thing. The pulley was down from the ceiling and Mary was hanging the wet clothes up carefully. There was a skill to spacing the clothes out properly, making the most of the space available. Each wooden rung was utilised to the maximum, making sure all the clothes from two washes were hoisted up to the ceiling and drying at the same time. In December it could take a couple of days to get it all dry. In the summer it could all be hung up outside in the drying green and be ready for ironing in one day, but if you tried to put it out in winter, it could easily freeze. It meant Mary would have to dodge the drips coming from the sodden clothes for the rest of the day whenever she was in the kitchen, but it was worth it to ensure her family had clean clothes.

She hadn't slept very well last night. The idea of Billy taking drugs had filled her with dread, even though Hugh had assured her that her son was way too smart to get involved in that kind of thing. Although she hadn't known about Kojak being the local dealer, she hadn't been surprised and chastised herself for being naive enough for the idea of dealing to kids being beyond him. The kind of stories she heard about Kojak were like some of the ones she used to ignore about Tommy. She wouldn't be surprised if her husband had been involved in something similar back in the day, although she didn't think drugs were as prevalent then as they were now. It may have been the swinging sixties elsewhere in the world, but in East Kilbride alcohol was still king when she was young. Drugs were something you read about in the news, not something you expected to be on the streets and readily available to children. Mary knew she would have to talk to Billy about the dangers, but she wasn't certain that he would probably know a lot more about it than she did.

Billy came running down the hall and stopped at the kitchen door. His face was fuming, and it looked like tears weren't far away.

"Is it true?"

"Is what true, son?" Mary had never seen Billy look so angry.

"Did he hit you?" Billy was shouting now.

"Who?"

"Dad! Is it true that he used to knock you about?" Billy looked frightened standing in the doorway.

Mary almost went into automatic denial but managed to catch herself. Talking to Hugh had made her realise that her little boy wasn't so little anymore, and maybe her protection of him was more detrimental than helpful. She looked out of the window, trying to hide the tears that were filling her eyes.

"Let me get the pulley up and we can talk. Go on into the living room and I'll be in in a minute." She looked at Billy and gave him a reassuring smile that wasn't fooling anyone.

Billy went into the living room, giving Mary time to gather herself before she had the hardest conversation of her life. Once she had secured the pulley, Mary took a deep breath and followed Billy. Billy was lying on the settee. Mary lifted his legs and sat down, placing his feet in her lap.

"What have you heard?" Mary didn't know where to start.

"Stuff. I just want to know the truth."

Mary took another deep breath. "Well, the first thing you have to know is that your dad loved you very much. I never lied about that. I never lied about anything. I just never told you the whole story..."

"Why?" Billy felt let down.

"Because you probably wouldn't have believed me. I'm not making excuses, Billy, but it's not been easy bringing you and Brian up on my own, especially when your dad was who he was. You must understand that when he died, the whole neighbourhood held him up as some kind of martyr. He was so well known around here that the stories making him out to be some kind of hero had started before his body was cold. If I had stood up and told the truth, I would have been ostracised by everyone. It was just easier to let the myth become the truth. And I didn't want you growing up hearing me complain about your dad. He was your hero. He was everybody's hero. If he was still alive it would have been easier because everyone would have seen him for what he was, but him dying the way he did would have made me sound like a bitch. Nobody would have believed me." Mary was speaking as softly as she could, hoping it would cushion the blows from her words.

"You should have told me..." Billy's voice was weak.

"Maybe I should have. I didn't know what was for the best."

"So, did he hit you?" The sensitivity in Billy's voice showed that he hoped he would get a favourable answer.

Mary thought again before she spoke. "He lived in a violent world, Billy. You've heard the stories, how he was the guy who started The Woodie, the first leader of the gang. You know the boys who run around in that environment now and they're bad enough, but when your dad was that age, it seemed to be much more violent. He built up a reputation and the only way he could maintain it was through violence. All the people who hailed him as a hero when he died were terrified of him when he was alive. He was a violent man because that was how he survived and sometimes he brought that violence home with him..." Mary couldn't stop the tears from rolling down her face.

"Did he hit *me*?" Billy sounded like her wee boy again.

"Never! I would have killed him myself if he had ever tried." Mary hugged Billy's legs tightly.

"He hit Brian..." Billy's voice was almost a whisper. Mary shuddered at the memory of Brian lying on the floor with blood streaming from the back of his head.

"He did it once. And that was the day he left this house for good. I swore that day never to let him hurt either of you ever again, and he never did. He died not long after that, but I swear if he was still alive today, he would never have laid a hand on either of you. I wouldn't have let him." Mary had never been so sure about anything she had ever said in her life.

"Did he cheat on you?" Billy didn't know how many questions he had, but they were coming thick and fast.

Mary was taken aback by the question. The truth was she had never suspected her husband of cheating on her when they were together, but over the years she had heard tales from others about the womanising that went on behind her back and she couldn't find a reason not to believe it. She never knew where he was, and he was absent from the house more than he was there. She had accepted it as a possibility but buried her head in the sand sufficiently for none of it to become a reality.

"Honestly? I don't know. Let's just say I wasn't aware of it at the time and I've no desire to find out if it was the case. Maybe you think I'm daft, maybe the whole world thinks I'm daft, but the truth is I'd rather not know, even if deep down I think it was something he was capable of. There's only so much heartache I'm willing to let that man inflict on me and I'm over it now, for the best part. I just don't want him inflicting you with the same heartache from the grave. He was your dad and he loved you, but he was a violent bully to almost everyone he knew, and I wanted to protect you from that. Maybe I was wrong to do that, but I would do it all over again if I could go back in time, because you and your brother were the only good things ever to come from him and I wouldn't change that for the world."

Billy sat up and threw his arms around Mary. They hugged each other tightly and let the tears flow. Mary felt relief flow through her body, the burden of protecting her son lifted from her now that he was becoming a man. Eventually Billy found his voice.

"Do you like Hugh?"

Mary released herself from Billy's embrace and looked him in the eye. "I do, but if you have a problem with that, it won't go anywhere. He seems like a good man and God knows I could do with a good man in my life, but you and Brian are enough for me if that's the way it has to be."

Billy buried himself in Mary's shoulder again. "He's alright. But if he ever treats you badly, you can't keep it from me this time.

You need to tell me. Nobody is going to treat you like dad did ever again."

Mary smiled as she hugged her son tighter. "Don't worry, no more secrets. Now, do you want a cup of tea? I'm choking for one..."

"I'll make it." Billy got up and walked through to the kitchen, leaving Mary to wipe away her tears.

It never ceased to amaze Mary how long it took either of her children to do the simplest of tasks. It was fifteen minutes before Billy returned with the tea, but she never complained. She heard tales from other mothers whose children wouldn't even know where the kettle was, never mind how to make a cup of tea. Both Billy and Brian could cook a basic meal, work the washing machine and use the iron if pushed, although it wasn't often she asked for their help. She was proud of how they were turning out.

"Do you know anything about guys your age taking drugs?" Mary tried to sound as casual as she could, but Billy almost stopped in his tracks at the mention of it. "Don't worry, Hugh assures me you're not involved, but I just wondered if you had heard anything about it?"

For a second Billy thought Hugh might have grassed him up about the acid and he was regretting giving his approval of Mary seeing him, but he quickly reasoned that her reaction would have been more extreme if she knew what he had been up to.

"What drugs?" Billy hoped she hadn't noticed his initial panic.

"Oh, I don't know, pot and things like that. It was just something Bunnet was talking about in the pub the other day. He seemed to think some of the boys on the floats might be involved..."

"I don't think so." Billy dismissed the theory as casually as his mum had been in bringing it up.

"If you hear anything, let me know. Or let Hugh know. It's probably not true..." It would take Mary a while to get used to telling her children the truth about things she would rather they didn't know.

"Aye, okay." Billy drank his tea and racked his brain to think of a change of subject. "When is Hugh coming round again?"

"We're going for a walk later. You can join us if you want..."

Billy laughed. "A walk? Nah, you're alright."

"Yes, a walk!" Mary laughed too. "What's wrong with going for a walk?"

"Nothing, if you're a pensioner!" Billy laughed.

"Ya cheeky wee git." Mary was feeling so happy now that everything was out in the open. "Oh, by the way, there was a note through the door for you. It's on the mantlepiece."

Billy got up and looked at the note with his name on it. 'Game of headers at the lockies at 3'. It was from Dick.

"What is it?" Mary had respected his privacy by not reading the note, but she was desperate to know what it said.

"I'm going out. Football."

"Football? You're turning down a walk with your mum and her boyfriend for a game of football?"

Billy smiled at Mary, happy that she was comfortable enough to call Hugh her boyfriend in front of him now. "It's hard to believe, but aye."

CHAPTER TWENTY-NINE

The Odd Brothers

WHEN YOU GO up Geddes Hill, there's a left turning about halfway that takes you behind the houses into a cul-de-sac of lockups. They are used by the residents of Whin Hill and Geddes Hill, although very few of them housed cars, not only because cars were a rare commodity, but because it was a pain in the arse to walk round there when it was easier to park in the street right outside your front door. Most of the lockups were used as glorified garden sheds, a place to dump the unused bikes, lawnmowers and other household shit deemed too precious to throw away but not useful enough to be needed on a daily basis. They were used as an extension to the street kids' playground as climbing frames, tennis courts and as the ideal place to play heady football.

The lockups, or the lockies as they were commonly known, ran in two rows facing each other with enough space to reverse a car out of each one. A gutter ran down the middle of the road, creating a natural halfway line, and the metal doors of each unit were the perfect size to represent a goal net. Each player defended their goal when the other player had possession of the ball. Who had possession was decided by where the ball ended up. Neither player was allowed into their opponent's half and only headers or volleys were allowed to score a goal. On any day, up to fifteen games of headers could be taking place at the same time. It was strictly a one v one game, although some of the younger kids could make it two v two without taking up too much room.

When Billy walked round, the whole place was deserted, which wasn't unusual considering the weather. Few cars had been driven through so the snow was undisturbed and seemed to add to the silence. Billy waited five minutes to see if anyone would turn up before deciding it was too cold to hang around any longer. As he started to walk away, he got a fright when Dick spoke.

"Alright?"

Billy looked up to where the voice was coming from and there was Dick, sitting on the roof of the lockies, smoking a cigarette.

"Fuck's sake, you gave me a fright. How long have you been up there?"

Dick smiled, the way he always did, and jumped down to join Billy. "A while. You're late. I didn't think you were coming."

"I only just got the note." Billy looked around. "Where's the ball?"

Dick looked around too. "I don't know. Have you not brought one?"

Billy laughed. "I don't have a ball."

"Naw, I don't either." Dick laughed too. "It'll be a short game then..."

"We'll get one." Billy gestured for Dick to follow him.

The back of the lockies looked onto the back gardens of the various houses they were built for. The boys climbed onto the roof of the row backing onto the houses of Whin Hill and began searching the gardens for any balls that had been booted over the top of the lockies. The younger kids were too wee to climb onto the roofs, so there was always a stray ball nestling in a hedge somewhere, lost when a spectacular attempt to recreate a Joe Jordan bullet header or a Peter Lorimer crashing volley had gone astray. Within ten minutes they had located one and jumped down into the garden to rescue it before the disgruntled householder found it and stuck a knife in it in a vain attempt to discourage the kids from having fun.

Back down on the ground, Billy took the ball and threw it in the air to begin the game. His header sailed over Dick's head and crashed off the lock-up door, the metallic sound filling the air. Billy laughed as Dick had made no attempt to save it at all.

"1-0."

Dick smiled and grabbed the ball to take his first go. He threw the ball too high in the air and had his eyes firmly closed as it came back down. He missed it completely, but managed to stop it rolling into Billy's half, meaning he could try again. He threw his second attempt even higher but this time managed to connect. The ball bounced off the top of his head and went over the roof behind him, rolling back down into the garden they had retrieved it from. Both boys laughed uproariously.

"You don't play football, do you?" Tears were filling Billy's eyes.

Dick was standing rubbing the top of his head to deaden the pain the ball had caused, happy to laugh at his own incompetence. "Nah, it's a fucking stupid game." The boys laughed even harder.

"I don't think it's worth climbing down to get the ball again, do you?" Billy didn't want to play either.

"Nah, come on." Dick climbed up to where he had been sitting when Billy arrived. Billy followed him and they sat in silence for a while.

"How do you think your gig went?" Dick offered Billy a cigarette, which he declined with a shake of the head.

"I don't know. I can't decide if it was a disaster or a triumph. Did you hear about it?"

"I was there." Dick blew a huge cloud of smoke, following it with a volley of professional smoke rings.

"Were you? I didn't see you…" Billy tried to remember the sea of faces in the crowd.

"For what it's worth, I thought it was a fucking disaster, but that's what made it so good."

Billy looked at Dick to check if he was taking the piss but the smile was warm, so he knew no offence was intended. "Who were you there with?"

Dick looked at Billy as though he was daft. "Nobody."

"Who do you hang around with?" Billy was realising he didn't really know anything about Dick.

"Well, today I'm hanging with you, but in general I don't really run with anyone. Not from round here anyway. I see my cousins sometimes…"

Billy smiled at Dick. "You're a bit weird."

"Just a bit? I'm losing my touch." Dick smiled back. "Is that what people think of me? A bit weird?"

Billy thought about it. "I don't know. You get called Dick, for fuck's sake. I think that's what people think. A bit of a dick." Billy smiled again, hoping he wasn't causing offence. "Why do you let them call you Dick?"

"I like it. My real name is Damian. Who wants to be called Damian? And what do you mean, 'let them'? It's not up to me what people call me. I couldn't give a fuck what they call me." Dick shrugged his shoulders and shivered involuntarily.

"Okay, what about the people who think you're a bit of a bugsy cunt?" Billy was determined to get a reaction.

Dick laughed out loud. "Bugsy? What are you? Seven or something?" Billy laughed too, glad he had got a response.

"So, what do people think of *me*?" Billy wondered if he would take Dick's answer in the same good spirit as he had.

"Oh, you're Tommy Loy's boy. The Golden Child. Nobody would dare call you anything in case your blessed father came back from the grave and kicked their cunt in." Dick was smiling, but there was a mocking sharpness in his tone.

Billy shook his head. "If only they knew the truth..."

"What do you mean?"

"It turns out my old man wasn't the hero everyone thinks he was. He was a thief, a bully and he used to kick fuck out of my mum on a regular basis. My brother too." Billy wasn't smiling now. He was looking up to the sky.

"Do you remember what I told you that night at the Genny's? You were off your face on acid, so I don't even know if you remember talking to me..." Dick was serious now too.

"Snippets. You said my dad shagged about. I asked my mum about it, and she didn't know anything, but she said she didn't rule it out." It was new information to Billy, but he didn't mind sharing it.

"Do you remember me saying why he was killed? That it was my uncle who did it?" Dick sounded sad.

Billy looked at Dick. There were tears in his eyes. "Are you my brother?"

Dick looked Billy directly in the eyes. "Yeah, I am."

"Fuck's sake." Billy broke down and started crying. Dick put his arm around Billy's shoulders and let him deal with it.

"Nobody thinks your dad was a hero, not really. He was a terror, by all accounts. He robbed anything that wasn't nailed down and punched everything that was. I don't remember him, but my mum has told me all about him. He treated her like shit too, by the way. Plenty of beatings. That's why my uncle hated him so much. Not that my uncle was any better. I remember him beating the shit out of me once because I spilled some milk on his carpet. I hope he rots in jail." Dick shuddered at the memory.

"When did you find out we had the same dad?" Billy took the

hanky that Mary always made sure he had out of his pocket and wiped his eyes.

"I've always known. My mum didn't sugarcoat things." Dick was proud that his mum treated him like a grown-up.

"Why didn't you say anything before?" Billy was beginning to feel that all he was going to do for the rest of his life was ask questions.

"My mum's shame, I suppose. She was ashamed that she was the fallen woman with the bastard child. All catholic guilt pish. I went along with it because I didn't want to upset her. It made no difference to me. He was dead anyway, so what was I going to get out of it if I went around broadcasting it?" Dick stubbed out his cigarette in the snow, pausing to enjoy the initial hiss as it hit the wetness.

"So why do it now?" Billy blew his nose.

"Oh, I'm not broadcasting it now either. I only thought it was fair that you knew the truth. I don't intend telling anyone else. Fuck that. Look at you. It's not exactly done you any good being recognised as the prick's son, has it?"

Billy and Dick both laughed. Billy looked at the sky again. Snow was starting to fall.

"I worry I'm just like him."

Dick laughed again. "You're not like him..."

"I think I might be. In the past couple of weeks, I've hit Cheesy more than once and I beat the shit out of one of my teachers because he was bullying me and belting the shit out of me all the time. I flipped. It's like the violence is in me and I can't stop it coming out." Billy was genuinely worried.

Dick let out a roar of laughter. "Everyone wants to hit Cheesy! He's one of life's punchbags. A bully who hasn't got the ammunition to back it up and by the sound of it, the teacher is the same. You're nothing like your dad, Billy..."

"*Our* dad..." Billy could already feel a connection.

"Aye, well, in name only. Although if anyone is showing the same attributes as him, it's more likely to be me." Dick was catching snowflakes on his tongue as he spoke.

"Rubbish. You're a good guy." Billy smiled at Dick.

"Not a bugsy cunt?" Both of them laughed. "Anway, about your band. I think you should get rid of the two pricks you've got playing with you and don't ever think about using that hellish bird again. And the name has got to go too. Fucking Handclap. Who came up with that?" Dick was happy to move the conversation on. He wasn't used to feeling the way he was now that everything was out in the open.

"Me!"

"Fuck that. I play guitar, pretty fucking well by the way, so all we need is a drummer, like every other band in this shithole of a town. And we need a new name." Dick was smiling again.

"You are fucking odd, brother." Billy couldn't help but smile back.

"That's it! The Odd Brothers! That's the name." Dick held out his arms.

"Okay! The Odd Brothers."

Billy and Dick hugged each other tightly.

CHAPTER THIRTY

The Eggy Stench

CHEESY'S ENTIRE BODY was aching. The cold was in his bones, and it took a couple of hours walking around each day before he got the feeling back in the toes of his right foot. He had a constant headache and the gap in his mouth where his two front teeth had been bled constantly. His idea of living down the Glen was beginning to look like a huge mistake. The temperature dropped to minus double figures most nights and the tent he had borrowed from Nicky did little to keep out the cold. On top of that, the place was full of noises. Animals scuttled by the tent every night, the birds never shut the fuck up and Cheesy was beginning to believe the whole place was haunted. Most nights he was woken by something or someone screaming, meaning he was lucky if he slept for more than a couple of hours a night.

The gig at the community centre had been a disaster. Apart from that cunt Billy Loy hitting him in the mouth with the microphone and dislodging his teeth, which was bad enough, that wee cow Lisa had rushed off after it without him and was refusing to speak to him. He had hoped she would let him stay with her because her parents were never there, but her big sister's boyfriend had answered the door the next day and made it very clear that he wasn't welcome round there. Cheesy had added him to the list. To be fair, there weren't many people who weren't on Cheesy's list now. When he got back on his feet, he would be busy bursting all the people who had done him wrong. Nicky was on the list now too. Cheesy had gone round to his mate's house the other day, hoping to scrounge a hot meal and some clean clothes, but the shitebag wouldn't even come to the door. His specky wee dad had come out and threatened to call the polis if Cheesy didn't fuck off and leave his son alone. If the wee wank couldn't take a doing when it was deserved, he wasn't worthy of Cheesy's friendship. The same went for all the other pricks who called themselves Woodie boys but shat themselves when challenged by the Blantyre lot. It would take time, but Cheesy would make sure every last one of them paid the price.

Top of the list was Billy Loy. He was a dead man walking. He was sailing through life just because his dad had been a Woodie legend, but he had never done anything to deserve the respect he got. The cunt wasn't even man enough to be a Woodie member himself. He had humiliated Cheesy with his lucky punch at the football a couple of weeks ago and using a microphone as a chib the other night was out of order. Cheesy ran his tongue through the gap at the front of his mouth to remind himself of how much he hated Billy. He looked at the kitchen knife sitting handily at the door of the tent to ward off any intruders and vowed he would make sure Billy knew what a chib really was when he got the opportunity.

The massive box of eggs took up a lot of room in the tent, but it was important to keep it dry if Cheesy was going to use it. He was formulating a new plan and the drugs inside the box were crucial to it working. The original idea to sell it off and use the money to get out of this hell hole had been harder to execute than Cheesy had thought. In his dreams, he planned to have all the Woodie boys selling it around town, giving him maximum profit without implicating himself at all. Kojak had put the word out that if anyone was caught with the drugs or was caught selling them, he would find them and break their legs, so there was no way any of the gang would take part in Cheesy's scheme. A new plan was required, and he had come up with one that would settle a few scores in one foul swoop. Cheesy had surprised himself at the genius of it.

Cheesy was going to plant the drugs on Billy and then grass him up to Kojak. Kojak would be so grateful, he would give Cheesy his job back on the milk float, maybe even take him on as an apprentice in the drugs game, and Billy would get the doing he deserved. It was foolproof, easy to execute and could be put into place quickly. Tonight was the ideal time to set things in motion. The snow was falling heavily again so the streets would be empty, giving Cheesy the cover of darkness and the quiet to take the drugs up to Billy's place and plank them there. He had thought about breaking into the flat by climbing up the outside verandas, but with all the snow it wouldn't be easy and the state his feet were in could be a hindrance. The last thing he needed was to fall from the top veranda and break his back, leaving him lying there with the drugs in his possession. He had thought it all through.

At the back of the flats there was a row of coal sheds, no longer used for that purpose, and each flat had their own shed. Cheesy would break into Billy's shed, plant the drugs and be gone in a matter of minutes. Cheesy knew from experience that the old wooden doors opened easily using nothing more than a screwdriver. He had been robbing them since he was a kid. Next day he would wait for Kojak at the end of his milk round and tell him all about Billy being the one who robbed him. By this time tomorrow night everything would be sorted, and he could look forward to getting out of this fucking tent.

Cheesy was right about how quiet the streets would be. The snow was thick, the streetlights giving the whole place a yellow sheen. Cheesy's foot was killing him, so he had to be careful walking and he made sure he stuck to the back streets where the grit lorries never went, so it was hard going getting from the glen to the other end of Calderwood where Billy lived. He had decided against taking the whole box of eggs with him. It was reasonable to assume whoever stole the drugs would just dump the eggs and only keep the boxes with pot in them. Cheesy had kept the eggs because he was hungry, but Billy wouldn't have done that if he was only interested in the drugs. One poly bag was enough to carry the pot and Cheesy congratulated himself on how clever he had been to think it through so well.

Cheesy wedged his trusty screwdriver into the shed door and it popped open with one twist. Nobody had coal fires anymore, so the sheds were used as storage space. In the dim light, Cheesy could see a few deckchairs and a couple of old car tyres piled up on top of a couple of boxes marked as bed linen along with an old tricycle. He placed the bag of drugs on the seat of the tricycle and popped the door shut again. He was gone within a minute.

Cheesy had planked two dozen eggs in his parents' shed when he had first robbed Kojak's float, thinking he would be able to come and go from the family home as he pleased when his mum and dad had calmed down a bit after him beating them up, but he hadn't been back since, reckoning they would need a bit more time before he would be welcome back. After planting the drugs in Billy's shed, however, the idea of returning to the tent straight away was too much to bear. At this time of night, both of his parents would be fast asleep after a hard day of drinking, so he grabbed the eggs out of the shed and went into the house via the back door, which was never locked. He took out the big pot and cracked a dozen eggs into it, adding some milk from the fridge, and whisking it all together with a fork. He didn't need to do anything quietly. He knew from experience, and by the number of empty Special Brew cans lying around the living room floor, that an earthquake wouldn't wake his parents. Ten minutes later he was sitting in the living room with all three bars of the electric fire blazing, tucking into the biggest, best tasting plate of scrambled eggs he had ever had. He decided to leave the dozen eggs left over for his parents in the fridge, reckoning that would go some way to appeasing their anger, but by the time he had finished his feast, the charitable thoughts he had been having were gone. His stomach was hurting, and he knew what was coming. He went back to the kitchen, put the big pot on the floor and dropped his trousers. Most of the diarrhoea made it into the pot but some managed to coat the linoleum around it too and some peripheral spray managed to find its way onto the back wall. The eggy stench was incredible. Cheesy carefully lifted the pot and placed it in the empty fridge beside the dozen eggs.

"Fuck them."

Cheesy headed out into the cold, mentally playing out how he would approach Kojak in a few hours, looking forward to the new start his careful planning would bring him.

CHAPTER THIRTY-ONE

Auld Perv

THE SNOWFALL MUST have been relentless during the night. Driving conditions were as bad as Bunnet could ever remember, which meant it was going to be a long morning. There were some streets it was going to be impossible for the float to get out of if he followed the normal route, so the boys were going to earn their crust today. They would need to carry crates further and fuller than usual, because if the float got stuck in the snow it would mean people not getting their milk and that would mean complaints. Bunnet knew most of his customers by name and he knew they would be loyal to him under most circumstances, but if they didn't get their milk, they wouldn't think twice about jumping ship to the rival dairy, and that could be a disaster. The rivalry between the dairies was fierce, and it wouldn't take much for one or the other becoming dominant. Bunnet liked to think the service he provided was second to none, but it wouldn't take much for people to change allegiance. Milk was an important factor.

None of this was helping his mood. He hadn't slept a wink last night. How could he be so blind to what was happening right under his nose? He knew Kojak was a wrong 'un, he had known that since the day he had taken him on as one of his boys, but he didn't think for one minute that he would be involved in drugs. In fact, Bunnet couldn't believe anyone round here would be taking drugs, let alone one of his colleagues being involved in dealing them. Drugs were for pop stars or low-life people in the American movies, not good working-class people in a wee town in the West of Scotland. Booze was the acceptable vice around here and Bunnet had seen it ruin enough lives over the years, people who had a weakness and couldn't handle it, but drugs were illegal. Where the hell was Kojak getting them? Was he growing them himself? Did you grow them?

There was too much Bunnet didn't know, and he was determined to get to the bottom of it.

The most disturbing bit of Hugh's revelation was that Kojak was peddling drugs to the boys. Bunnet was confident none of the boys on his float would be involved. Two of them had potential careers in football and they were all just too sensible to get involved in anything like that. When he took a boy on, Bunnet always made it clear that he wouldn't tolerate any trouble. If he heard that any of them had so much as not done their homework, he would be on them in a flash, and over the years he hadn't had to sack many boys. He was proud that most of them had left school with at least a couple of O Levels under their belt and, as far as he knew, had all gone on to decent jobs. He had turned a blind eye to some of them being involved with the local gang because that was just part of growing up, part of the Scottish culture. You couldn't teach them about the Scottish clans in school and not expect them to go out and create their own. Most of their parents had grown up in a gang culture and helped pass on the folklore it created, but it was something they grew out of. As far as Bunnet knew, drugs weren't something you grew out of.

The other thing keeping him awake was Brenda telling him about the prostitute ring centred around the bus station. Bunnet didn't often use the buses, he preferred to walk wherever he was going if he wasn't driving the float, but they were the lifeline of the town. East Kilbride was in the arse-end of nowhere when you thought about it, so the bus service was an essential part of life for most people. The idea that prostitutes were peddling their wares in front of decent people going about their business was disgusting. And the thought of decent young girls like Maggie being forced to sell themselves to God knows who, filled him with dread. Bunnet had never taken the time getting to know Oggy because he always felt there was something about him that he didn't like. He had assumed his dislike came from Oggy being from Hamilton, an out of towner, but now Bunnet was berating himself for not finding out more about him. Being a good judge of character was something Bunnet prided himself on, so ignoring his first impression that Oggy was trouble and not doing something about it was a lesson he wouldn't let happen again.

Although the snow had been falling all night, the sky was clear now and the temperature had plummeted. The boys were taking every opportunity to jump in the cab to sit with Bunnet in the hope of thawing out a bit before they next had to load a few crates and set off to the streets the float wouldn't be going down.

"Tell me, do you know anything about drugs being sold around here?" Bunnet would ask each boy individually, hoping they would open up if nobody else was there to hear their answers. "Don't worry, I know you wouldn't be involved, but I've been hearing stories that some of the boys on other floats might be."

"Aye, loads of people do it." Ian was the best footballer in town, and everyone had really high hopes that he would make the grade at Motherwell. There was even talk that he might get called up to the Scottish schoolboys' team.

"What drugs is it they do?" Bunnet was surprised at the casual way Ian had confirmed his fears.

Ian laughed. "Everything."

"What kind of things?" Bunnet was out of his depth. He wouldn't know a drug if it walked up and slapped him.

"Glue, Zoff, speed, sulphate, grass, leb, black, oil, acid, poppers..."

"Jesus Christ!" Bunnet wasn't sure what he had expected but the ease in which the list tripped off the boy's tongue and the seemingly endless variations he was naming shocked him. If Ian knew all of this, why the hell didn't he? "Where does it all come from?"

"I don't know..."

Ian moved out of the cab and jumped off the float with a double crate, running freely despite the snow. Bunnet didn't expect any of the boys to divulge the source of the drugs. He knew Kojak had a temper on him and most people were wary of him, so it would be unfair to push them. It didn't matter. Hugh had already confirmed it and now Bunnet could see for himself that he wasn't talking about a couple of pills or a few joints. This was serious, and Bunnet couldn't let it continue.

Kojak had taken the risk of driving down to the bottom of Waverley to deliver to the flats at the bottom of the street. It was the last street of the round and the going had already been too slow. All the boys had finished and opted to walk back to their houses, desperate for heat, leaving Kojak to do the flats on his own. He couldn't complain – it had been freezing sitting in the cab, never mind running around in the stark elements – but now he was regretting letting them go before he was finished. He had tried three times to drive back up the hill, and there was no way it was happening. With all the milk delivered, the float was too light to give any kind of purchase in the snow, the wheels spinning wildly as he went backwards instead of up the hill. He would have to phone the dairy and get one of the lorries out to tow him back to the top, and then he would have to listen to Bunnet go on and on about the right way to drive in the snow. His mood couldn't get any worse, but the idea of having to listen to Bunnet lecturing him could be the thing to tip him over the edge.

Kojak heard a float coming down Alloway Road and readied himself for the onslaught of Bunnet's tedium. He already knew he should have taken the extra time to use the flatter route down Alloway Road, so he didn't need the old pest telling him so. The float stopped and Kojak looked up, hoping his expression would warn Bunnet off. To his dismay, it wasn't Bunnet. It was Oggy, and that was even worse.

Oggy was pissing himself laughing. "Are you stuck? Ha! Ya fanny."

"Do yourself a favour and jog on, Oggy, I'm really not in the mood." Kojak looked around for something to busy himself with, but he had nothing.

Oggy climbed out of his cab and walked over to Kojak, not even trying to hide his delight at the sight of the stricken float. "While I've got you here, I need a word."

Kojak walked forward, clenching his fists. "I'm not joking, Oggy. Fuck off now or I won't be held responsible for my actions."

"Naw, you fuck off, ya prick." Oggy wasn't laughing anymore. "Another one of my girls nearly fucking died last night because of you."

"Fuck off. Who?" This was all Kojak needed. The news that Linda had died wasn't out yet so another one could be disastrous. He was getting enough earache from Greer about the stolen gear without his clients all dying on him.

"Karen Black. She overdosed down at the bus station. It was lucky one of the other girls found her lying on the back seat of the

181 bus or you would have another death on your hands." Oggy was raging.

"I've already told you, it's nothing to do with me if the junkie wee slags can't handle their gear. Anyway, it's only you saying Linda died. I've not heard anything about it. For all I know, you're making all this shit up..." Kojak couldn't think why that would be the case but it was the best he could come up with when he was so cold and tired.

"She's still not been found. Fuck knows what nick she'll be in by now..." Oggy shivered as the vision of Linda lying on the sofa flashed into his head again.

"Bollocks. There's no way that wee Maggie didn't go straight round there after she heard about Linda. She probably found her alive and well and hiding from you, ya leechy cunt." Kojak had been bracing himself for some fallout after Maggie had been told about Linda, but nobody had said anything.

"Maggie's not daft. She wouldn't have gone near. In fact, Maggie's fucked off. She probably got such a fright she's sitting in her mum's house going cold turkey as we speak. Your dirty drugs are affecting my business and it's going to stop." Oggy was ready for Kojak to pounce, confident he could handle it.

"Can I have a word?"

Neither Kojak nor Oggy had noticed Bunnet park up behind Oggy's float. He was already approaching them when he spoke. Both men stepped back from each other, annoyed that they were being disturbed.

"Not now, Bunnet." Kojak could feel the anger rise to a dangerous level.

"Aye, now. I know what you two are up to and I'm not having it." Bunnet was level with Oggy and Kojak. He had a serious look on his face. "Are you stuck?"

"No. Now fuck off, Bunnet. Trust me, now isn't a good time." Kojak was certain he would deck the old prick if he started on about road safety.

"Make time. I might have been a bit naive as to what you two were up to, but I've got it now and I'm here to tell you it stops immediately." Bunnet was using his stern voice he kept for any of the boys who stepped out of line. Oggy and Kojak looked at each other, confused at what Bunnet was talking about and then looked back to him.

"What the fuck are you talking about, old man?" Oggy knew Bunnet was respected around the dairies, but he had never had much to do with him.

"Prostitutes. You." Bunnet nodded at Oggy. "And drugs. You." Bunnet jerked his thumb at Kojak. "I've heard all about it and it's got to stop."

"I don't know what you've heard, Bunnet, but..." Kojak couldn't help but show Bunnet a bit of respect. He had been a grown-up when Kojak was a boy and even though he was a boring old fucker, he had never done anything wrong.

"Don't try and deny it, laddie. I've been told. You're selling drugs to the boys and you," Bunnet turned back to Oggy, "that young neighbour of mine, Maggie, she told me all about you and the damage you're doing to vulnerable young women. I'm not having it. It stops now or I'll be forced to do something about it."

"And what are you going to do about it?" Oggy took a step towards Bunnet.

"I'll go to the polis." Bunnet's confidence took a dent as Oggy approached him, realising suddenly that he would never be a match for either of them if they got physical.

"The polis?" Kojak stepped towards Bunnet too, his face going red.

"Let him." Oggy put an arm out and stopped Kojak from getting too close to Bunnet. "Maggie told me all about you. How you wouldn't leave her alone. Always trying to get her to suck your withered old cock for free, being violent towards her. In fact, she told me it was *you* who sold her drugs." Oggy turned to Kojak. "I'm sure it wouldn't be difficult to make sure some drugs were found in his house when Maggie went to the polis and told them all about it." Kojak nodded, the threat in his eyes still piercing into Bunnet. "In fact, I've got ten girls who would queue up to tell the polis all about how you've been harassing them and hitting them, ya fucking auld perv!" Oggy spat the last words straight into Bunnet's face.

All the confidence was gone from Bunnet now. "Nobody would believe you."

"Fucking open your mouth and we'll see what happens. Even

if the polis didn't believe it, do you think anyone would want you living round here anymore? What do you think would happen to an auld perv if word got out?" Kojak was almost frothing at the mouth now.

Bunnet couldn't believe what he was hearing. He couldn't believe how helpless he felt. "How can you even suggest this after all I've done for you over the years, laddie?"

Kojak exploded and punched Bunnet hard in the face, knocking him to the ground. Oggy had to use all his strength to stop Kojak from pouncing on the older man and inflicting more damage. Kojak took a few steps back and instantly regretted his actions. Oggy leant down and helped Bunnet to his feet. His nose was bleeding, and his left eye was already swelling badly.

"Do yourself a favour, Bunnet. Walk away, get in your float and fuck off home. We're willing to let this slide but if we hear about you going anywhere near the fucking polis or any of my girls, it's the end for you. I'll make sure you're driven out of this shithole of a town you love so much and then I'll find you wherever you go, and I'll ruin you all over again."

Bunnet was in shock, but he didn't pause. He ran over to his float and drove off. Oggy turned his attention to Kojak.

"You didn't need to hit him; he was already shitting himself."

"It's the last time the auld cunt calls me laddie." Kojak had taken enough.

"Stay away from my girls, Kojak." Oggy used all the menace he could muster.

"Go fuck yourself." Kojak was never going to waiver.

"This is the last warning you're getting." Oggy walked off towards his float.

"You don't fucking warn *me*, I warn *you*!" Kojak shouted after Oggy as he walked away. He turned and kicked the wheel of the stranded milk float in frustration. Surely his luck would have to turn soon.

CHAPTER THIRTY-TWO

Mrs McGowan

CHEESY WAS WATCHING as Kojak struggled to get the float back up the hill on Waverley and reckoned he could use this as an opportunity to garner more brownie points in his quest to get his job back. He went to the back of some houses and found a shovel in the second shed he broke into. By the time he returned to his hiding place, however, both Oggy and Bunnet had arrived and Cheesy chastised himself for letting the opportunity to help pass him by. What happened took him by surprise. Oggy and Kojak appeared to be squaring up to each other until they both turned on Bunnet, and Kojak flattened the old guy with a right hook. Bunnet dragged himself up and ran back to his float sharpish, closely followed by Oggy, leaving Kojak still stranded at the bottom of the hill. Kojak looked really pissed off, so Cheesy knew he would need to play his part carefully. Kojak had climbed back into the cab and was readying himself for another attempt at getting up the hill when Cheesy approached.

"Need a hand?" Kojak physically flinched, not expecting to see anyone around at this time of morning.

"Fuck's sake, ya wee prick, you gave me the fright of my life there." Kojak's nerves were in tatters.

"Sorry." Cheesy was pissed off at the way Kojak talked to him but he held his tongue. "I thought you might need a hand getting back up the hill?" Cheesy held up the shovel for Kojak to see. Kojak looked around, wondering where Cheesy had come from.

"What, you just happen to be walking by with a shovel?" Kojak didn't trust anyone.

"I reckoned there would be a load of people stuck after all that snow, so I'm wandering around with my shovel offering a service, for the right price." Cheesy smiled, partly hoping it would endear him to Kojak and partly because he was so proud of himself for thinking as quickly as he had. He even parked the idea of digging people out in the back of his mind, thinking it may be a good business opportunity if this plan failed.

"What the fuck happened to your coupon?" Kojak had taken a while to realise there was something wrong.

Cheesy had forgotten about his missing teeth when he offered the smile. If Kojak was to believe him, he couldn't say it was the result of Billy Loy smashing his face in with a microphone in case he took that as a reason for Cheesy grassing him up.

"Dentist." Cheesy knew it wasn't a good reason for having no teeth, but he hoped it would be enough for Kojak. Kojak took a deep breath and looked up the hill again, deciding if he could afford to turn down the use of the shovel.

"Fucking butchers these dentist cunts. Alright, get digging." Anything was worth a try if it meant he didn't have to phone the dairy for help.

Cheesy should have known that Kojak wasn't going to do any of the manual work. He sat in the cab and watched as Cheesy dug a channel for each wheel, the float slowly making its way up the hill. Kojak even shouted at him to hurry up a couple of times when Cheesy had stopped to get his breath back, but he took the barracking in silence, knowing it would be worth it to put the main part of his plan into action. After about forty-five minutes of hard labour, the float was at the top of the hill and Kojak was able to get enough purchase to head off back to the dairy.

"Right, that's you. You can grab a pint of milk off the back if you want." Cheesy knew Kojak had no intention of paying him for his help.

"Could you give me a lift up to near Geddes Hill? I reckon there'll be plenty of people getting stuck up there..." If this didn't work, the plan was doomed.

"Fuck's sake, Cheesy, I'm not a taxi..." Kojak had no shame and it didn't cross his mind that he should be grateful.

"I know. I'm not saying you should take me up there, but you'll be passing it on the way to the dairy anyway..."

Kojak thought about it before grudgingly nodding for Cheesy to jump up into the cab.

"How's things, anyway?" Cheesy needed to get a conversation

going. He was struggling to come up with a way into talking about the missing drugs.

"Shite. You?"

"Aye, shite."

"Good." They both laughed. If Kojak was honest, he missed Cheesy. He was a thieving wee bastard, but he was reliable, and he was a good Woodie boy. "Tell me, have you heard of anyone trying to sell gear round here? Apart from the usuals, I mean."

"Nah, just the usuals." Cheesy knew this was his way in, but he would need to play it cool. "Although I was surprised you had that Billy Loy working for you now..."

"Billy Loy?" Kojak had taken the bait. All Cheesy had to do now was reel him in.

"Aye, you know, Tommy Loy's boy?"

"He's selling gear?" Kojak looked surprised, but Cheesy could see the cogs turning in his brain.

"Aye, just pot, but he's dealing. He tried to rope me in to help him but there was something dodgy about it. I don't trust him..." Cheesy was playing a blinder.

"Where's he getting his gear from?" Kojak was struggling to hide his excitement at this revelation.

"I thought it was you. He said it was your gear..." Cheesy delivered the clincher as cooly as he could.

"The cheeky wee fucker." Kojak stopped the float and turned to face Cheesy. "When was this?"

"I don't know, a couple of weeks ago. I don't think he's sold much, though; nobody trusts him. I think that's why he tried to rope me in. He showed me his stash. It was all in egg boxes, so I just presumed he was working for you now."

"Fucker!" Kojak shouted and thumped his hands on the steering wheel. His eyes were darting around, thinking fast about this new information. "Where does he live?"

"Geddes Hill."

"Right, I'll take you right up there and you're coming with me while I pay him a visit." Kojak started driving again. "Wee fucker."

He couldn't believe he hadn't seen it coming. Tommy Loy's kids were trying to step into their old man's shoes. They must be stupid to think Kojak would sit back and let them. Cheesy settled back in the cab and opened his pint of milk, trying not to let his smile spread too broadly.

Brian Loy was working his first week of night shifts and he was struggling to get a grip on it. Trying to sleep at 9am was beyond him, but he had to try and get his head down because if he didn't, he wouldn't be worth a damn when his shift began later that night. Some of the journeymen had told him not to worry about it, because everybody who worked the night shift in The Rolls Royce had a cubby hole somewhere in the factory where they could get their head down and sleep for a few hours every shift, but he couldn't believe that was true. The men were enjoying taking the piss out of Brian as the new boy, sending him for tartan paint, left-handed hammers and the like. The other day one of them had sent him to the storeroom to fetch a long stand and he had wasted half of his day waiting in there, before one of the older storemen told him there was no such thing as a long stand.

"They've sent you for a long stand son. A 'long' 'stand'? How long have you been standing there?"

"I don't know, about three hours?" Brian had no idea.

"Aye, well, I reckon you've had a long enough stand now." The old fella smiled at him kindly.

When he had finally made it back to his workbench, his gaffer had given him a bollocking for being so naive while all the others pissed themselves laughing. He wasn't going to be caught out with the nightshift malarkey. Billy was away to school, but Mary was home from her cleaning, and he could hear her and Hugh laughing in the living room. He thought about going through and asking them to keep it down, but it wasn't them keeping him awake and he didn't want them to think he was being petulant because Hugh was hanging around more. It had been a while since he had heard Mary laugh, so he wasn't going to throw a spanner in the works, not even a left-handed one.

Brian must have nodded off, but the urgent banging on the front door forced him up and out into the hall before his eyes had properly focused. The angry banging continued until he opened the door.

"Where's your brother?" Kojak was stood there with some wee toothless guy behind him, grinning like an idiot.

"What?" Brian had no idea what was happening.

"Your fucking brother!" Kojak was shouting and flecks of spit sprayed everywhere.

"What?" Brian was waking up, but he felt sure he had missed part of the conversation.

"Out the fucking way." Kojak went to barge past Brian.

"Whoa, what the fuck..." Before Brian could finish his sentence, Kojak headbutted him, catching him on the side of his jaw. The wee toothless guy followed Kojak into the hall and grabbed Brian by the hair, pulling his head down and kicked him in the face. Brian was unconscious before the second and third kicks struck. Kojak burst into the living room and stopped in his tracks when he saw Hugh sitting on the sofa with Mary. For a second, he thought he was in the wrong house.

"What the fuck are you doing here?" Kojak had to make sure this was the right flat. Hugh stood up, looking just as confused as Kojak was.

"What the fuck are *you* doing here?" Hugh looked bewildered. While the two men looked at each other, wondering what was going on, Mary jumped up and walked towards Kojak.

"What are you doing in my house? Get out."

Cheesy followed Kojak into the living room, causing Hugh to do another double-take. "What the fuck is going on, Kojak?"

"Where's Billy?" Kojak was back on track now that Mary had come forward.

"Why? What's it to you?" Mary knew not to give anyone a straight answer when you had no idea what was going on. She had learnt that from her husband, and it was a natural instinct now.

"He's stolen something that belongs to me, and I want it back." Kojak was struggling to stay in control. If he didn't get answers quickly, he was ready to start smashing the place up.

"Don't be ridiculous..." Mary was having none of it, without even knowing the full story.

"I think you're barking up the wrong tree here, mate. Billy wouldn't steal anything..." Hugh could see that reason may not be the best weapon when it came to Kojak, but he knew he had to try.

"Don't fucking 'mate' me. Just because you're shagging the maw disnae mean her son isn't a wee cunt." Kojak was shouting again.

"That's it, get out!" Mary went to push Kojak out of her living room, but Hugh knew enough to stop her. He grabbed her by the arm and pulled her back next to him.

"What's he supposed to have stolen from you?" Hugh was determined to give reason another go.

"He robbed the eggs off my float, and it had my stash in there." Kojak wasn't going to answer many more questions, but Hugh being there had thrown him off track.

"When?" Hugh couldn't see the reasoning behind Kojak's accusation.

"Last Saturday. The wee cunt robbed the float while I was in Sadlers Wells..."

"Don't be ridiculous..." Mary was shouting now too. Hugh turned and indicated for her to be quiet.

"He couldn't have. He was on my float last Saturday. I think I would have noticed..." Hugh gave a weak laugh, hoping it would be enough to lighten the mood.

"You don't know what they're up to when they're off delivering, Shagger. Stop trying to stick up for the thieving wee bastard. Where is he?"

"He's at school. Where *he* should be too." Hugh nodded at Cheesy. "What's he doing here?"

"Fuck off, Shagger." Cheesy was enjoying every minute of this, but Kojak turned and scowled at him, letting him know he was talking out of turn, and he should shut up.

"Just let me search the flat..." Kojak didn't want to have to batter Hugh on the same day as he had hit Bunnet.

"You are not searching my flat..." Mary would take whatever was coming before she let Kojak go through her home.

"He keeps them in the shed." Cheesy was getting impatient. He wanted Billy caught.

Kojak glared at Mary and Hugh before turning and walking out of the living room. Mary shrieked and ran out after him, Hugh following on, hoping Billy hadn't been so stupid. Brian was coming round as Kojak and Cheesy stormed past him and started walking down the stairs.

"Oh my god, Brian!" Mary ran to her son and helped him onto his feet. "Right, that's enough."

Mary and Hugh ran down the stairs after Kojak and Cheesy,

reaching the sheds just at the same time as they did. Kojak held out his hand to Mary.

"Key."

"Fuck you, ya baldy twat." Mary didn't care if the neighbours heard her speak like this. They probably all thought she had a potty mouth anyway.

Kojak turned to Hugh. "Listen Shagger, if you don't keep her in line, I will. Now give me the fucking key for the shed."

"No chance." Mary held up her keys and made a show of putting them down her bra, hoping that would be enough to stop Kojak from going any further. Kojak took a step towards Mary, the look on his face telling everyone that nothing was stopping him. Before he could get close, Cheesy piped up.

"I'll open it." Cheesy slipped his ever-present screwdriver out of his sleeve and walked over to the shed door. As easily as he had done before, he popped the door open and stood back, inviting Kojak to look inside. Right at the front, on top of the tricycle where Cheesy had left it, was the poly bag full of egg boxes. Kojak lifted the bag and looked inside, smiling back at Mary with satisfaction. Mary's reaction surprised him. She burst out laughing. Kojak looked from Mary to Hugh and back again.

"What's so fucking funny?" Kojak wondered if Mary knew the danger her family was in now that he had found his stolen drugs.

Mary dug in her bra and brought out the keys. She walked over to the shed door next to the one Cheesy had opened and slid the biggest key on the chain into the lock. The door opened to show that the shed was completely empty. She turned back to Kojak and smiled again.

"Whoever's trying to set our Billy up obviously isn't as clever as they thought. That's Mrs McGowan's shed you've just broken into. As you can see, ours is empty." Mary started laughing, more with relief than anything. Kojak turned and looked at Cheesy. The colour had drained from his face.

"Hold on, now that I think about it, that Saturday your stuff was stolen, it definitely wasn't Billy." Hugh knew there was something not right about Kojak's theory. "That was the morning he couldn't even do his own round because he was still off his face on the acid you sold him. He spent the whole round curled up in a wee ball in the cab. He was never out of my sight."

"What?" Kojak looked back at Cheesy, who was slowly beginning to back away.

"What?" Mary was staring open-mouthed at Hugh.

"Think about it, man. None of the boys could have done it while they were doing their round. Who had the opportunity? And who's enough of a stupid wee fanny to plank them in the wrong place?" Hugh was trying to ignore the death stare he was getting from Mary. Kojak was still staring at Cheesy. If looks could kill, Cheesy was getting the last rites.

"Ya fucking wee..." Kojak lunged for Cheesy but he was already running. He was gone before Kojak had taken two steps. He stopped and turned back to face Hugh and Mary.

"There! Phew! Now we know the truth. Billy would never steal anything. He's a good lad. You've got your stuff back, nobody's been hurt, apart from Brian a wee bit, but I'm sure he'll be fine..." Hugh couldn't stop talking.

"If I find out your boy had anything to do with this, I'll be back." Kojak was making sure everyone knew how close they had come to him causing serious damage.

"If you come anywhere near this house again, I won't be held responsible for my actions. Now fuck off. And if I hear about you selling drugs to kids again, I'll go straight to the polis." Mary was pointing at Kojak with the big shed key.

Kojak laughed to himself, but he wasn't so sure Mary wouldn't do what she said.

"You do that, and it'll be the last thing you ever do. I promise you that." Kojak sneered, leaving everyone sure he meant what he said.

CHAPTER THIRTY-THREE

Tarzan's Feet

SCHOOL WAS A lot quieter for Billy since his run-in with Mr Todd. Toddy had been off sick since it happened, and Billy had a sense that the other teachers were a bit more wary of him now. He had no idea if Toddy had told anyone what had happened, but there had been no fallout apart from a few spiteful looks from the other Techie teachers which Billy couldn't decide were a result of him dealing with the bully or if they were the same looks he had always got. Billy hadn't told anyone about it, apart from Dick, so there hadn't been any rumours going round one way or the other. As far as Billy was concerned, it was as though it never happened.

The big talking point today had been the ambush of the number 126 bus. The 126 was a small, 32-seater that serviced the areas of East Kilbride away from the main roads. Billy had no idea why, but it was known locally as the Jimmy bus. It was used mostly by pensioners who couldn't manage the walk to the main thoroughfares, and it ran the length of Morrishall Road as part of its route. There was a mini-roundabout at the school gate, which meant the bus had to slow down to a crawl to get round, especially when the weather was so bad. A group of kids decided to build a wall of snow across the road at one side of the roundabout which would make it impossible for the bus to continue its journey after the roundabout. There wasn't enough space on the roundabout to reverse back, so when the driver realised he couldn't proceed over the snow wall and couldn't reverse, there was nothing he could do but get out of his cab and try to kick the wall down. The second he got out of his cab, every kid in school started to bombard him with snowballs, forcing him to scuttle back to the safety of his bus. This left the bus stuck on the mini roundabout with no chance of escape. The noise of snowballs bouncing off the windows and roof of the bus was deafening as the bewildered passengers cowered in their seats. The onslaught was relentless until the school bell rang, and the kids returned to lessons, delighted with their ingenuity and regaling each other with tales of their throwing skills and the fear in the eyes of the pensioners on board. It had helped break up the day nicely.

At home time, Billy and Danny were leaving via the Morrishall exit when Billy spotted Dick standing at the gate, his usual smile spread across his face. Dick went to the Catholic school, St Brides, or that was where he was supposed to go. Like a lot of kids aged fifteen, Dick had failed all his O Level prelim exams, disqualifying him from taking the full exams later in the academic year. This meant there was no point in him going and the teachers didn't see any point in having a group of kids being forced to attend when they had no future there. If they were forced to attend, they would just cause chaos because it made no difference to them if anyone learned anything or not. It was easier to turn a blind eye to their truancy and concentrate on the pupils who had a chance of gaining a few qualifications. Billy had no idea what Dick did to fill his days, but whatever it was, it was probably more exciting than school.

"There's Dick." Billy waved over and Danny screwed up his face.

"Why are you waving at him?"

"He's a good guy. He's a punk." Billy hadn't told anyone about his new family member yet.

"Dick? He's a fucking tramp, not a punk. There's a difference, Billy." Danny thought Billy was going mad.

Billy laughed. "Shut up. Alright, Dick?" Dick started to walk towards the boys.

"Alright, man? Learn anything good today?"

"The whole school snowballed the fuck out of the Jimmy bus. It was cool." Billy was excited, but felt a bit silly saying it in such a childish way.

"Nice one." Dick looked around at the masses of snow surrounding the mini-roundabout and nodded in approval. "Have you asked him yet?" Dick nodded at Danny and gave him his smile.

"Not yet." Billy had been waiting for the right moment.

"Asked me what?" Danny was immediately on the back foot.

"Dick and me are starting a new band, The Odd Brothers, and we want you to play drums." Billy spoke in a matter-of-fact way.

Danny looked confused. Apart from the fact that he couldn't

play drums, or have a drum kit, or had ever even mentioned that he might want to play drums, he couldn't believe Billy would want to be in a band with someone like Dick. Nobody liked Dick. He was a dick, for fuck's sake.

"Are you joking?" Danny looked at Billy as if he had just announced he was an alien.

"No, he's fucking brilliant on the guitar. Me on bass and you on drums would be amazing..." Billy's enthusiasm was genuine.

"Who told you he was brilliant on guitar? Him?" The contempt in Danny's voice was hard to ignore.

"Me! I was down at his place and heard him play. He can play the whole Clash songbook!"

"You were in his house? Fuck me, are you sure you're not bugsy now?" Danny didn't think about Dick's feelings. It was how everyone treated him.

"Wow, you Proddies love the old bugsy thing." Dick was laughing but it was hard to know if he was sincere or not.

"Did you fuck his maw?" Danny laughed at his own joke.

"What?" Billy didn't see what was funny.

"His maw's a prossie!" Danny couldn't believe Billy didn't know. "She's a junkie as well. If Kojak isnae feeding her drugs, Oggy's in there feeding her cock."

"Watch your mouth." Dick spoke quietly, the smile no longer on his face.

"Fuck off, Danny, that's out of order." Billy was amazed his friend could be so cruel.

"It's not. His maw's as hard as Tarzan's feet and he hangs about with those Blantyre nutters, the ones with guns. They killed your dad!" Danny was determined to push his point home.

"We don't all have guns, but I can get one if you want..." There was a hint of a threat in Dick's response. He was ready to defend himself.

"See! Fuck that, Billy. Sort yourself out, mate, and get the fuck away from him. And his skanky brass maw." Danny considered his case closed.

Billy didn't know what to say. He didn't even know where to look. He hadn't met Dick's mum when he was in their house and although he had heard a couple of boys talking about her in the same way as Danny was, he had never considered any of it to be true. His silence was enough for Dick.

"Fuck the pair of you." Dick stormed off. He was used to this kind of shit, and he never let it bother him, but he thought Billy would be different. They were brothers, after all. He felt tears beginning to flow as he ran as fast as he could away from the one person he thought might show him a bit of respect.

Dick didn't stop running until he reached his street. He pulled up sharply when he saw the milk float sitting outside his block of flats. He walked slowly into the close and opened the front door to the flat as quietly as he could. From the front door he looked down the long hallway into the living room and his breath was knocked out of him. His mum was on her knees, her face in Kojak's groin as he stood facing her. Kojak's trousers were at his ankles, and he was holding the back of her head as he thrust himself into her mouth. Kojak slowly turned round and noticed Dick standing at the end of the hallway. He didn't bat an eyelid and continued pushing himself into Shirley.

"Get to your room, Dick. I want a word with you when I'm done."

It was the casual way Kojak had dismissed Dick's presence that lit the flame. There was no panicked reaction to being caught doing what he was doing. He didn't care that Dick was there and he didn't care that what he was doing was wrong. Shirley turned to look at her son and there was nothing in her eyes. It was as if she had no idea what she was doing or who else was in the room. Dick snapped. He started running down the hall towards the living room, screaming at the top of his voice. As he got within five feet, Kojak pushed Shirley away and readied himself for the impact. Dick put his head down and connected with Kojak's stomach at full pace. They both crashed into the fireplace, scattering the clock and the letter rack full of final reminders. Kojak quickly punched Dick a few times in the kidneys, leaving him flat on the floor, windless. He followed up with kicks to the face and head. Dick was literally seeing stars, like they did in the cartoons he enjoyed watching, and he struggled to remain conscious. Kojak was breathing heavily from the force of the impact to his solar plexus and the exertion he had put into beating Dick. He realised Shirley was screaming now, still kneeling where he had left her, so he turned and volleyed her in the mouth to shut her up. She fell sideways and cracked her head off the wall, landing in a heap and whimpering quietly. Kojak turned to Dick again and lifted him up by the front of his shirt. Blood was coming from his mouth and nose and his eyes were swelling.

"You ever try that again and I will fucking kill you, ya spawny wee cunt. Do you get it?" Kojak slapped Dick's face, sending blood and saliva all over the room. Dick tried to nod but he wasn't sure if he was doing it right. His head was spinning. "Now, tell me where Cheesy is hiding out. I know you know. And don't say he's at home because I've been there."

Kojak went to slap Dick again, but he wondered if another blow might knock him out. "Where's Cheesy?" Kojak shouted right into Dick's face.

"Down The Glen! In a tent!" Dick shouted back as if his life depended on it. Kojak threw Dick back down to the ground and walked over to Shirley.

"Sort yourself out, Shirley, and make sure your ugly wee sprog keeps his mouth shut about this. If I have to come back here again, I'll sort you both out for good. Understand?" There was madness in Kojak's eyes as he loomed over Shirley.

Shirley nodded her head, unable to talk or at least say anything that would have made any sense. Kojak dusted himself down and looked around the room to make sure he had done everything he needed to do before leaving. He took a deep breath and left, shouting as he walked down the hall.

"What is it with cunts today?"

Once Dick had heard the front door slam shut, he crawled over to where Shirley was lying and held her head in his lap. He stroked her hair and shooshed her crying.

"It's okay, Mum. I'm here. That's it done. I'm going to look after you now." He meant every word of it.

CHAPTER THIRTY-FOUR

Last Straw

BRENDA HAD REALLY enjoyed her scrambled eggs. Cooking was something she had never really had time for before, but she enjoyed it very much now she had more time. None of it was what you would consider Cordon Bleu or anything like that, just some stew, a chicken casserole or a nice pork chop, but it beat the Fray Bentos pies or tins of mince she had got used to over the past few years. It meant she was putting on a bit of weight, but she couldn't care less. There was no need to stay slim anymore if she didn't want to. She had cleared out her wardrobe too. The short skirts, tight blouses and high boots she had worn every day were sitting in a bin bag by the door. Her intention was to take the bag down to the bus station one night and let the girls there have a rummage through and take what they wanted, then bin anything that was left over, although she hadn't got round to doing it yet. Speaking to the girls depressed her. Giving up working the streets had given her a new lease of life and she felt like she was thriving. She had bought a couple of nice trouser suits to wear while she was working in the pub and a couple of plain dresses for everyday wear. When she had looked at herself in the mirror while trying them on, she couldn't stop laughing. She looked like a different person.

Working in the pub was brilliant. She didn't make half the money she did from soliciting, but Brenda didn't care. She had always been a good saver, so money wasn't a problem. She had enough in the bank, along with her pub wages, to see her through to retirement. She was even thinking about having a week away somewhere in the summer, down the west coast or maybe even England. She had always fancied seeing London and there was a cousin she had lost touch with living in Brighton. If the address in her old diary was still current, she might bite the bullet and go down for a visit. She smiled at the thought of it, knowing it was probably a pipedream. As far as she could remember, her cousin had been a bit of an arsehole, but it was nice to think she could do it if she wanted to.

Working in the pub had opened a social life too. Most of the punters were decent people and she could have a good laugh with them. Brenda tried to think about the last time she had laughed working at the bus station and gave up after ten minutes. Laughing hadn't been a big part of her life down there. A few of her old punters came into the pub, but most of them kept their heads down, not wanting anyone to know they had used her services in the past. A couple had tried to take liberties, squeezing her arse when she was collecting glasses or cornering her in the snug when it was empty, but she had made it very clear to them that she had moved on from that life now, usually with a swift knee to the bollocks to hammer the point home. She didn't deny her past occupation, but she tended not to bring it up in conversation unless someone else did. In general, nobody judged her and some, like Mary, even told her how much they had admired the way she always handled herself. Brenda was proud of what she had achieved, but she was glad that it was all in the past now.

Brenda took her empty plate through to the kitchen and started cleaning the dried egg from the pot when the doorbell rang. She dried her hands and moved through to the hall, but she stopped short of opening the door when she saw the outline of the figure on the other side of it. She thought about creeping back into the living room and pretending not to be in, but it would have been pointless as her outline would have been as visible as the person on the other side.

"Who is it?" Brenda noticed the fear in her voice and scolded herself for being so weak.

"It's me."

"What do you want?" Brenda sounded better this time, more controlled.

"I don't want anything. Come on Brenda, I just want to say hello."

"Well, you've said hello."

"Please Brenda. I need to speak to you. I want to apologise. It's not easy to do that through the letterbox."

Brenda took a deep breath and opened the door. Oggy was

standing there with a bottle of milk in his hand. He held it out to Brenda and smiled.

"Peace offering."

Brenda turned away without taking the milk, leaving the door open as the only sign that she was letting Oggy come in. She went into the living room and stood to face him with her arms folded, hoping she wasn't giving away how nervous she was. Oggy came in and put the milk on the coffee table.

"Is it okay if I sit?" Oggy pointed to the settee.

"If you think you'll be here that long..." Brenda was trying to play it cool, but she wasn't convinced it was coming across that way.

Oggy sat down and looked around the room, nodding and smiling. "You always keep this place really nice, Brenda."

"What do you want, Oggy?" Brenda wasn't going to make this easy. She remained straight faced and stayed standing.

"As I said, just to say hello. To make sure you're doing okay. Are you doing okay? I hear you're working in the pub..." Oggy looked like he hadn't slept properly for a while. Brenda fought the urge to show sympathy.

"I'm fine. I've moved on. New job, new life."

Oggy nodded again. "I've missed you."

Brenda let out an ironic laugh. "No, you haven't, Angus. You might miss controlling me, but you don't miss *me*." It had been a long time since Brenda had called Oggy Angus.

Oggy looked hurt. "That's not fair. I do miss you. I miss our chats..."

"You mean you miss me doing your job for you. Looking after the girls. Making sure you don't have to deal with any trouble." Brenda had realised after she stopped, how much of the welfare responsibilities she had taken on as Oggy's interest in anything other than getting paid had waned.

"You didn't look after the girls." Oggy let his mask slip for a moment and then caught himself before he said anything to alienate Brenda further. "I valued your insight. You know I couldn't be there all the time, I needed you to keep me up to date with what was happening. I looked after you..."

"You did at first. Now you just abuse everyone..." There was hate in Brenda's voice.

"Christ, Brenda! I don't abuse them! They do that themselves." Oggy realised he had raised his voice, but Brenda was being unfair. "Honestly, Brenda, you've no idea what it's like. Every one of them is on smack now. Every one of them. I can't keep up with them. They turn up when they like, they all look like shit and when it comes to collecting the cash, I've got to run around after them, hunting them down before they throw it all away on heroin."

"Oh, poor you."

"It's not just the money. I swear to God, I'm watching them fade away. I'm scared stiff I'm going to find one of them dead one day." Oggy looked closely at Brenda to see if there was any reaction. If she knew about Linda, Oggy would be able to tell. She didn't flinch.

"Do your job, then! Your job is to look after them." Brenda wasn't going to let Oggy feel sorry for himself. "You take their money, but you don't do anything for them. Talk to them. Help them get off the drugs..."

"Och, behave yourself. What can I do to get them off that shite?" Oggy thought Brenda was being unreasonable.

"Scare off the dealers. If they can't buy it, they can't take it. If a punter was abusing them, you would scare him off. What's the difference?" Brenda was in full flow.

Oggy laughed. Either Brenda was taking the piss, or her career change had addled her mind. "Scare off the dealers? You do know it's Kojak who supplies them?"

"Well, if you can't do the job, you should give it up. You can't keep taking their money and not do what they're paying you for." Brenda was beginning to enjoy showing Oggy his shortcomings.

"I've told him to stay away, but you know Kojak. The only way he's going to listen to me is if I smash his brains in, if he's got any brains." Oggy held out his hands. "Two girls have gone off radar recently and I'm pretty sure others are going to follow. I wouldn't be surprised if Kojak isn't pimping them out somewhere else..."

"What do you mean, off radar? Who?" Brenda showed concern for the first time.

"Linda and young Maggie. I haven't seen either of them for days." Oggy looked at Brenda again, hoping mentioning Linda by name might get a response.

"How hard have you looked for them?" Brenda sounded worried.

"I've got another job, Brenda. I've not got time to be going round their houses. They've not been round the bus station in a while, that's all I know." Oggy could see that Brenda didn't know about Linda. She would have said something.

"Fuck's sake, Angus, that's what I'm talking about. That's your job! Get your arse in gear and get round to their flats to make sure they're okay." Brenda couldn't believe Oggy was being so careless.

"I wondered if maybe you could go and see..." Oggy couldn't help sounding sheepish.

"Fuck off! I knew you had an ulterior motive for coming here. I'm out of it, Angus. It's your job. Grow a pair of bollocks and do it yourself." Brenda should have seen it coming.

Oggy stood up angrily and started towards the door. "You really are a useless old cow; do you know that?" As he got to the front door, Brenda shouted after him.

"You forgot to say sorry to me!" Brenda's voice almost cracked with emotion.

Oggy restrained himself from going back and giving her another slap. "Go fuck yourself!" He slammed the front door and ran down to his car.

Oggy got in the car and punched the steering wheel. He still had options, but they were beginning to run out. Brenda was a selfish bastard. She was always harping on about looking after the girls and doing the right thing by them, yet here she was not giving a fuck. She had abandoned them and was unwilling to help, even though Oggy had clearly given her reason to be worried about Linda. Oggy would make sure she paid for her disloyalty once all of this had blown over. People weren't taking him seriously enough and that was dangerous.

Oggy had three options left as far as he could see. He could go to Linda's flat and 'find her' but that would leave him open to questions about his relationship with her and he could do without that kind of heat coming down on him. He could phone the police anonymously and tell them he thought Linda was dead, but he reckoned the police would ask even more questions and it wouldn't take long for one of the other girls to point the finger in his direction. Neither option would be good for him. He couldn't believe a woman could be missing this long and nobody had noticed. Where were her friends, her family, the people who should be the ones breaking her door down when she wasn't answering their calls? It was clear Linda wasn't being missed, so why should he be the one to put his neck on the line? He could still see her blue lips, still smell the stench of her rotting body. He had already been through enough. It was up to somebody else now.

The third option was the only logical one left to him. Oggy needed someone to find Linda and for that person to implicate Kojak in her death. That would put a dent in the baldy prick's ego, maybe even get him sent down, and more importantly, let Oggy sleep at night without Linda filling his dreams. It was Kojak's drugs that killed her. He should be the one lying awake at night, preferably in a jail cell, not Oggy. It made sense that Maggie should be the one to find Linda. The fact she had known about Linda being dead for a while and had done nothing about it made her culpable, in a way. Oggy was sure it wouldn't take much to pressure her into doing what he asked. Oggy reckoned she was in hiding, probably at her parents' house. All he had to do was go to the flat and have a look around. He was sure there would be something there to give him a clue as to where her parents lived. If that didn't work, he would ask around the other girls. She had a kid. People with kids couldn't stay underground for long.

Oggy drove up Maggie's street and suddenly remembered that Bunnet lived there too. The last thing he needed was that nosy old fucker poking his nose in again, but he reckoned his threats, and Kojak hitting him, would be enough to stop him in his tracks. Just in case, Oggy parked further up the street and slipped in the back door of the close. He tried three keys before he found the right one to open the door. He slipped in quietly and was immediately struck by how cold it was in there. If felt even colder than it was outside, but if Maggie hadn't been there for a while, there wouldn't have been any heating on. The living room looked exactly like it had when he and Kojak had been there before. If he hadn't seen it before, he would have said someone had broken in and trashed the place, but that was the way Maggie lived. He hoped she had gone back to her parents. At least the baby would be better off being there. Oggy looked around for some letters or something with an address on it. There would be nothing tying her to this address because she wasn't the official tenant, so anything he could find would give him a clue as to her previous whereabouts. He searched as much as he could without touching anything. He would need to get a team of cleaners in to fumigate the place when he had someone else lined up to move in.

"Fucking manky wee tart."

The kitchen wasn't as bad, but the sink was full of dirty cups and teaspoons blackened on the base from preparing her drugs. There was something in the bin smelling bad enough to ensure Oggy wasn't going to have a rummage through it in the hope of finding something useful. Oggy almost gagged and opened the kitchen window, even if it meant the flat got even colder. There was nothing in any of the drawers apart from a couple of tea towels that looked brand new and unused.

Oggy moved through to the hall, having a brief look in the empty cupboard, before entering the bedroom. The curtains were still closed so he flicked the light on and stopped. Maggie was on her knees next to the baby's cot. She looked like she was praying, head down with her arms in front of her. She wore a nightie that had seen better days and a pair of fluffy slippers like the ones Oggy's gran wore. She called them her baffies. Everything was still and the silence was deafening.

"Maggie?"

Then Oggy noticed the syringe lying on the floor next to her.

"Maggie?"

Oggy walked over slowly, not really wanting to get there. The cold of the room was seeping into his bones, and he could feel the blood drain from his face as he touched Maggie on the shoulder. She felt colder than anything Oggy had ever felt before.

"No!" Oggy tried to stifle his gasp for air, but the noise coming from him was unstoppable. His natural urge to escape kicked in, but before he got to the hall something stopped him. The baby. Oggy walked over to the cot, trying to force himself to look but his brain wasn't letting his eyes go there. He almost had to turn his face round with his hands to look down into the dirty bed.

The baby, Adam he suddenly remembered from somewhere, was lying on his back. At first Oggy thought it was a doll, because the head seemed too big for the body, but the expression on the face was never going to be used for a doll. The eyes were open, and it looked like he was screaming, but no sound came from his blue lips. Oggy suddenly felt like he hadn't taken a breath for too long and started to hyperventilate. He stumbled out of the bedroom and out of the flat. He started running and was halfway down the street before he realised, he was running the wrong way. He stopped and threw up on the road, bending over and feeling like his entire stomach was spilling out. Nobody was around, the snow no doubt keeping most people indoors. Oggy wiped his mouth on his sleeve and tried to walk calmly back up to where his car was parked, but after only a few steps, he was running again. He slipped on the snow and went down but was back up and running again in one single movement. He got in the car and started it before burying his face in his hands. He took a deep breath and gathered himself before putting the car in gear.

"That's it, Kojak. Last straw."

Oggy drove off, knowing exactly what he had to do.

CHAPTER THIRTY-FIVE

Don't Be Daft

THE PHONE WAS ringing by the time Kojak finally made it back to the house. He thought about ignoring it but it could be the dairy telling him about something he had to deal with before the next day's delivery so he couldn't afford to let it go.

"Hello?"

"Kojak?"

"Aye." Kojak didn't recognise the voice.

"This is Sid. From The Parkville. Do you know who I mean?"

"Aye." Sid was one of the young guys Greer employed to ferry the drugs around. Kojak had dealt with him a few times, transferring his weekly delivery from the back of a van to the milk float in the hotel car park.

"Listen carefully. You need to check in with your customers. The last couple of deliveries you received were tainted." Sid spoke quickly.

"What do you mean, tainted?" Kojak could really do without any more hassle.

"It wasn't cut properly. It was eighty per cent pure." Sid's phone voice was monotone.

Kojak chuckled. "Eighty per cent pure? Fuck me, Greer must be spitting feathers. Somebody's going to get their arse felt…"

"Greer's gone." Sid cut Kojak off quickly.

"What do you mean he's gone? Gone where?" Kojak didn't like the sound of this.

"He's gone. He won't be coming back. Don't make me spell it out." Sid left a silence to let his words sink in. "He was too busy testing the product to keep an eye on what was going on. It's what happens."

"Fuck's sake." Kojak felt a shiver go through him. "So, is that it? Game over?"

"Of course not. There's somebody new in the driver's seat, that's all." Sid sounded like he considered Kojak to be an idiot.

"Who?" Kojak wondered if this was some kind of job interview. With all the trouble he had been having dealing with his own shit, he wasn't sure he could be arsed taking on the whole operation.

"You won't know that. Things are being tightened up. You'll only deal with me from now on." Sid's tone didn't change at all.

"Aw hold on, man, I don't deal with people I don't know..." This was the last thing Kojak needed.

"You know *me*."

"Barely. No offence, mate, but I'm used to talking to the organ grinder, not the monkey. I need to know who I'm dealing with." Kojak was being treated the same way he treated the boys on the float, and he didn't like it.

"You're fucking dealing with me!" Sid raised his voice for the first time. "There's no discussion here, Kojak. You're a very small cog in a very big machine here. Small cogs can be replaced very easily, do you get me?" Sid waited for an answer, but Kojak remained silent. "Do you get me?"

Kojak recognised the threat in Sid's voice. If these people could get rid of a guy like Greer, they wouldn't bat an eye lid at dealing with him. "I get it."

"Good. Now check your clientele. We've had quite a few reports of casualties all over the place. Nobody was used to shit that pure." Sid resumed without the anger.

"And what do I do if any of them are fucked?" Kojak immediately thought of Linda.

"Get new customers. I couldn't give a fuck." Sid was losing patience. "And what about the gear you lost? The new boss will be very upset if I have to tell him you haven't dealt with that yet..."

"It's sorted. I got it back." Kojak could tell Sid was going to be as much of a pain in the arse as Greer had been.

"You've dealt with whoever had it?" Sid sounded doubtful.

"It was just a local toerag. A young fella. I got every bit of it back, don't worry about it." Kojak tried to brush Sid's doubts aside.

Sid took a deep breath, as though he was dealing with a petulant child.

"Deal with the toerag, Kojak. The new boss wants everything running like clockwork, with no fucking glitches. The slightest thing warrants broken bones at least. Make sure it's the toerag whose bones are damaged, because I don't want to have to do it for you. If I have to do your job for you, the boss might wonder if we need you at all. This is serious now. No more Mr Nice Guy like it was under Greer. Got it?" Sid had gone monotone again, but the threat in his words was loud and clear.

"I'll deal with it." Kojak knew there was no point arguing. If these people thought Greer was Mr Nice Guy, there was no doubt Kojak wasn't going to be able to stand up to them.

"Good. I'll be in touch."

The line went dead, and Kojak flopped down onto the sofa. How much more shit could he take? At least five of his punters had been missing recently, if you included Linda. The idea that they could all be fucked up or even dead was hard to comprehend. He would have to go round them all and make sure they were okay. When he thought about it, Shirley had been more out of it than usual when he saw her today. She was already smashed, and he had given her another bag in exchange for the blowjob. He would go round later and take it back off her. She hadn't finished the blowjob anyway, so he would be justified in his actions. Before he did that, he would need to deal with Cheesy. He knew if he waited long enough, the wee fucker would show his face and Kojak intended giving him a slap somewhere public, in front of his mates to humiliate him, but after the phone call he realised there was an urgency now. It would have to be done out of the way too, because a slap wouldn't be enough now. Kojak thought about the number of times he had threatened to break someone's legs over the years, usually for minor things. Now the threat would have to be followed through. At least Sid hadn't demanded more. Cheesy had fucked up, but not as badly as Greer apparently. Kojak thought about his old nemesis and smiled. Fuck him.

Cheesy was in the tent going through what he should do next. His feet were throbbing, and he had a blinding pain in his head like he had never experienced before. The one thing he knew was that he couldn't live like this for much longer. As far as he could see, his options were shrinking. Kojak would be after him now and for all his bravado, Cheesy knew he was no match for him, especially in the condition he was right now. The only way he could win that fight would be if he took him by surprise, and it would need to be a permanent solution. Cheesy picked up the kitchen knife and ran his finger down the blade. If he planned it well, he could take care of Kojak and Billy fucking Loy in one night and then disappear. He could hitch a lift down to London and start a new life there. Lots of people did it. There were squats in London, he had seen it on the news, where all sorts of people lived together for no rent, and it looked like a real laugh.

Without realising he was doing it, Cheesy had moved the knife to his left wrist. Cutting himself there would end all the pain. It would teach his useless fucking parents a lesson. They would be fucked up if he killed himself. Everybody would. They would all realise how badly they had treated him, how they had all disrespected him, and he wouldn't have to feel anything anymore. He tried to think of a time he had been happy and couldn't remember a single one.

Suddenly, the tent flaps were wrenched open, and Kojak was standing in front of Cheesy with a baseball bat in his hand.

"Hello Cheesy."

The grin on Kojak's face was sinister enough to send Cheesy into panic. In an instant, Cheesy flew at Kojak with the knife in his right hand and plunged it into his left shoulder. Kojak screamed and ran backwards, giving Cheesy enough room to get out and start running. He ran into the trees and started down the steep slope towards the river, but he was running too fast and lost his footing. Cheesy was in the air for a split second before he hit the first tree, spinning him round 180 degrees before he hit the second one. After that he seemed to hit every tree and rock on the way down, none of the impacts enough to stop him falling further into the darkness. After what felt like an age, Cheesy came to a halt as he landed in the water. He couldn't breathe, knowing he had broken ribs on the way down and no matter how much he tried, he couldn't get to his feet. He tried to focus on what he had to do to get further away. He could hear Kojak make his way slowly down the slope, cursing loudly every step of the way. Cheesy had left the knife sticking out of Kojak's shoulder so he had no way of defending himself if he couldn't get away. A single shaft of light came through the trees and Cheesy could now see that he was at the bottom of The Horseshoe Falls. Even if he could get to his feet, there was no way he could climb up there with his busted ribs. He felt his legs, hoping to rub some life into them, but his last hope disappeared when he realised the right one was pointing in the opposite direction it should be. Cheesy gave up and started sobbing.

Kojak didn't realise he had been stabbed until he was halfway down the slope, the handle catching his eye as he carefully made his way from tree to tree. It wasn't until he got to the bottom and was standing over Cheesy that he reached up and pulled the blade out of his shoulder. The pain made him roar, but once it was out, he didn't feel a thing. Rage and adrenalin hid any pain, although he knew it would kick in later. Kojak looked down at Cheesy and barely recognised him. He was covered in blood from countless injuries and his face was swollen like a football. Kojak shook his head in disappointment.

"You're a stupid wee cunt, Cheesy, do you know that? I was going to break your legs and you've already gone and done it for me." Kojak laughed at his own joke while Cheesy made one last futile attempt to move. "And now you've stabbed me!" Kojak put his hand to his shoulder then looked at it. There was blood on his hand but not as much as he was expecting. Kojak shook his head in disappointment at Cheesy. "You couldn't even do that very well."

"Ambulance." Cheesy felt the taste of blood in his mouth when he spoke but didn't have the energy to spit it out. Kojak laughed again.

"That's very thoughtful of you, but I don't need an ambulance, mate. It's gone straight through without hitting anything. I'll be fine."

"Me!" Cheesy tried to scream but only managed to cough, sending his whole body into spasm from the pain in his ribs.

"Don't be daft. You don't need an ambulance either." Kojak stopped smiling and held up the knife. "Pathetic creatures need to be put down."

Before Cheesy could attempt saying anything, Kojak plunged the knife into his stomach, twisting it round and up when it would go no further. Cheesy went stiff and blood gurgled in his throat, his eyes almost popping out of his head. His flooded lungs ensured there was no more noise.

CHAPTER THIRTY-SIX

Do Something

BILLY WASN'T FEELING very good about himself. Danny was his mate, but Billy should never have let him talk to Dick the way he had. Dick was his brother, even if he had only known about it for a short while. If anyone had treated Brian like that or talked about Mary the way Danny had done about Dick's mum, Billy would have knocked them out, no questions asked. He wouldn't blame Dick if he didn't want anything more to do with him, but he had to try and tell him that it would never happen again.

Billy rang the bell to Dick's flat, but he didn't hear anything from inside. He was about to walk away but decided to give the door a loud bang with his fist, just in case the bell wasn't working.

"Who's there?" Dick's voice sounded small, frightened even.

"It's Billy." Billy waited for the door to open, but there was still no movement inside. "Come on Dick, let me in. I know I've been an arsehole. I just want to explain..." Billy tailed off because he didn't really know what it was he wanted to say. He was about to give up when the key turned in the lock and the door opened. Dick was already walking down the hallway towards the living room. Billy pushed the door open and moved into the hall. "Can I come in?"

"If you want." Dick didn't even turn around to look in Billy's direction.

Billy walked down to the living room, trying to think about how he could make up to his new brother. How do you start this conversation? Dick was standing with his back to Billy, staring out of the window that looked into the primary school. He obviously wasn't going to make this easy for Billy, and he was quite right.

"Look, man, I'm really sorry about all that shit Danny said about you and your mum. I should never have stood there and let it happen." Billy hoped he was making a good start.

"It doesn't matter." There was a tremor in Dick's voice that let Billy know it plainly did matter.

"It does matter, and I promise I'll never let anything like that happen again. Danny's a mate, but he can be a real prick at times. From now on it's me and you, nobody else. The Odd Brothers against the world." Billy hoped adding a bit of levity to the situation would lighten the mood.

"Really?" Dick turned around to face Billy. His left eye was almost closed, it was so swollen. There was dried blood around his nose and there was a bruise down the right side of his jaw. Billy's breath was taken away.

"What the fuck happened? Did somebody do that to you?" It was a stupid question, but Billy had blurted it out before he could think. The desire to protect Dick overwhelmed him and he had never felt that before. At least the stupidity of the question had brought a smile to Dick's face.

"Naw, I did it to myself. I often beat myself up for fun." Dick couldn't help himself.

"Who did it? Tell me! I'll kick their fucking cunt in..." Billy meant what he said.

"It was Kojak." Dick stopped Billy in his tracks.

"Kojak?" The disbelief in Billy's voice was unavoidable. "Why?"

Dick walked over to the settee and plonked himself down. The pain in his ribs made it difficult to sit down properly. He thought for a second, looking at Billy to decide if he could trust him with the truth.

"Kojak's a drug dealer, I'm sure you know that, and your arsehole mate Danny was right, my mum's a heroin addict. He's here all the time, selling her shit and making her do stuff. I came in the other day, and I had had enough. I went for him, and he kicked fuck out of me. He hit my mum too."

Billy was standing with his mouth open, struggling to take in what Dick was saying. His mind was racing, searching for a smart solution he could offer that would solve the problem, but he was coming up with nothing. "We need to tell someone..."

Dick laughed, shaking his head at Billy's naivety. "Who?"

Billy searched for an answer. "I don't know, what about Oggy? Maybe he could have a word with Kojak, warn him off. You've been on his float for years, that's got to count for something..."

Dick laughed out loud. "Oggy? He's as bad as Kojak. The other thing your prick mate was right about is my mum's on the game. She does it to pay for the drugs. Oggy's her pimp and although I've never seen him do it, I'm pretty sure he's given my mum a slap or two in the past as well."

Billy looked as though he may pass out. He floated over and sat down next to Dick on the settee, not even trying to hide his dismay at Dick's revelations.

"Don't worry about it. It's over now." Dick was looking into space, as though he was talking to himself.

"How?" Billy wondered if he had missed an important part of the story.

"Because if either of those fuckers come round here again, I'm going to fucking kill them." Dick spoke in such a matter-of-fact way, so sure he had come up with the solution to all his problems.

"No offence, mate, but the state of your face from your last attempt tells me that's pretty unlikely." Billy didn't want to burst Dick's bubble, but there was no chance he would ever be big enough to take on Oggy, never mind Kojak.

"Don't worry about it. I'll be ready next time." Dick didn't look at Billy. He stared at the fireplace in front of him with a steely resilience in his eyes.

"Dick, you can't do this yourself."

"Listen, Billy, I've been doing everything for myself my whole life. I love my mum, but she's in a state most of the time. My dad, our dad, was never a part of my life and by all accounts he was a useless cunt anyway, so it's always just been me. Honestly, it'll be fine." There was a calmness to Dick now.

"I'll help." Billy was determined to show support, but Dick laughed again.

"No way. This isn't your fight, mate. It's bound to get messy and there's no way I'm being accused of dragging you down with me. Me and my mum will deal with it."

"You're not dragging me down! We're brothers." Billy was keen to show support, but he could hear it in his own voice that he didn't think he would be any use against such a formidable enemy.

"We're only half-brothers, and this doesn't involve your half."

Billy was defiant. "I'm not leaving you to deal with this on your own…"

Dick stood up slowly, trying to conceal the pain he was in. "I'm afraid you are, mate. I don't want you here."

"What?" Billy was surprised.

"I've told you already Billy, you're nothing like your dad. This kind of thing isn't you. Yeah, I've no doubt you can handle wee arseholes like Cheesy, but Kojak and Oggy are beyond you. I've been round guys like them my whole life, all the Blantyre mob. Leave it to me and then once I've dealt with them, you and me can start that band and take over the world." Dick sounded grown up.

"But they'll fucking kill you." Billy knew Dick's assessment of how useful he would be was accurate, but he wanted it to be different.

Dick smiled his smile. "They won't. I promise you." Dick held out his hand and helped Billy out of his seat. He ushered Billy down the hall and out of the door.

"I must be able to do something to help." Billy was numb and feeling useless.

"Just go home. Honestly, don't worry. I'll be in touch." Dick continued to smile as he closed the door. Only when Billy couldn't see him anymore did he allow the mask to slip. Dick closed his eyes and slid down the wall, allowing tears to form in his eyes, but not letting them flow.

Hugh was sitting in the pub, looking at his watch nervously. Mary had refused to see him since Kojak had burst into the house and threatened them. She was angry at him for not telling her about Billy taking acid. He had tried to assure her it had only happened once and he hadn't wanted to betray the boy's confidence while they were trying to get him used to the idea of Hugh being on the scene romantically, but she had been too upset to listen. She had finally answered the phone today and agreed to meet him in the pub, although the conversation had been brief and curt in its manner.

Brenda finished serving some punters at the other end of the bar and came down to join him.

"I had a visitor the other day." Brenda looked nervous, checking to see if anyone else was within earshot before she spoke. Hugh raised his eyebrows in response. He had his own troubles, but Brenda had always been good at listening to him drone on about his problems, so he couldn't just ask her to leave him alone. "Oggy."

"Aye? What did he want?" Hugh wasn't sure he wanted to know.

"Just to say hello he said, but I think there's something going on." Brenda was talking conspiratorially.

"Really?" Hugh tried to show interest, but he wasn't convinced he was doing a good job.

"He was all cagey and saying some of the girls had gone missing. He was trying to get me involved, but I was having none of it." Brenda seemed defensive.

"What do you think it was all about?"

"I don't know, but when he realised I wasn't going to help him, he reverted back to his usual, telling me to go fuck myself, and when he left, I watched him get in his car. He was raging, banging the steering wheel and everything. I think something's happened. He was moaning about Kojak selling the girls drugs. I'm frightened he's losing control. He can be a right nasty bastard when he loses control. I don't know what to do..." Brenda had another look round the bar to make sure nobody was listening.

"Well, do me a favour, Brenda, don't mention it to Mary when she comes in. We had our own run in with Kojak, accusing Billy of stealing his drugs. He beat up young Brian and threatened us. I say we leave those two nutters well alone and hope they run each other out of town or something..." Hugh looked at his watch again, hoping Mary would arrive soon. He wondered if he should have suggested the snug instead of the bar, so they could have had a bit of privacy.

"Come on, Hugh, we all agreed. We can't let them drag the whole community down..." Brenda tried to re-ignite the spirit they had all felt the other day.

"But they're not, are they? They're dragging the druggies and the prossies down. No offence, Brenda, but you're out of that game now, just let them get on with it. It only affects us if we get involved." Hugh took a drink of his pint, more to stop him from talking than anything else. The last thing he needed was more trouble from Kojak or Oggy or anybody else until he had sorted things with Mary. Brenda looked at Hugh like he had kicked a blind puppy.

"Well, it sounds like Mary might be very interested in hearing about it. You need to grow a pair, Hugh." Brenda stormed off.

"Brenda..." Hugh's plea was useless. Brenda was already serving one of the old regulars further down the bar, all the time looking back at him with daggers in her eyes.

Hugh needed the toilet now, but he daren't move from his seat in case Mary came in and thought he had stood her up. Brenda stayed down the other end of the bar, laughing at a joke one of the old fellas was telling for the millionth time. Hugh didn't know how she could be bothered using the energy required to keep old guys like that happy. She would get no thanks for it in the end. Just as he decided he must go and empty his bladder, Mary came bustling into the bar. Hugh stood up and smiled as much as his squeezed prostate would allow, but his face dropped as he realised Bunnet was coming in with her. Bunnet had a huge bruise on the side of his face that wasn't there when Hugh had seen him at the start of his run this morning. Hugh muttered under his breath as Mary and Bunnet approached. "Oh, what the fuck now?"

"Brenda!" Mary shouted to Brenda and motioned for her to join them at the other end of the bar.

"Hi darling, what can I get you?" Hugh tried to ignore the urgency in Mary's demeanour and the fact that Bunnet was there too.

"Whatever." Mary dismissed Hugh's attempt at a hug. "I ran into Bunnet outside. Look at the state of him."

Hugh looked at Bunnet. He was being sheepish and trying not to return his gaze. "What happened to you?"

"Kojak and Oggy beat him up." Mary couldn't wait to deliver the news.

"What?" Brenda was quick to join the conversation. She couldn't help but give Hugh a told you so look.

"They beat you up? Just like that?" Hugh couldn't hide his dubiety. He had to quickly change his response as he noticed Mary and Brenda glaring at him disapprovingly. "Dirty bastards. What happened?"

"I dug them up this morning at the end of my run, about all this drugs and ladies of the night stuff, and they went mental. Making all kinds of threats and the next thing I'm on the ground. Psychopaths the pair of them, totally out of control." Bunnet was trying to stay cool, but Hugh wondered if he might have beaten him up himself if he had actually used the term 'ladies of the night'.

"That's the last straw. Kojak beat up our Brian too. They've gone too far." Mary was fizzing. Hugh saw a way into her good side.

"Oggy was round threatening Brenda the other day too."

Brenda shot Hugh a look but wasn't about to put him on the spot. The situation was too serious now.

"Really? Are you okay, love?" Mary grabbed Brenda by the arm, concern bursting out of her.

"Yeah, I'm fine, but I think he's out of control." Brenda loved Mary in that instant. Nobody had shown her that much concern since she was a kid.

"But what can we do? We can't go to the polis. You heard Kojak the other day. We can't do that." Hugh was hoping to bring a bit of reality to the table, but he sensed nothing was going to stop Mary now she was on a roll.

"They said if I went to the police, they would spread it around town that it was me supplying the drugs and harassing the girls. I think they meant it." Bunnet looked genuinely concerned that this could be a possibility. Hugh started laughing.

"I don't think you need to worry about that, Bunnet." Hugh's laughter was cut short by the scathing looks he received from both Mary and Brenda.

At that moment, Billy came running into the bar. His face was as white as a sheet, and he was panting as though he had been running.

"Mum! I need your help!"

"What is it?" Mary's panic instantly matched that of her son's.

"I think Dick's going to be killed." Billy was struggling to get his breath back. Mary looked confused.

"Who's Dick?" Mary searched her memory for which of his friends he was talking about

"He's my brother." Everybody looked at Mary then, sensing her confusion, back to Billy. "He's... my half-brother. Dad and his mum were together at the same time as he was with you."

Mary felt her face redden, but she was determined not to make a scene. She knew this day might come and now it was here, she was going to help her son deal with it. "And what's wrong with him? Is he injured?"

"No, well yes, but he's okay just now." Billy was all over the place.

"Alright, calm down, buddy. Dick? Are we talking about Dick off of Oggy's float?" Hugh took hold of Billy by the shoulders and tried to concentrate his racing mind by looking him in the eye.

"Yeah. Oggy or Kojak are going to kill him. Kojak beat him and his mum up the other day and Dick says if either him or Oggy come to his house again he's going to kill them. His mum is on drugs and she's a prostitute. Kojak and Oggy beat her up all the time and Dick's had enough." Billy was almost hyperventilating.

"Who's his mum?" Brenda asked Billy, but it was Hugh who answered.

"Shirley Graham? He's probably right about her..."

"I know Shirley. He's right. She's really vulnerable. I can imagine those two scumbags abusing her, no doubt." Brenda started to get a bad feeling about it all.

"I'm not kidding, Mum, Dick's going to challenge them, and he won't give up. They're going to kill him if we don't stop it." Billy was calming down now that he had told someone. All he needed was some support and he was ready to fight for Dick. "He's in his house now, waiting for them to come round, we need to get there and help him."

"Right!" Mary moved round to the centre of the pub and raised her voice for everyone to hear. "Listen up, everyone!" The old guys sat at their tables raised their heads. "You all know Kojak and Oggy, they come in here, they deliver our milk and some of you might even consider them friends. What you might not know is that they're involved in drugs and prostitution and God knows what else. They're roaming around, beating up women, kids and they're out of control. They even beat up Bunnet this morning! You all know Bunnet!" Bunnet doffed his bunnet as everyone looked at him. "They beat up my son Brian the other day..."

"What?" Billy was startled at this news.

"He's okay, mate." Hugh put a reassuring hand on Billy's shoulder.

"They're a blight on our community and it's time we did something to put an end to it. There's a young boy in his house just now, scared stiff because these thugs are coming round to batter him and his mum for nothing other than standing up for themselves.

We can't let that happen. It's time for us to do something. Who's with us?"

The pub had been silent while Mary was giving her rally call. The punters all looked round at each other, then went back to their pints and newspapers. It was as though nobody had said anything.

"Right! That's it! The pub's closed! Get the fuck out of here, every last one of you useless old cunts!" Brenda had taken enough. She started running round the tables grabbing the glasses from the tables and pouring the beer onto the floor. Suddenly the place was in uproar.

"Ho! Ya fucking mad bitch. You cannae be doing this..."

"Fucking watch me! Now get the fuck out! All of you!" Brenda in full flow was something to behold. The old guys didn't stop shouting their insults and threats of calling the manager but none of them were brave enough to stick around. Within two minutes, the place was empty, apart from Brenda, Mary, Hugh, Bunnet and Billy.

"You go home, son. We'll take it from here." Mary gave Billy a hug.

"No chance. He's my brother. I'm going." Billy looked about two feet taller than he had when he first came running into the bar. Mary looked at Hugh and Hugh nodded to her. There was no way anyone was going to stop the lad. Mary looked round her merry gang and gave them all a reassuring smile.

"Okay, let's go do something."

CHAPTER THIRTY-SEVEN

Bang

DICK WAS WORRIED about his mum. She had barely left her bed in the past 24 hours, even failing to make it to the toilet on a couple of occasions, leaving Dick to clean up after her. She would only drink orange juice and coffee and hadn't touched the beans on toast Dick had made for dinner. She kept drifting in and out of consciousness and her speech was really slurred, although it was improving as the day went on. She was asleep now and Dick was dozing on the settee in the living room when he heard a crash coming from the bedroom. He ran through to find Shirley lying on the floor, trying to get up. Her skin was yellow, and the whites of her eyes were bloodshot. A small cut on her forehead where she had banged it earlier was bleeding again.

"What are you doing, Mum? Get back into bed." Dick lifted Shirley with ease, her skeletal frame weighing nothing at all, and lay her down on the bed.

"I need more aspirin. My head is splitting." Shirley rubbed her face with her hands, trying to clear her head.

"You've had loads already. We don't have any left." Dick lifted the empty box on the bedside cabinet and shook it to make sure he was right.

"Be a love and pop out for some more, will you?" Shirley sat up and tried to muster a smile.

"No way. I'm not leaving you alone." Dick could see that Shirley was looking stronger than she had been for hours, but he was still scared of leaving her on her own.

Shirley managed a weak chuckle. "Don't be daft. I'm fine. It's just a cold or something. Some aspirin and a strong coffee will sort me out."

"No, it won't, Mum. I'm not stupid. I know it's not a cold. It's the heroin." Shirley looked shocked. "Oh, stop pretending, Mum,

I'm not a wee boy anymore. I know it's heroin and I know it's killing you, even if you don't seem to realise it. You might not care what happens to you, but I do. I'm not going to sit here and let you kill yourself. You need to give it up..."

Shirley started sobbing. Thick mucus started running from her nose, but she couldn't find her handkerchief. Dick handed her the toilet roll he had place next to the bed.

"I'm so sorry I've let you down. What kind of mother lets herself get in this state? I should be looking after you, not the other way around. I'm so ashamed of myself. Maybe you'd be better off if I wasn't here..." Shirley wiped her nose and looked at the contents of the handkerchief. The sight made her more upset.

Dick stood up angrily. "Don't you dare talk like that! I don't mind looking after you. We can call the doctor! He'll help you get better. You just need to stop taking that stuff."

"It's not that easy..."

"Yes, it is! Stop taking that stuff and stop working down at the bus station. I've spoken to Sid. He says I can start working with him as soon as you're feeling better, you won't need to do any of that anymore. I'll be making enough money for both of us..." Dick's exasperation was beginning to boil over.

"No!" Shirley shouted and reached over to grab Dick's arm. "You're not working with that lot. They're trouble. You'll end up involved in all sorts. Do you want to end up like your Uncle Sammy? In jail for the rest of your life?"

"They're not like Uncle Sammy..." There was no conviction in Dick's voice. He knew exactly what his cousins were like.

"Damian! Promise me! Stay away from the Blantyre side of the family. They've never done anything for us except bring trouble to our door." Shirley was desperate to protect her son.

Dick couldn't remember the last time his mum had called him Damian. He looked away from her, unable to make the promise she was asking him to. Shirley slumped back onto the pillow, the exertion of shouting leaving her exhausted.

"Please go and get some aspirin, son." The pain in Shirley's head was threatening to burst out of her eyes.

"You need to eat something." Dick was glad to get away from the subject of his dodgy relatives.

"Oh, I couldn't..." The very idea of food made Shirley's stomach churn.

"You can't keep taking aspirin on an empty stomach, Mum..." Dick wasn't about to give in.

"Okay!" Shirley was getting angry. "You jump out and get some aspirin and pick up some soup while you're there. I could maybe manage some soup..."

Dick was hesitant. "What kind of soup?"

"Anything. Tomato." Shirley had taken enough. She needed the painkillers before the pain killed her.

Dick stood up, encouraged by the idea of Shirley eating something. "And I'll get some rolls. You can't have soup without a roll." Dick delivered the final sentence in a sing-song fashion, the way Shirley used to.

Shirley smiled at Dick using one of the mantras she had used throughout the years when she had struggled to get her fussy toddler to each much of anything. "That's right, you can't have soup without a roll."

"Okay. And you'll be okay while I'm gone? I'll only be ten minutes at the most." Dick was already putting his coat on.

"I'll be fine." Shirley needed a break from talking.

"Okay. I won't be long." Dick darted out of the bedroom and set off down the hall.

"Don't forget the aspirin!" Shirley shouted after Dick, but she wasn't sure if he had heard her, he was moving so fast.

Kojak's shoulder was aching. It had stopped bleeding, but it was hard to judge how much blood he had lost because he was covered in the stuff. Most of it was probably Cheesy's, or at least he hoped it was. He couldn't go home looking the way he was in case any of the neighbours saw him and called the police. He was sure some of the nosy fuckers would take great delight in grassing him up the first chance they got. He parked round the corner from Shirley's place because no houses looked onto that part of the road. He moved as quickly as he could towards the flat, pausing at the corner to peek round, making sure nobody was in the street. As he looked, Dick came out of the flats and took off in the other direction, heading towards the shop.

"Thank fuck." Kojak could do without the whining wee shite, so he was delighted to see him leaving. He still had his baseball bat with him, but he hoped Dick going out meant he wouldn't need to use it. He trotted round and was in the flat without anyone seeing him. He took Dick heading to the shop as a good sign that Shirley wasn't lying dead from an overdose and hearing her voice as soon as he stepped inside her flat came as a relief.

"What have you forgotten?" Shirley sounded rough, but at least she was alive. Kojak walked into the bedroom and was shocked at the sight of her lying in the bed. She looked like a corpse, even if she was still alive.

"Jesus Christ! What's happened?" Shirley jumped up as though a ghost had walked in. Kojak took a second before he remembered he was covered in blood and probably wasn't looking his best either.

"I've had a wee accident. I'm fine, but I need some help getting tidied up. Are you okay?" Kojak wondered if Shirley would be of any use to him, but she was up and out of the bed in an instant. Kojak was always amazed at how perky junkies became when their dealer walked into a room.

"I'm fine, baby. Where are you bleeding?" Shirley felt better already, knowing another hit wasn't far away. She was taking Kojak's jacket and shirt off before he could answer. "Oh, nasty. Is that a stab wound?" Shirley ran her finger over Kojak's shoulder, making him groan quietly.

"I'm fine. I just need it cleaned up and a dressing put on it. Can you do it?" Kojak had doubts, but he had to hope Shirley wasn't too far gone.

"Of course I can, baby." Shirley led Kojak through to the kitchen and opened the cupboard under the sink. She took out a box with a green cross on the side and took out some bandages.

"I need you to give me back the last bag of gear I gave you Shirley. It's bad shit. If you use it, it could kill you. I'll get you more, but I need that stuff back." Kojak hoped bringing it up now wouldn't hinder the attention his wound required.

"Nah, it was fine, man. It's all gone." Shirley was working remarkably quickly and tenderly on Kojak's wound.

"You've done it already?"

"Yeah. It was heavy shit alright, but it was great. I could do some more if you've got it..." Shirley kept working on Kojak's shoulder.

Kojak looked at Shirley and wondered if she had looked in a

mirror recently. "You're a fucking machine Shirley, but you need to slow down a bit with this shit. You look like death."

Shirley laughed. "Says the guy covered in blood. What happened anyway? Who did this to you?"

"It doesn't matter. He won't be doing it again." Kojak didn't want to mention Cheesy. He knew his body would be found and there would be pressure on Kojak from everywhere, but he could only deal with one thing at a time.

Billy was frustrated at how slowly the adults were walking down to Dick's flat. He kept running ahead and coming back again to try and get them to hurry up. They were all talking too much and not getting their arses in gear.

"Come on!"

"Slow down, son. We need to get a plan. We can't just go storming in there. I know he's your friend, but his mother might not take too kindly to us turning up at her house uninvited." Mary had been full of adrenaline when they left the pub, but the closer they got, the more uncertain she was about what they could realistically do. Brenda had closed the pub, but not one of the regulars had come with them to help, preferring to stay in the car park and moan about their lost pints. She looked around at her fellow vigilantes and her enthusiasm took another hit.

"He's my brother, not my friend." Billy could sense the adults were gearing up to let him down. Mary looked to her friends, hoping they might have an idea.

"Maybe we should just phone the police…" Hugh was way out of his comfort zone.

"And say what? We think a couple of bad guys might be on their way to beat up a child and his mum? I'm not sure they're going to drop everything and slap on the blues and twos on our say so…" Brenda was always the voice of reason.

"The police won't do anything. I wouldn't be surprised if those two hoodlums had the police in their pockets anyway. It's up to us…" Bunnet saying 'hoodlums' sounded ridiculous, but now wasn't the time to point it out.

"So, what do we do then?" Mary stopped, not willing to go any further without a proper plan.

"We kick fuck out of them!" Billy shouted.

Mary gave a nervous laugh. "Okay, firstly, I'm not happy with you using that kind of language and second... I don't know..."

"Billy's right." Bunnet looked to Hugh.

"Oh, I can see the value of Billy's opinion, but I'm not convinced me and you getting a doing from Kojak and Oggy is going to do anything for our cause." Hugh looked from Bunnet to Mary and back again. "I'm a lover, not a fighter and Bunnet's black eye already shows he's not up to the task..."

"There's five of us here, not just you two." Brenda had never backed down from a fight in her life.

"Six. Dick's there too." Billy needed them to hurry up, not stop for a discussion.

Hugh laughed nervously. "I'm sure Dick's really fired up, but he can only be about six stones in his stocking soles, so I'm not sure he's going to make much of a difference..."

"Look! Do what you want! I'm going now and I'm going to help my brother." Billy started walking away.

"Wait, Billy." Mary looked pleadingly at her friends and then started to follow her son. "We're coming son. Wait up."

The others all set off after Mary, Hugh shaking his head in disbelief that he had got involved in the first place.

Oggy had been looking for Kojak all day, driving round all his usual East Kilbride haunts. He couldn't get the picture of Maggie's baby lying motionless in his cot out of his mind. Kojak was going to pay for this. It was his fault Maggie and Linda were dead and even if he hadn't physically done anything to the baby, it was down to him that he was dead too.

Oggy pulled up outside Shirley's flat and decided he would stop his search here. It would only be a matter of time before Kojak turned up there to supply her with more of his death powder. Oggy could sit tight and wait for him to arrive, it could maybe even give him the element of surprise. Oggy was confident in his own strength, but he had to be wary of Kojak. He was a fighter, with a fierce reputation, so Oggy would need to be at the top of his game if he wanted to take him down.

Oggy opened the door to the flat as quietly as he could and crept up the hall. He could hear voices in the living room, but they were talking quietly so he couldn't make out who was in there. He burst through the living room door to see Shirley tying off a bandage on

Kojak's shoulder. They both jumped in surprise at Oggy's sudden entry.

"Oh, for fuck's sake, Oggy, you gave me the fright of my life. Listen, I've been sick, so I haven't been out earning the past couple of nights. You're going to have to wait for your money..." Shirley was obviously scared of Oggy. The difference between how she reacted to him being there as opposed to when Kojak walked in was like night and day.

"Shut up, Shirley." Oggy was staring at Kojak, trying to understand what was going on. The sight of him half-naked, with a bandage on his shoulder, threw Oggy off a bit.

"Don't talk to her like that." Kojak was at the end of his tether as far as Oggy was concerned. He had heard enough and if Oggy started again, Kojak was going to have to deal with him. Maybe today was a turning point and he should deal with everyone who had been bugging him recently.

"Shirley, leave." Oggy didn't take his eyes off Kojak.

"What do you mean, leave? This is *my* house..." Shirley stood between the two men, facing Oggy.

"Get the fuck out, Shirley." Oggy's tone made it clear he wasn't messing around.

"I'm warning you, ya prick..." Kojak took a step towards Oggy, but Shirley put her hand up to stop him.

"You've no right to come barging in here..." Shirley didn't want Oggy spoiling her chances of scoring more drugs from Kojak.

"Maggie's dead!" Oggy shouted at Kojak. Kojak took a step back, shocked at the news.

"What?" Shirley turned to look at Kojak then back to Oggy.

"Her baby's dead too." Oggy struggled to stop his voice from cracking.

"Oh my God..." Shirley put her hand to her mouth. "What happened?"

"He killed her. And Linda." Oggy was still staring at Kojak.

"Nothing to do with me. It's not my fault they can't handle it. Shirley's okay, she had the same stuff, probably more." Kojak gestured to Shirley but regretted it when he looked at her. Shirley was far from okay.

Oggy glanced round the room and spotted the baseball bat by the side of the chair. He looked at Kojak and smiled before they both lunged for it, getting there first. In the same move, Oggy swung the bat towards Kojak's head.

"No!" Shirley moved to protect Kojak, taking a direct hit from the bat on the side of the head, sending her sprawling on to the settee. Kojak lunged at Oggy, driving him back onto the dining table. The baseball bat got dropped in the tussle as the two men grappled with each other, each landing short punches as they fell onto the floor.

Dick was feeling better as he left the shop. If he could get Shirley to eat some soup, he was sure it would help give her the strength to face up to her problems. With his help, she could get off drugs and they could start building their life again. Working for Sid would be dangerous, but as soon as they were back on their feet, Dick was pretty sure he could get a job at the dairy, maybe even have his own milk float one day. He could look after Shirley properly and get out of the dingy flat and into a nice house somewhere. As he turned into the street, his heart stopped. Oggy's Ford Capri was sitting outside the flat. Dick started running, dropping the shopping bag as he went. The blood was pumping in his ears as he ran into the flat, the noise of crashing furniture greeting him as he ran up the hall. He flew into the living room as Kojak smashed one of the dining chairs over Oggy's back, the two men not even noticing his arrival. Dick looked over and saw his mum lying on the settee, a trickle of blood running down her face. Dick felt his world collapse.

Dick ran out of the living room and into his bedroom, scrambling in the bottom drawer of his wardrobe. After what felt like an age, he found what he was looking for.

Oggy and Kojak were knocking lumps out of each other. Kojak's shoulder wound wasn't hindering him in any way, but it had started bleeding again and both men were covered in it. Neither had noticed Dick coming into the room and leaving again, such was the intensity of their fight. The living room looked like a bomb site, with broken chairs and blood everywhere. Neither man had the upper hand, and they were still exchanging blows when Dick ran back into the room.

"Haw, cunts!"

Kojak and Oggy stopped in their tracks as they spun round to see Dick standing in the middle of the room with a gun in his hand, pointing it straight at them.

"Fuck off, Dick, this is nothing to do with you." Oggy didn't believe the gun was real and went to fly at Kojak again.

"Make one move and you're dead." Dick was firm but calm as he spoke.

Oggy looked at Dick again, taking a closer look at the gun in his hand. "What is that? A fucking peashooter? Get out of here, Dick, before you get hurt."

"That's not a peashooter." Kojak hadn't taken his eyes off the gun since Dick had shouted his warning. The worried look on his face made Oggy think again.

"Eh?" Oggy looked from Dick to Kojak and back again, beginning to realise Kojak wasn't faking his fear.

"Put the gun down, Dick. There's no need for that." Kojak had seen guns before, and he knew the one in Dick's hand was real.

"Stop being a wee fanny, Dick, and give me the gun..." Oggy wasn't having it. There was no way a wee guy like Dick could have a gun, never mind use it. The wee prick was a punchbag to everyone he came in contact with. There was no way he had the balls to threaten anyone, never mind fire a gun.

"I swear to God, either of you move and I'll blow your fucking heads off." It was as though Dick was reading Oggy's mind and he wanted to show what was happening was real.

"Dick! Stop it!" Billy was standing in the doorway, aghast at what was happening before him. Mary, Hugh and Bunnet came into the room and couldn't believe their eyes at the devastation.

"Oh, for fuck's sake, what is this? A bastard social club? Get the fuck out of here, all of you..." Oggy wondered if the blow on the head he had taken from the dining chair was causing him to hallucinate. He looked to Kojak, hoping he would back him up, but Kojak still had his eyes fixed firmly on the gun in Dick's hand. There was a weird look in his eyes. He looked scared.

Brenda came in and ran over to Shirley, who still hadn't moved since being struck by the bat. "Shirley! Wake up! What have you done to her?" Brenda looked at Oggy and Kojak with hatred.

"Dick, this isn't the way to go, son. Put that down and we can talk about this." Bunnet tried to exert the authority he usually had over the boys who worked on the milk floats. The boys respected him, although the events of the past few days had left him wondering if he was living in a dream.

Dick hadn't taken his eyes off Kojak and Oggy, even when everyone else had arrived. "Nah, we've done all the talking we're going to do. These two need to be taught a lesson."

"Let's kick fuck out of them then. We can take them." Billy was struggling to know what to do. He finally asked the question everyone, including Oggy and Kojak, had been wanting to ask. "Where did you get a gun?"

"Remember I told you I get up to some serious shit with my cousins? Well, looking after a gun every now and then is about as serious as the shit gets." Dick gave the quickest of glances to Billy, the smile on his face lighting up when he saw his brother.

"Oh my God. All of this has to stop! We need to phone an ambulance." Brenda was kneeling next to Shirley on the settee. She looked up to the others with tears in her eyes. "I think Shirley's dead."

"Aw, for fuck's sake," Oggy threw his hands up in the air and rolled his eyes, as though nothing was going right for him. He showed no remorse, only annoyance at the latest thing going wrong for him. "This is not my day..."

Dick let out a single, desperate sob. "Fucking right it's not."

The gun exploded twice in rapid succession, making everyone throw themselves to the ground, their hands automatically covering their ears. The room filled with acrid smoke and when Billy finally looked up from his hiding position, only Dick was left standing, still pointing the gun at the same point as before. Billy looked over to where Kojak and Oggy lay on the carpet. Neither were recognisable, a bullet having hit each of them in the face. Blood and brains covered the walls.

"Are they dead?" Hugh couldn't stop himself from talking, even though he knew it was a stupid question. The sight of Kojak and Oggy lying there didn't seem real. It was like he had walked into the middle of a film. He couldn't stop thinking about the scene in *The Godfather*, where the two guys were shot in the restaurant. It was like that, but there was a lot more blood, and the smell was something you didn't experience in the cinema.

Mary got up and started walking towards Dick, tears streaming down her face. Dick snapped out of his trance and turned to face the others, pointing the gun at them now that Kojak and Oggy were no longer the main threat.

"Stop. Don't come any closer, Mrs Loy." There were tears in Dick's eyes, but he remained remarkably calm.

"It's okay, son, it's over. You can stop, you're safe now."

Mary didn't move again, but she hoped her soft tone would calm the boy enough to put an end to the madness. Dick walked over to Shirley and stroked her hair, keeping the gun pointed at the others. He checked her pulse and his face dropped even further as he realised Brenda's prediction was correct. His mum was dead.

"Dick." Billy looked at his brother pleadingly. "Come on. It'll be okay. We're here for you."

"I don't think things are going to be okay, somehow." Hugh spoke without realising he was doing it out loud.

"Shut up, Hugh! You're not helping." Mary slapped Hugh on the arm.

"Please, Dick. Give up." Billy was crying.

Dick smiled at his brother again. He lifted the gun to the side of his head and spoke before he pulled the trigger for a third time.

"Bang."

Manufactured by Amazon.ca
Bolton, ON